PENGUIN BOOKS

CANTERBURY BEACH

ANNE SIMPSON's first book of poetry, *Light Falls Through You*, won the 2001 Gerald Lampert Memorial Award and the 2001 Atlantic Poetry Prize. In 1997 she won the Journey Prize for her short fiction. She lives in Antigonish, Nova Scotia.

CANTERBURY BEACH

ANNE SIMPSON

Penguin Books

PENGUIN BOOKS

Published by the Penguin Group

Penguin Books Canada Ltd, 10 Alcorn Avenue, Toronto,
Ontario, Canada M4V 3B2

Penguin Books Ltd, 80 Strand, London WC2R 0RL, England

Penguin Putnam Inc., 375 Hudson Street, New York,
New York 10014, U.S.A.

Penguin Books Australia Ltd, 250 Camberwell Road,
Camberwell, Victoria 3124, Australia

Penguin Books (NZ) Ltd, cnr Rosedale and Airborne
Roads, Albany, Auckland 1310, New Zealand

Penguin Books Ltd, Registered Offices: Harmondsworth,
Middlesex, England

First published in Viking by Penguin Books Canada, 2001
Published in Penguin Books, 2002

1 3 5 7 9 10 8 6 4 2

*Publisher's note: This book is a work of fiction. Names,
characters, places and incidents either are the product of the
author's imagination or are used fictitiously, and any
resemblance to actual persons living or dead, events,
or locales is entirely coincidental.*

Manufactured in Canada.

NATIONAL LIBRARY OF CANADA CATALOGUING IN PUBLICATION DATA

Simpson, Anne, 1956–
Canterbury Beach
ISBN 0-14-029816-9
I. Title.
PS8587.I54533C26 2002   C813'.6   C2001-903886-0
PR9199.4.S527C26 2002

Visit Penguin Canada's website at **www.penguin.ca**

Paul

End

Whan that April with his showres soote
The droughte of March hath perced to the roote,
And bathed every veine in swich licour,
Of which vertu engendred is the flowr;
Whan Zephyrus eek with his sweete breeth
Inspired in every holt and heeth
The tendre croppes, and the yonge sonne
Hath in the Ram his halve cours yronne,
And smale fowles maken melodye
That sleepen al the night with open yë—
So priketh hem Nature in hir corages—
Thanne longen folk to goon on pilgrimages . . .

Geoffrey Chaucer

SETTING OUT

VERNA ∾

Like the earth, she could be depended on. Her children could not.

It was the time of year when things pushed up out of the ground, leaves shook in the breeze, a fuzz of green clung to the land. All of this had happened quickly, because only a few months ago Verna had woken to snow. She'd looked out the window and seen a thin layer of snow over the brownish grass, on the crocuses, on the driveway, as if someone had iced a cake with a meagre hand. May had been a cold month, and the first part of June wasn't much better. Now it was almost the beginning of July. She'd seen grosbeaks and purple finches on and off throughout the winter, but now she saw robins. Warblers. A ruby-crowned kinglet perched on the clothesline pole. There were even hummingbirds drinking up the cherry red liquid that she put in a feeder in the backyard. When they came, she looked up from whatever she was doing in the garden and watched their tiny, jewel-like bodies. They hummed, they glistened. They were a signal for Verna that the weather had finally turned; it was time to make the trip to the cottage she and Allistair had made each summer, give or take, for forty years.

The sky was a perfect, limitless blue the day they left. There was nothing as fine as a morning like this, thought Verna, sitting in the back of the car with her arm resting on a pillow. She'd brought it in case Allistair wanted to nap in the car, but he was wide awake in front, attentive to Spike's driving even as he gazed out the window. She reached over and put her hand gently on his shoulder. He turned briefly to her, smiling, thinking she was going to tell him something. But she wasn't. They passed a single elm, bare of leaves and diseased, but still standing in the marsh that opened into the sea. Its branches were spread out in a wide fan.

It was strange to think she'd been married to Allistair for so many years. Sometimes she would look at him as he ate his custard or tapioca pudding, considering it. Love was only one of the things that held people together, she thought, but habit was the thing that clinched it. They'd had four children, five if she counted the one she'd lost: Neil, Spike, Evelyn, and Garnet. Garnet. But she wasn't going to think about him just now. She folded her hands in her lap and watched a woman pulling a lawn-mower around the side of a house. The wheel of the lawn-mower got stuck on something in the grass. The woman bent to the grass, pulled up a shiny object, and tossed the silvery thing out of the way. It might have been a broken fragment from a lawn ornament. Part of a mirror ball. Verna watched the arc it made in the air. Glittering, falling.

The trip to Maine would take a day and a half, even though they could get there in twelve hours if they pushed it, but they were planning to do things in a leisurely way, stopping at the Bell Motel in St. Stephen for the night and going on to the cottage the next day. Verna loved it there, even though they only went for a few weeks each summer. Why did they have to go all that way, Allistair had asked her, when they lived right beside the ocean? But it wasn't the same, she said. The beach just wasn't the same at home. There weren't the tides. Well, they could see high tides at Truro, if it was tides she wanted. But it wasn't that. It was the place they'd gone almost every year since their honeymoon.

She turned to see if Robin's blue car was still behind them. Why Neil hadn't come with Robin was still a mystery, even if he'd said he would drive down the following week. Verna was disappointed, but she didn't say anything. She knew more than Neil thought she did. He and Robin were apart more often than they were together. And Neil had his eye on another woman. Carolee. It had to be Carolee. Verna had felt it coming, or something like it, even before the day last week when Robin had asked her to go kayaking. There was a pitch to Robin's voice then that made Verna worry. Robin and Neil should have had children by now: they'd been married ten years, living in that big house they'd built at Seabright. It needed children. Blond children, like Robin. Freckled over the nose, like Neil.

Evelyn had a child. She could have brought Luke with her, but he was sixteen and wanted to stay at his father's and keep playing baseball. They all knew he was staying because of that girlfriend who was skinny as a string bean and always had her hair in her eyes. Verna hardly saw Luke now, but she remembered when he used to sit on her lap as she told him stories and he dug in her black purse for humbugs. She missed his silky skin, the pictures on her refrigerator, the knock-knock jokes he used to tell her. He was her only grandchild. And he hadn't come with them.

She noticed the way the trees had been slashed away from the verge of the new road at the top of Mount Thom. The spruce had fallen this way and that, some like great spears. Why did she worry about them? Why did she spend all her waking hours thinking about the children? Once she'd mentioned it to Allistair and he told her, as he had before, that they could look after themselves. He'd set down his coffee mug on the kitchen counter and reflected on the weather outside. On his mug was a little picture of a bald-headed man in a fiery place with a devil standing in front of two doors. On one door were the words, "Damned If You Do," and on the other, "Damned

If You Don't." They didn't need their hands held, Allistair was saying. Then he went out, careful to make sure the screen door caught on the latch so it wouldn't go swinging in the wind.

On the descent from Mount Thom it was possible to see clear across to Bible Hill. At least Verna thought so. The slopes close by were a velvet green, but farther on they became a softer grey-green and then blue-green. Hills swathed in spruce. A bald eagle glided like a swimmer, making a wide circle over the nearer ridge. A slow, effortless movement. Who did she worry about more? Spike didn't stick to things. He fell in love with nearly every woman he met. On the other hand, Neil seemed to stick to things with a vengeance. Only at the bitter end of something would he call it quits. Like his father. The eagle skimmed over a clearing on the right and perched on a limb of a dead tree.

It wasn't just the boys. Evelyn could take care of herself and Luke, but she picked odd partners to live with. *Partners.* That was Evelyn's word. And Phonse Lafontaine, of all people. But he was a kind man, even if some people said he was two sticks short of a cord. And then Robin, who should have been an artist and instead was an information officer at the hospital. Why would anyone want to be an information officer if she could be painting irises in a vase? It was as if they'd all deviated from the path their lives were supposed to follow. Verna knew, as she'd always known, the way her life would go. From the time she'd married Allistair, she'd known her family would be her true work. Sometimes she'd wanted other things, but she'd always come back to this one immutable fact.

There was a trailer ahead with two bicycles and several lawn chairs roped to the back with bungie cords. The green-and-white straps of a lawn chair fluttered in the wind like flags. Verna had heard once about a lawn chair flying off a camper and killing the driver in the car behind. She could feel the lawn chair slicing through her own neck, her body sailing out the window in two pieces. She closed her eyes and when she opened them again Spike was passing the trailer, which had moved slightly, like a lumbering bear, to the shoulder of the road. She wasn't going to die before they got there. Allistair wasn't going to die, either. They would all get there in one piece. They'd celebrate their fortieth anniversary with photographs taken on the lawn in front of the cottage, as they lifted glasses of champagne to the camera. They'd received cards from the Lovells in Vancouver, from the Chiassons in Sydney. Cards with shiny lettering, with rings, hearts, and elegant inscriptions about love. One was a pop-up card with two rainbow-coloured cars touching fenders as they unfolded. A little heart sprang up at the same time with the words, "Love takes us down the road." Verna put this card behind the others, standing them on top of the bureau behind the bottle of Oscar de la Renta perfume Allistair had given her for Christmas. She gave a little sigh of pleasure.

"Any sandwiches back there, Mum?" asked Spike.

"It's only ten o'clock." But she'd already taken the lid off the cooler. "Egg salad, chicken salad, and somewhere down below there's cheese and ham. If I can just lay my hands on it." She dug down farther in the cooler and pulled up the bag of sandwiches. "You and food. Honestly."

"It's the triathlons." He bit into the ham and cheese sandwich she handed him. "Any pickles?"

She gave him a few pickles on a napkin and watched him from the back seat. She remembered a vivid flash of red: Spike's cowboy shirt as he stood up beside Neil on the barn roof, daring him to jump. Neil stood up awkwardly, aiming his BB gun at Spike, his little face pinched and white. He didn't like heights. It wasn't a real barn, just big enough for bicycles and a lawn-mower. But the drop from the roof to the woodpile would break a leg, crack a skull, puncture a lung. Spike came down and said Neil could stay up there for good if he wanted, but Verna told Spike to button up his lips. Then she told Neil to sit down. He sat, the black-and-white cowboy boots sticking out on either side of the roof. Sharp, pointed. She went up the ladder to get him, but he didn't want to come down. He sat up there for the rest of the afternoon and all through supper while the others ate their tuna casserole. When it was time for chocolate pudding, Allistair got up from the table and walked out the back door. He climbed the ladder. He held out his hand to Neil, who scrambled over the roof, still clutching his BB gun, quick as a squirrel.

They worried her sick, she told Allistair that evening. And it wasn't just barn roofs. It was just that they could crack themselves wide open. They were fragile. But they were stronger than she realized, Allistair told her. And pig-headed. She lay in bed after he said this, lying still, listening to the comforting, rasping sound of his breath, evenly rising and falling, and the slow creak of the barn door which she'd forgotten to close properly. She knew it would keep her up all night so she went out in her thin nightgown, her feet making impressions on the damp grass. She banged the barn doors firmly together at the same time and wedged a stick in the hasp where a padlock should have been. Maybe it wasn't that they were fragile, she thought, clasping her arms around herself in the cool air. Maybe she was the fragile one. She gazed up at the sky, flecked with brilliance. When she'd been little, it had seemed to her that the night sky was a blanket, or a cloak. She knew that there was an entire world behind it; some glowing, magical place, glimpsed through tiny holes. But there was always the darkness flung over it, like blindness.

SPIKE ∾

"Well, now, that boy's going to be the handsome one," Aunt Kathryn had said once, when she brought Spike a present for his twelfth birthday. She was speaking to his parents, appraising him, with her head on one side.

Maybe she thought he hadn't heard her, because he'd been busy unwrapping the present, even though he knew what it was before he opened it. She always bought him a book. This time it was *Everyday Life on the Canadian Prairie Farm*. It had black-and-white photographs of men on tractors. A little boy sailing a toy boat in a slough.

"Thank you," he said. She kissed him on the cheek and her lips were dry.

Since that time, he had always been the handsome one, whether he liked it or not. Neil was good, Spike was handsome, Garnet was naughty. As he grew older, Spike considered this. When someone said he was handsome it wasn't necessarily a compliment. It was a way of saying that being handsome accounted for some things, like his confidence.

Still, it had its advantages, being good-looking, even if people made a point of trying to take him down a peg or two. It didn't work most of the time, because he liked people on the whole and they liked him. He could charm them out of it. Then they would see that he didn't need to be taken down a peg or two. This tactic worked best with women. It worked with men, too, but it took a little longer. But it didn't work with some people.

Janelle had said she didn't much like him at first.

"Why?" he asked when she told him.

"You're so full of yourself."

"What do you mean?"

"Just that you think about yourself all the time."

"I think about you all the time," he said. "Come here."

She went over to him and he kissed her.

"There, you see. I wasn't thinking about myself."

"Yes, you were."

He could say what he liked; it didn't make any difference.

He glanced around, one hand on the wheel. It was flat
and would remain flat until they reached Folly Mountain,
and even then it wouldn't do much of anything except
rise and fall. Northern Nova Scotia could be barren, he
thought. Cold in winter, and windy or rainy the rest of
the time. He'd left and gone to live in Toronto because
he wasn't going to spend the rest of his life in some little
town the rest of the world couldn't pronounce.

In the little rectangle of mirror he could see his mother's
white head as she bent over the cooler. Her hair used to be
blonde. She was smaller now than he'd ever seen her. Or
maybe she just looked small and a little stout in comparison
to his father. It was the same face he knew well, wrinkled
now around her eyes and mouth. She moved again, out of
the mirror's rectangle, so he couldn't see her. She was just
barely into her sixties. There were women her age who ran
marathons. But it wasn't his mother so much as his father
who had aged in the past year. It was his father's hair, especially, because it had always been so dark and thick. Spike
smoothed his hand over his own hair.

If Spike lived close enough, he would have gone out of
his way to see his parents. Evelyn was always saying that
she was the one who looked after them, but she worked in

a gift shop and taught literacy in the evenings, which
didn't leave much time. It was Phonse who looked after
everything. He was something of an oddball, but then Evelyn was always picking up strays. First she'd gotten married
too young and nothing came of it, except a baby. Now she
was with Phonse, but who could tell if she'd get it into her
head to leave him, too? She saw herself as the responsible
one. But Neil had always been the responsible one.

"What have you got against me?" Evelyn had asked
him once.

"Nothing," he said, looking at her. She could have
been nice-looking if she'd tied that long hair up. It was
dark and thick like his, but sort of frizzy, and she didn't do
anything with it. She was putting on a little weight. And
she always wore those socks and sandals. "I don't have
anything against you."

"We're poles apart," she said.

"I wouldn't say that." He got along with her most of
the time. He got along with all of them.

"You always have to be the centre of attention."

"No, I don't," he said thoughtfully. "You do. You just
don't know it."

She laughed, looking up at the ceiling. "I can't believe
you. You don't know anything."

Spike let it drop. She would start one of her argu-
ments, and he couldn't be bothered arguing. They used to
argue about who would do the dishes, who would weed
the garden. But now it was other things. She didn't know

much about men, for instance. Spike had made mistakes with women, but she'd made just as many with men. He noticed these things.

Evelyn and Robin were like night and day. Robin didn't wear socks and sandals. She could have worn silk suits. She could have worn anything. Robin was wasted on Neil, but then that marriage was a mistake, as Spike could have told her from the beginning. He could have told Neil. It wouldn't have made any difference, though, because they'd been in love. And anyway, maybe Spike was just jealous. Robin was a smooth-skinned woman with fair hair, but she was always pulling it back and braiding it, instead of letting it down. She got on with things briskly, with no idea how she affected people. She didn't intend to affect people.

And here they were, almost all of them, together. Except Neil, who had some lame excuse. And Garnet. There was no telling what he would do. Spike glanced in the mirror to see if he could see the blue car. They'd probably be telling jokes and giggling. The one about the pope and the Buddhist and the man with a penis shaped like a pretzel. He smiled. No, that wasn't something they'd talk about. Anyway, he couldn't see them because of the semi blocking his view. Now that they were going up Folly Mountain he could accelerate and leave the truck behind. When they came to the top of the hill he could see the lake below, blue as a bit of cut-out sky. He thought of the beach in Maine and the froth of waves against shore. Something waiting for him. It was a great day, he thought, stretching. They couldn't have asked for anything better.

EVELYN ༄

"They're a species unto themselves," Evelyn said. "I mean, even Phonse."

"Hard to figure out." Robin took her right hand off the wheel, flexing her wrist. "My father was like that."

"Dad's the same," said Evelyn.

Robin passed a truck and drew back into the right-hand lane, where she had a good view of the lake below Folly Mountain. A motorboat was unzipping it from top to bottom, the water parting in two blue halves.

"He's kind of needy sometimes," said Evelyn. "I don't know how to put it. More than Mom. She gets stubborn about things, though. She didn't want me to go to Indonesia." She looked out at the lake as they drove down the hill, past the roofs of cottages visible through the trees. A teenager was circling around on a jet ski boat, making little white doodles on the water. A bulldozer was clearing some land near the shore. People wrecked things, she thought. They wrecked all kinds of things. She looked away from the lake.

Evelyn was unique, Mrs. Dyson once said to her mother. Evelyn was sitting on the landing, listening to them and lining up buttons from the button jar. A pink one, a rhinestone one, a daisy one. They satisfied her, lying in neat rows on the stair runner.

"She can be difficult," her mother said.

"Gaby was like that sometimes." Mrs. Dyson's teacup clinked against the saucer.

"But she's got strange ideas."

"It's just her way of looking at things," said Mrs. Dyson. "She's unique."

"Yes, well," said her mother. "That's the truth."

Unique, thought Evelyn, taking out a shiny black button. It was a good word. Like *unicorn*. She took out a round glass button and put it against one eye, squeezing it so it would stay there. The glass was faintly yellow, and when she looked through it everything looked different.

It seemed to her that her family did everything to make sure Evelyn wasn't unique. She had to wear smocked dresses. Even the girl in her reader wore smocked dresses. She wore saddle shoes like the other girls in her class. In winter she had to wear a woollen cap with ear flaps exactly like the ones her brothers wore. She hated it. It smelled of mothballs. Once, walking home from school, she had taken it off and given it to a brown spaniel puppy, who probably chewed it to pieces. Neil and Spike had been walking with her, and Neil told her she was a stupid idiot.

"I don't care," she said, running away from them. Her hair flew behind her wildly. Her ears were cold. "I don't care about any of you." She ran all the way home, knowing that one of them would tell on her, that her mother might make her go back and fetch it, that sooner or later she would have to wear a cap with ear flaps again. For the moment, though, she was free. She put out her arms and became an airplane. She dipped her arms. She flew. She wasn't like the rest of them at all.

On the trailer in front was a sticker of a mermaid with lime green hair. She had a lime green fishing pole. She also had large breasts. "Goin' fishin'?" said the sticker.

People made mistakes. Getting married to Duncan was a mistake, Evelyn thought. But she'd married him anyway. She had a will of iron. Sometimes it was a good thing, she thought, gazing at the mermaid's lime green hair. Sometimes it wasn't.

Anyway, she had Luke. Or she would have him for a few years more and then he'd go off on his own. He was already starting to live his life the way she lived hers. Making wilful choices. He didn't listen to her any more. He knew what was right and wrong, but it didn't stop him from doing stupid things. That time he'd been drinking with the guys and gone off in Mike Murphy's pickup, when he was so drunk he drove into a ditch. They were just lucky it wasn't a telephone pole. That's what she told him. If he was an idiot now, he'd be an idiot later. She told him that, too, although by then he'd turned away from her. She could see what he was thinking. She was overreacting as usual. He wasn't going to get himself killed. So she went over and shook him by the shoulders.

"Wha-at the—" he said.

"I just want you to listen," she said. "I don't want you to die on some road between here and nowhere."

"I'm not going to die," he said, shrugging free from her grasp. "Don't worry."

"Well," she said more calmly, "I do worry."

She had meant to say she loved him, but he didn't like it when she said that. He used to like it. When he was small, she tucked him in and tickled him, so that the sheets and blankets were in a jumble and she had to tuck him in again. She told him she loved him best in all the world. She kissed him. He looked up at her almost sorrowfully, she thought. He loved her, too, better than best in all the world.

Some nights she would go in while he was sleeping. He'd have thrown off most of the blankets, and one foot might be off the bed, an arm spread wide. As if he'd fallen there. As she pulled up the blanket, he'd turn and curl himself into a ball, one arm clutching a dirty-white polar bear. She couldn't bring herself to leave. She sat on his bed, smoothing the damp hair off his face, looking at him. For those few moments, as she stroked his hair, he was hers. He belonged to her. Not for long, because she would have to teach him that he didn't belong to anyone. So he could grow up and leave her.

The trees at the side of the road wavered. Then she blinked and they straightened themselves into serried ranks. She'd deal with it when the time came.

ROBIN ✄

Everyone expected Robin and Neil to have children by now. Verna. Allistair. Even her mother and Jerrold. Except she couldn't imagine that Jerrold cared. She'd never even met him.

But they didn't have children. And it became more and more unlikely as time went on, especially now. They didn't even talk about having children any more. They had talked about it once. They had tried to deal with it, as Neil put it, so that they could reach a compromise. She thought about that. A compromise. What did that mean? Having half a child? A leg. An arm. What exactly did that mean?

She sighed. She didn't want to think about it. Sometimes when they had talked about it she felt a dull pain in her stomach. It was psychosomatic, she knew, but it was strange the way it happened. At one time she'd gone to see a therapist about things like that.

"It's repressed feeling," said the therapist.

"Maybe it is," said Robin.

"Of course it is," assured the therapist. She was a large, comforting woman with round glasses and short grey hair.

She lit candles every session because she felt that it was calming and helped people centre themselves. In her small office there were plants everywhere. A rubber tree. Ferns. Geraniums that bloomed and flourished in the middle of winter. This woman had three children of her own, though they were grown. She cooked, she gardened, she lived a robust life in the country.

"Have you ever thought that something is holding you back?" she said to Robin.

"I've thought about it. I've thought that I should just ditch my job and do what I really want to do, whether Neil likes it or not."

"Would he object to what you really want to do?"

"I don't know," said Robin, considering. It would throw him off. She wasn't sure it would be helpful to either of them if he were thrown off.

"Maybe you should think about it a bit," said the therapist, shifting her weight to get up. "What I want you to do this week is really consider things." She put out the four candles, and a thin scribble of smoke drifted up from each one. "And when you come back I want you to talk about it."

But Robin didn't go back. She was getting into deep water and she knew it. Besides, she didn't like being admonished by the therapist, whose own life appeared so tranquil. She was envious of the woman's plants. She was envious of the candles, which the therapist had made herself. She was envious of the authority in the therapist's voice when she talked about relationships. Anyway, Robin had never mentioned what was really bothering her in those sessions. She already knew how the line of questioning would go.

So what you're saying is that you've always wanted children?

Yes.

But Neil doesn't want them?

Not Neil, no.

How do you want to resolve this?

She glanced at a dead porcupine by the side of the road. The fringe of sharp quills, the bloody mess. She should have been able to feel something for it, but the feeling was absent. When she was little she cried at the sight of such things, but she didn't any more. They passed it, and there were other bloody bits strewn along the side of the road.

Robin lifted her hair with one hand and held it on top of her head.

"It's getting warm," Evelyn said.

She'd never said anything about wanting children to Evelyn. Evelyn often talked about Luke as if Robin wouldn't understand. As if Robin had no idea of the work, the responsibility, the care involved in bringing up a child. Evelyn didn't know she was excluding Robin, but at a certain point Robin could feel a door being closed in her face.

Maybe it didn't matter. Maybe it was just one of the things that didn't matter. But all around her, she could

feel doors being closed. She noticed it with Neil. Like last
week when he didn't tell her why he'd come home late.

"What'd you make for supper?" he asked, opening the
oven door.

"Fish sticks," she said.

"You're kidding. You made fish sticks? They're covered
in grease."

"I know," she said, licking her fingers. "I like them."

Then he'd put on an apron and made himself linguine
with cream sauce. He took off his apron and poured himself a glass of wine when he was done. He poured one for
her, too.

"Want some?" he asked. "It's better than fish sticks."

"All right."

She had been a good cook once. He'd come over every
night to eat meals and sleep in her bed that first summer.
She imagined there had been something exotic about it
for him, something illicit. He used to talk to her about
sex. He'd be eating grilled salmon and talking about posi-
tions they might try. She told him to eat up. She fed him
second helpings, sometimes more.

"It's good," he'd tell her. "Really good."

That was before he learned to cook. Now she found
things in the kitchen cupboards she hadn't bought. Pine
nuts. Peanut oil. Balsamic vinegar. He cooked meals for
her.

"How is it?" he asked, waiting for her to take a mouth-
ful of linguine.

"Fine," she said, wiping her mouth.

"Fine?"

She'd needed to go away. Not that she was in the mood to celebrate anyone's wedding anniversary. But if it hadn't been this trip, it might have been another. She might have taken a bus all the way to New Mexico or Florida. Key West. She'd never been there. Her life was slipping away and there were places she'd never seen. Tropical wonders, white sand, huge flowers cascading from trellises. She could wear them in her hair. She could dance on the beach. She could imagine all kinds of possibilities.

There was a patch on the road ahead that shone like water. It was an illusion, she knew, and when they approached, it disappeared. It became asphalt again. The trees were exactly the same as the ones they'd left behind. Same spruce, same aspen, same birch. Yet something had opened up. The sky spread itself wide in blue abandon, and the land rolled away, stretching itself out towards the ocean. Something was out there waiting just for her. It was there. She could feel it.

A L L I S T A I R ∽

Allistair had owned MacDonald's Construction for thirty years before he sold it the year before to Ed Legris, who changed the name and had a heart attack six months

later. Allistair could see a disaster coming. Ed didn't
understand the business, whereas Allistair had always had
a knack for it. He'd made a very comfortable living doing
it, maybe because he understood what people wanted: a
solid foundation, a good roof, a warm house in winter.
Each week for more than twenty-five years there had
been an advertisement in *The Tartan* displaying a smiling
house with cartoon arms holding a banner: "MacDonald's
goes the extra mile, building homes to make you smile."

But in the last few years Allistair had no longer been
able to predict what people wanted. They wanted big
houses even if they couldn't afford them. Sometimes he
drove around town on a Sunday thinking about houses
people couldn't afford. It seemed to be a sinful waste of
money. Nobody needed a house with a portico of soft,
reddish terracotta, with fake-gold light fixtures hanging
over the front door. They didn't need houses with four
and a half bathrooms. What were they going to do with
four and a half bathrooms? Allistair thought of his grand-
parents' house in Baddeck. The house had been in the
family for years, a white frame house with a red front door
that no one ever used because they always went to the
back door. It was a solid, honest house.

The house where he and Verna lived was well built,
with a red mansard roof, white clapboard siding, and big
windows. It had an expansive kitchen, which had never
been renovated in all the years they'd lived there. They'd
talked about it, but nothing had ever been done. They

had moved in five days after Allistair had turned thirty-three, in the heady days of his new business, when he and Verna had been married almost nine years. They still had the black-and-white photograph Les Dunphy had taken on moving day of Verna with a polka-dot scarf around her head, holding Garnet on the sofa in the front yard. She was smiling, which made her squint a little, but her face was radiant. Allistair had told her shortly after they'd gotten married that her face was like a shiny pearl, and she'd laughed and laughed as she looked in the mirror, turning her face this way and that. What a card he was, she told him. It had been easy to make her laugh. Beside Verna, Spike was only a blurred shape in the photograph. He'd been bouncing up and down. Allistair was standing next to the sofa holding a box and grinning. Neil was in front, on the ground, busily poking the earth for worms as Evelyn looked over his shoulder. That photograph was vivid in Allistair's mind, not so much because it marked that particular day in his life, but because Garnet was in it. A bundle in Verna's arms.

The day they'd moved Verna had wanted to leave their double bed on the screened porch just for one night, so she put Garnet's bassinet in the hall where they could hear him. They'd made love quietly, because both of them imagined the neighbours would hear. Verna had strong legs and round breasts, on which tiny golden hairs surrounded the nipples. In the morning, he'd woken and walked around the bed, surveying Verna asleep. He touched a

knuckle of her left hand, but she hadn't woken. *Verna,
Verna.* With a face like a pearl. He thought about the day
he'd asked her about getting married. They'd been swimming and she almost drowned him. No, she hadn't almost
drowned him. It was just a little joke. She didn't want to
talk about getting married. Why hadn't she? She knew
they'd get married, but she didn't want to think about it
just then. She wanted to swim. But he wanted to make
love to her whenever he saw her, not just that one time at
Arisaig. It had driven him crazy. He wanted to get married
so it wouldn't be a mortal sin. He also wanted to get married because he wanted to wake up beside her warm body
every morning, and he thought about this more than he
thought about mortal sin, but he didn't tell her.

He picked up Garnet, who had begun to make soft
noises in the bassinet, and talked to him about the weedy
patch that he intended to turn into a first-rate vegetable
garden. He pointed out the little barn with the cupola on
top. He discussed Garnet's future, advising him not to
build houses when he grew up. It was a fine thing to do,
but it wasn't the only thing. There were things Allistair's
own father had talked about, like knowing about the
world. Collecting knowledge. Allistair collected knowledge just as his father had done. There were things to find
out about, like stars or birds, he told Garnet. Even sala-
manders. He smiled, rocking his son as he walked across
the grass, which grew in unruly abundance over the edge
of the lawn and down the hill to the orchard at the back.

The gilded blades of grass were distinct, separate. He paused, looking over his land. His small, untidy kingdom.

From the back seat, Allistair peered around Spike's shoulder so he could see the gas gauge. He sat back, satisfied. Spike was telling him about a new thing he was into: making balls that were covered with little bumps and ridges so that they were easier for kids to catch. He was sure it would take off. Allistair knew it would take off, too. Spike had the Midas touch. The trouble was that he didn't stay with these things very long.

"I've got a picture of my house." Spike pulled it awkwardly from his wallet, one hand still on the steering wheel as he unfolded it and gave it to his father. "That's the place I bought near High Park."

Spike handed the photo back to Allistair, who smoothed out a white crease in the middle. The house was larger than he'd expected, with a dark-green front door, brick, three storeys, covered with ivy. But it was in Toronto. They'd wanted him to settle down in Halifax, closer to home.

"Need to get that ivy trimmed back," said Allistair. "I'd get rid of it altogether."

"But you like it?"

"It's a good size. What'd they want for it?"

"They were asking close to eight hundred thousand. I brought them down around seven eighty-five."

Allistair looked back down at the photograph. Almost a million dollars. For a house.

"How much did you put down on it?"

"Well, Jeff and I had just sold those sporting goods stores in Oakville and Mississauga, so I had a little extra to put down on it."

"Cash?"

"I put down some cash. There's still some to pay off."

It wasn't bad at all. But it was hard for Allistair to think in terms of hundreds of thousands of dollars in a way that made it sound like loose change. Cash, no less. It dazed him, scandalized him. But he felt a little glow of pleasure at the same time. This son was smart. Sometimes a smart-ass, but smart nevertheless. They were all smart. Though something was up with Neil and Robin. They thought he didn't see these things. They thought he was oblivious. But he wasn't. He could see into their lives clearly, as though he were standing on a train looking backwards. He could see them playing on a green lawn beside the vege-table garden that Sunday morning years ago when he called them for church. He could see each of them: Evelyn in her blue dress with the white collar, holding a jar, Neil with the trapped toad in his cupped hands, and Spike with the lid, waiting to clap in on the jar. Garnet crawling towards them on the grass. Allistair had called to them, but they hadn't heard. He saw their flushed cheeks and glistening hair, and it seemed that he was moving away from them, knowing he would recede in the distance, in the far distance, without being able to touch them.

SNOWMAN

Verna used to watch Colwell getting into his truck almost every morning. She'd be making coffee and look up as he swung into his truck. Nothing to it. She'd finish making the coffee, start to hum. Everything was as it should be. He was a good neighbour, just as they were good neighbours to him and Liz. But one day Verna poured some coffee into her cup, listening to a twangy song on the radio. *Lester loves a la-a-a-dy and the lady loves him to-o-o-o-o. Lester's past is sha-a-a-dy but the lady is no fool.*

She kept humming that song. Once it was in, it stuck. And she kept thinking about Colwell Dyson. He had kids of his own, and one of them was already in junior high. Liz cut Verna's hair. She'd even given her a home perm once, which Verna had regretted. Verna could think about his wife all she wanted, but when she began to think about Colwell, she thought about laying her head against his chest. She thought about his arms, his hands.

She thought about his feet. It was ridiculous. But after a while there was nothing she could do about it.

She was happy with Allistair. But every morning she timed the coffee-making so she could watch Colwell leave. She saw him out in the yard with Allistair discussing the sag in the barn roof. One Saturday when Allistair was chopping wood with him, first in their yard, then in Colwell's, the sound of the chainsaw ripped through her head. It went on and on, so the children didn't hear what she said and crayoned all over the kitchen table until she banged it with the palm of her hand. The crayons jumped. The purple and red ones fell on the floor and broke. The chainsaw stopped, and first Evelyn started to cry, then Garnet.

Colwell used to come over after supper now and then for a cup of tea with Allistair. They had strong, sweet tea after supper, never coffee. Sometimes Verna ironed in the kitchen while he was there, and sometimes she fussed over the lunches. Her hands were always busy. One night Colwell told Allistair that his wife was sick. He spoke to Allistair but he was telling Verna, too. He was looking straight at their Irving Fuel's calendar, at the picture of Margaree Valley in the fall, with the trees all plumed in scarlet and gold. He didn't glance at either one of them. He asked them to look out for Liz. They didn't know what he meant so they both nodded and Verna went back to scrubbing the roasting pan. He and Allistair didn't speak for a while and she glanced up.

Colwell was still staring mutely at the calendar. She looked at it, too, though she'd seen the picture every day for at least two weeks. There was a church in the valley, a stream, with two boys fishing. Far off in the distance were blue hills, smoky blue, perhaps in the east, perhaps in the west.

Verna kept turning in bed that night, dragging the blankets little by little away from Allistair, and he finally got up and took an extra quilt off the chair, flinging it over himself. She looked at his face as he slept again. He always slept an easy sleep, his cheeks flushed, his mouth completely without expression. She ran a finger tentatively across his nose. He turned his head into the pillow. She thought about Colwell, wondering if he wore striped flannel pyjamas, if he snored, if he continued to sleep with his wife when she was sick. Sick with what? She imagined him sleeping on the threadbare green couch in the living room downstairs, the one with the leaves and flowers carved on the woodwork. Upstairs his wife would be still as a wax figure, completely still, with the sheets and blankets drawn up to her neck.

In one of her dreams she saw Colwell standing beside a river. The river was deep and extremely clear. She could see rocks on the riverbed, jewel-like rocks, and the fish moving between them. The fish were a brilliant reddish orange. They may have been carp, maybe Oriental carp. They moved in folds, in flashes. Colwell called to her but she couldn't make out what he was saying. She put out her hand, which was useless, because he had no way of taking it from that side of the river, at such a distance.

Verna had an idea that dreams could be picked up by other people. Not always. But sometimes she really believed people dreamed together. It was a bit like trees changing colour in the fall. Where did the trees get the idea of changing colour? She never wanted to believe that it had to do with a lack of light. It was a whiff of something in the air. In a mysterious, accurate way trees knew what other trees were up to. It might not seem to have anything to do with anything else, the way one tree turned yellow-orange, a wild yellow-orange, among the sober green. But then all the other trees turned, too.

The next time Colwell came over for tea he watched her as she tidied up the kitchen. He looked at the back of her legs when she stretched up to put the dessert dishes away. She blushed. And she left the kitchen and sat in the living room by herself, doing the mending, when she really wanted to be in the kitchen where it was warmer, where the light made a ring around Allistair and Colwell, sitting together at the table. She sewed a blue button on Evie's overalls, a neat tuck in Garnet's torn undershirt, a wobbly seam in her plaid shirt, which felt like the raised back of a caterpillar when she ran her finger over it. She heard bits of what they were saying. *Liz never went out like that in her life before.* Her darning needle went in and out of

Neil's sock. She went over the same place in the sock until it was finished. *Her dress turned inside out.* She took out some black wool and threaded the needle again. Colwell's voice was lower. *Her slippers. Walking all the way down Hawthorne Street in her slippers.*

She didn't see Liz for a while. She was busy taking Neil and Spike to hockey, picking up Evelyn at Brownies, doing baking for the Christmas bazaar at the church. The next time she did catch a glimpse of her, Liz looked as she always did, in her double-breasted grey fall coat with her red-patterned scarf. Verna checked for anything amiss, like slippers or even a fallen hem, but there was nothing. Perhaps she'd been hoping for something. Maybe, in an indirect way, it was Verna's fault. It was possible.

Colwell came over for tea at least three times a week now. This was fine with Allistair. Sometimes Verna would stay in the kitchen for a while, making the tea and arranging, on one of her mother's Royal Doulton plates, the fine sugar biscuits and the chocolate-cherry squares she'd started making again. When Colwell was right there in the kitchen she'd consider his big hand as he took the teacup from her. It wasn't an attractive hand. The fingers were short. She didn't look at his face as she handed him the cup. She didn't look at Allistair's face either.

She'd think about Colwell's fingers on the inside of her arm. She imagined him touching her, right along there, all the way from the wrist to the elbow. And she daydreamed about making love with him, like Deborah Kerr and Burt

Lancaster in *From Here to Eternity*. Then something would pop into her head, like the fact that Neil needed new winter boots, or that she'd forgotten to call D'arcy MacIsaac about getting a new trap for the kitchen sink. And she'd see how silly it was: Colwell embracing her on the beach, sand in their eyes as they tried to kiss each other.

Liz took herself off to live at Arisaig in the old house that had belonged to her parents. She wanted to be alone for a while. Colwell was sitting at the table as he told them this, his hair wet and dripping down his collar. It was one of those black, wet nights in November when everything was slicked down by the rush of rain. He wiped his hand along the inside of his collar. When Verna poured him tea his hands weren't quite steady. Just yesterday Liz had gone. Up and left, taking the truck. And the cat, too. She'd left a note saying Colwell could come and get the truck when he chose. That was all. Nothing about the kids. Of course, it was just Gabriella and Clayton at home, and Gaby could do most things round the house. But what was he to do?

He looked up at Allistair and Verna, as if they'd know straight off. Allistair said Liz would be all right in a while, just give her a while. Verna didn't say anything. She patted him on the shoulder, a gesture of sympathy. But it wasn't really a gesture of sympathy. It was just that she'd wanted to touch him for a long time and now she could, in passing, for an instant. She wasn't thinking about Liz.

And later, when Allistair opened the back door and then went out to fasten the flapping tarpaulin over the wood-pile, she stood beside him for a moment. Colwell was lacing up his boots, but he stopped. He looked at her and put his hand on her back, right in the small of it. That was all. Then he finished lacing his boots and when Allistair came back he was bent over.

Verna thought about that for a long time. She'd be making a meat loaf and thinking about Colwell. She'd break an egg into the mixture and think of his leg over hers, his chest close against her skin. She thought about his hands and each of his fingers. She thought about his mouth. By the time she'd put in the mustard, the vinegar, a little Worcestershire sauce, she was exhausted. She smiled at the pear tree outside the kitchen window. They'd made love over and over. And afterwards the meat loaf came out of the oven perfectly done, with juice dribbling from it onto the plate. But she'd never liked meat loaf much.

One morning Verna did a great load of laundry through the wringer washer until her hands felt raw. Then she took the things outside and hung them up one by one on the line, though she knew everything would freeze solid: the pyjamas, the tablecloth, the tea towel with the picture of the Grand Canyon that her sister, Theresa Anne, had sent one Christmas. She had to go in once, stepping over Garnet and his toy train, to warm her hands under the hot water faucet. When she went out again, she could see Colwell in his backyard, not doing

anything, just staring at her. She walked down the steps.
He didn't move.

He stood with his arms at his sides, slackly. She stood
next to the vegetable garden where she could have walked
through the little hacked-off stalks, the dead leaves. The
ground was frozen and her shoes wouldn't have left a mark.
Everything she wanted to say was tumbling around in her
head: that she wanted him to touch the small of her back
again, that she had begun humming snatches of a song over
and over, even though she was sick of it. He looked straight
at her. She wanted him. She could feel his gaze on her face,
on her reddened hands holding a damp towel. He had grey
eyes, but they were darker from a distance. When he smiled
his teeth were a little uneven in the front, but he didn't
smile, he just looked at her. It was difficult to meet that
gaze, but she couldn't look away. The wind lifted the hair up
on the top of his head. His golden brown hair, soft and fine
as a child's. It came to her that she would not go to him,
that she would not touch his hair ever in her life, and that
the two of them would go on like this, side by side, never
saying a word. In the hours they stood there it might begin
to snow and she imagined it falling on them, still as they
were. It could fall and keep falling all through the day and
in the end it would cover them. They could lie down in it.

But it wasn't snowing. They'd been standing there a
minute, maybe half a minute. Colwell took a step towards
her. Verna stayed where she was. He buttoned his jacket,
an old plaid jacket with a red button that had been sewn

on later, when the first one had fallen off, and she watched his fingers, clumsy with cold, trying to fit the button through the buttonhole. Then she bent down and picked up a tin pail that Garnet must have left at the edge of the garden. There was a little green car inside the pail that clinked as she picked it up. It must have been while she was looking at it that Colwell went around the side of his house. When she looked up, he'd gone. She could feel tears glazing her eyes, and some crazy thing inside her, jumping like a frog. She went back to the house and sat down in the hall next to Garnet, watching his little fingers laying out track, her face wet and her mouth twisted up in a knot for fear she'd cry out.

Verna didn't like driving when it was dark, especially at the beginning of winter, but she went out that night anyway. There could be patches of black ice and she'd never see them. She told Allistair she was just going over to Gracie MacKenzie's for the craft group, and all he'd have to do was get Neil and Spike into bed after they'd done their homework. It frightened her, lying like that. She drove slowly, peering out the windshield, thinking she could see the sheen of ice at each bend. She thought that she'd miss the place because she'd only been there once before. First she went right by it, past the church and Harley's Variety before she swung around. Then she went down the long drive to the house, stopped the Chrysler, and sat there for a while with the lights out.

The sky was dull and smooth, with nothing to show distance or depth. Her feet were numb with cold as she got out of the car because the heater wasn't working well. She knocked several times, until the porch light went on and Liz opened the door, gesturing impatiently for Verna to step inside so she could shut out the chill air. It was almost as though Liz expected her.

"I haven't gone around the bend or anything," Liz said, leading her down the hall to the kitchen. She lifted the cat off the table and swept away the hairs. "I'll go back home in a few days." She filled the kettle and put it on to boil.

"Well, they miss you," Verna said.

"Maybe. They're a little worried." She leaned against the counter, her hands on the edge of it. "But I had to go away for a while. All I wanted to do was sleep. So that's what I do. I sleep and then when I get up it's time to make supper. Then I sleep again until morning. I've never slept so much in all my life."

"It's what your body needs."

"Well," she said, one side of her mouth crooked up, "it's what my body does."

She got up to make the tea, putting things on a tray. The cups were chipped but they were good china, patterned with roses and tiny gold leaves. She put sugar and milk in Verna's, though she didn't ask for it.

"I've been dreaming," Liz said, "sleeping that much. Once I dreamed the house was flooded and there was nothing I could do. Most of my dreams aren't frightening, though. They're just scattered bits of this and that all run together."

"Dreams are like that. Sometimes I think we're all dreaming each other's dreams."

"Yes," she said, pondering. She drank some tea and Verna sipped hers, surprised by the warmth and sweetness. "That's just it." The cat jumped into Liz's lap. It was a brindled cat: white, brown, and orange.

"I dreamed about Colwell." She patted the cat as it wound itself into a ball on her stomach. "I dreamed that he came into the bedroom and he was just standing there. I didn't know why. It wasn't as if he scared me or anything, it was just that I didn't know what he wanted from me. I had no idea." She stopped talking and stroked the cat. Verna watched her fingers, which were long and tapered at the ends. She kept stroking and stroking the cat, running her hand over the white, the brown, the orange fur. She was crying.

"He loves you," Verna said.

"Yes, I guess he does."

Her hand stopped moving over the cat's body.

"But I don't crave him. Usually I can't get enough of him. But not now."

Verna drank the last of the tea and set the cup on the saucer. "That's to be expected," she said.

"Do you crave Allistair?"

Verna's face flushed. She wasn't prepared for this.

"Of course you do," Liz said.

Verna didn't say anything.

"I'm sorry," she said. "I didn't mean to pry."

"No," Verna said. "I do, but I've never put it quite like that."

"Well." Liz got up abruptly, and the cat had to twist and jump quickly to the floor. "I'm glad you came. Most people are afraid, as if I've turned green or something. But I always thought you're the kind who's not really afraid of anything."

Verna didn't watch for black ice on the way home. She was thinking about Liz and the things she knew. She thought Liz could read her thoughts, the way she'd talked about Colwell. But what business did Liz have asking about Allistair? Then she recalled Liz's hand stroking the cat, that distracted, sad hand. She drove unsteadily, thinking about Liz, about Colwell. How things arise out of sadness. Craving. Did she crave Allistair? Verna thought of the way Allistair stood with his back to her when he was putting on his pyjamas. His body was young and firm, his back straight. She liked the way they rolled, hastily, crazily, across the bed, without caring. Once, years ago, they'd been out by the tourist park at Arisaig when there was no one around. They were sitting on a picnic blanket and she had moved the bag of sandwiches out of the way so they could lie back. His body was warm against hers. Behind him was the Northumberland Strait, the blue, ruler-straight line of ocean that she could see behind his neck

and under his arms when he moved, so it was there, and
then not there, there, and then not. Yes, she craved
him.

Maybe there was a time when she could have left Allistair for Colwell. Or a time when he might have left Liz
for her. But neither one of them did. And in the last few
years Colwell had suffered two heart attacks and Liz was
worried the next one would do him in. It grieved Verna.
They'd become old. And it could be that Verna had
imagined things back then. Perhaps Colwell had never
really touched her at the small of her back. Perhaps he
had never stood in his backyard looking at her. She could
have made it all up, because Allistair always said she had
a wild imagination. She could have dreamed it. It all ran
together now anyway, so that she recalled the dream of
the snow that day together with the dream of Colwell
buttoning up his jacket. She saw the things hanging on
the line: Evie's dress, Neil's striped Sunday shirt, Allistair's socks. She saw them frozen and stiff. And she saw
the snow falling light as breath, in its soft, insistent way,
as if it had something to tell her.

FORTUNE

Allistair drove the Chrysler up the driveway towards the house and backed up beside the porch, putting his arm along the seat and looking over his shoulder. "Chantilly Lace" was on the radio; he was singing along to it. He hoped Verna had made a dinner of pork and beans. There was a garble of children's voices and Spike was running across the Dysons' yard next door. Evelyn called, "Neil's in the tree house."

The laundry billowed out white, gingham, striped. Its clean scent came through the half-open window of the car. Reversing the car slowly, he tilted over something hard, perhaps a tricycle, before the car bumped down again on solid ground. He opened the door quickly, seeing a child's body by the rear wheel. A small hand, plaid shorts, black sneakers, an undone lace. Even as he tugged at him he called his name. *Garnet.* He was lying still. Over his white T-shirt, not quite long enough to cover his belly, was a picture of a red lobster with goggle eyes and waving antennae. His chest may have been rising and falling but Allistair couldn't tell. All he saw was the picture of the lobster with the mark of the tire tread across it, like a brand.

Allistair's grandmother once read him a story from a leather-covered book with gold-tooled binding. Each page was edged with gold. The story was about a prince rescuing his brothers, saving the kingdom, and winning a princess. But his grandmother said it was a story about finding fortune. When she finished reading it she looked at him, tamping the tobacco down in her pipe, and said that it would happen to him sometime. She had an odd smile that turned up on one side and down on the other, because she'd had Bell's palsy. Her dress was pink and white, patterned with windmills. There were two ducks in front of each windmill. He concentrated on the ducks so that he wouldn't look at her mouth slipping down on the left side.

When Verna Desormeaux leaned over the counter at the Snow King fourteen years later and kissed him, Allistair remembered what his grandmother had said. He didn't expect it to happen. It was just another shift at work and he was finishing up, wiping the counters and tables. He had to mop the floor, too, turn out the lights, and lock both doors, but Jeannie Archibald and Verna were sitting at one of the tables, giggling. He had to work around them. Jeannie had eyebrows that arched up as if he'd insulted her. Verna had a smooth face and dark eyes that could have been grey or blue. He went back to the cash to count the bills and looked up to find her standing in front of him. She leaned over, in full view of Jeannie, so that her lips brushed against his. It was hardly a kiss, and even before she turned away it occurred to him that Jeannie had set her up to it. Maybe bet a dime that Verna couldn't do it. He could hear Jeannie chuckling as they left, a snicking sound that reminded him of scissors.

Verna didn't show up at the Snow King again but he thought about her. He'd discovered something, like the first time he'd had a swig of his grandfather's Glenfiddich. He almost hated the sweet, rich burning inside his mouth, down his throat. But he wanted Verna. He wanted her so much that he asked Sharlene MacIsaac to the May dance and then he didn't know why. They stayed out in his brother Frank's truck at the far end of the parking lot where he could get her to roll up her sweater and hitch up her skirt, which was as much as she would do. So they sat up after a while, Sharlene pulling down her sweater with one hand and patting her hair into place with the other, saying she wished she had some spray to get it back into shape. They drank rum, hidden in a paper bag, until she threw up out the window and he drove her home. Then he cruised down Main Street and along Church, through the university and out to the Trans-Canada. There was nowhere to go. He started along the Lochaber Road absently, slowing down to pass a girl. She turned, looking straight at him, though she couldn't see anything in the glare. Verna. He stopped for her, leaning over to open the door, and she got in. They went all the way to St. Joseph's without saying much of anything until he pulled into the lane at her place.

"I'm not seeing Bart Chisholm any more," she said.

She had her hand on the door handle.

"I'll come around tomorrow night and see what you're doing, then," he said.

Fortune had fallen into his lap.

He told Verna he wanted to marry her. They were sitting by Lochaber Lake, flinging stones into the water. She couldn't make them skip but kept trying. He gave her some bigger stones and showed her how to flick her wrist. It was warm; he wiped his forehead. He'd get enough work doing carpentry from spring to fall, he told her, and then maybe he'd do odd jobs through the winter. She piled up a little tower of stones beside her. One day he'd start a construction business and have guys like Shane McCormick and Ed Duggan work for him. Guys that knew the business. She toppled the tower of stones with her finger, stood up suddenly, and took off her blouse, her shorts. She was clad only in her brassiere, her blue panties with forget-me-nots. Then she splashed quickly into the water, and when she was out far enough she ducked under, coming up with her head, her blonde hair gone dark, sleek and shiny. Laughing.

He scrambled up, taking off his clothes as fast as he could and almost tripping himself getting out of his

trousers. Then he ran into the lake, hooting like a crazy
man. She splashed his face, so he dove under her white
legs and tried to catch her by the feet. But she swam
away, then dove and yanked at his ankles with unex-
pected force, pulling him down. It was only for a
moment, but he flailed his arms in the weedy darkness,
and when she let go he shot out of the water, gasping.
She surfaced at his back, gulping air.

"No," she said.

The things Allistair regretted flew at him, white and
huge, a sheet on a line, ballooning into his face. All the
time, he could hear his voice calling Verna's name as he
pulled the sheet down. Then he heard a strangled sound
and turned to find her kneeling over Garnet, rocking a
little. She had half-lifted him so his head was in her lap.
Allistair went towards her, slowly, with an end of sheet
still wound around his right foot until he kicked it loose.
She rocked back and forth, a strand of hair brushing Garnet's face as she moved. On the asphalt were his son's
legs, feet turned out, as if he were sleeping.

Verna always maintained she picked Allistair and he didn't
have much to do with it. She knew she wanted a small
wedding so that the whole damn county wouldn't be there,
a simple ring, same as her mother's, and a promise from
him that they wouldn't have more than two children. She
didn't want to spend her life cleaning up after children.

They did have a small wedding, with just enough family on
both sides to keep everyone happy, except that Verna's
mother's cousin Donalda, who had a tongue she could cut
herself on, made a fuss about not being invited. Allistair
got Verna a wedding band from MacKenzie's that matched
her engagement ring, the one with a small sapphire and
two diamonds, which she said was adorable, just absolutely
adorable, so he didn't mind the fact that he'd be paying
them both off one month at a time. But as for children,
they had four, not counting the one she miscarried
between Neil and Spike. The last one was Garnet, named
after his father, who was definitely the last one, Verna said,
or she'd move out and leave him.

Garnet had hair that shone, yellow as butter. Verna
called him her little cupcake, her little dupdake. He woke
a lot in the night during the first year and Allistair got up
with him, just as he had with the others, and rocked him
in his arms, crooning "Love Me Tender." He'd fall asleep
and then Allistair put him gently back in the crib, drawing up the blankets. That was when Garnet's eyes would
open, dark and wide, and he'd have to pick him up again
and start all over. He'd give him a bottle and then hold
him against his shoulder until he burped, sleepily. Then
he'd try to put him down again. Sometimes it worked and
he would creep stealthily back into bed, warming himself
against Verna's body. But he would still be awake, taut as
a stretched elastic, waiting until he could hear the steady
rise and fall of sleeping breath from the crib.

Allistair didn't mind being awake in the middle of the night. He'd just got the contract to do up the Prince Edward Hotel. And here they had a big house already and a Chrysler parked out front. He had a second-hand truck, too, but he parked it by the barn. Every Saturday he washed the car with Neil and Stephen, just so that he could see it shine whenever he glanced out a window. These things surprised him. But all of it had started with Verna, when she'd kissed him that first time, like lightning slicing a tree wide open.

At the hospital they told Allistair that his son could have broken his neck. They showed him the X-rays, which Doc Welsh slapped up against the light on the wall. He told him to look closely and he did, examining the collarbone wings, the hoops of rib, the faint, curved spine. Garnet was lucky, Doc told him, because there wasn't one fracture, not one break anywhere. He'd be all right. Right as rain. Then he clapped Allistair on the shoulder and said that it was a good thing, because, after all, things might have gone differently. But Allistair stood looking at the X-rays, hardly hearing what he said. The white against the black shocked him. They were small bones, a child's bones, and the spaces between them were shiny and dark, filled with nothing at all.

Garnet didn't remember what happened. He grew tall, his hair gradually darkening, and played on his own most of the time. Sometimes he tagged after Neil and Spike, even when they yelled at him to go home. He climbed the fence at the baseball diamond and hung there, upside down, for an entire inning. "You're weird," Neil would tell him. "You're an idiot," Spike would say. He often sat in the crook of the oak tree, snagging toys in the grass with his fishing line. Once he caught it in Evelyn's hair, so she stamped her feet, yelling at him and tangling her hair so much that Verna had to cut out the hook.

One summer night Allistair found the window open in Garnet's room and his bed empty. He checked under the bed and in the closet. He looked out the window, scanning the porch roof. Then he ran outside, expecting to see his inert body lying on the grass, but there was nothing except a rustle in the oak tree and a flash of white. When he stood under it he could see Garnet's pale feet. Allistair told him to come down, but he didn't move for a moment. Then he scrambled down, shaking the branches, and Allistair held him close.

"I'm afraid," Garnet said.

"Of what?"

"I don't know."

The night pressed against them. There was a rectangle of light from the hall window, but it wasn't enough to dispel the dark. Allistair picked him up and carried him into the house. It was difficult taking him up the steps and by the time he reached the landing his breath came in little gasps. He was losing something, but it wasn't anything he could name.

The car lifted and jolted back down to the ground. Allistair was afraid even before he opened the car door. The feet were like his own, bare and crooked outward. The hand was that of a man. Allistair tugged at him, but it was much more difficult to pull such a heavy body, such long limbs. He knew his son's face, though it was older, but he didn't know what to say so that Garnet would open his eyes. He could only lay his hand on the tire tread mark across his chest.

Garnet left home when he was eighteen. He worked as a stevedore in Halifax, at a time when there was more work in that sort of thing. After a while he moved to Boston. Once he sent a letter saying he had married a girl called Cinta at the city hall and he would bring her home to visit. He enclosed a photograph of her sitting on the front steps of the library in Boston. Verna didn't comment on her long legs, the skimpy sundress that showed her breasts, snug as two loaves of bread, her wide-brimmed hat, her eyeliner, and the earrings that dragged down the lobes of her ears. The girl seemed to be smiling, but it wasn't easy to tell if it was a smile or just the set of her lips. Allistair scanned the photograph for clues about Garnet, but there wasn't anything, not even a ring.

Neil visited Garnet once in Boston but when he came back he didn't say much. He just mentioned that Garnet

and Cinta drank too much. He didn't say that he'd found
Garnet fully dressed in a bathtub with the tap going, with
the lukewarm water rising all around him. But they found
out these things soon enough, after the letter that came
from Cinta, with its long sentences and misspelled words.
She'd always loved Garnet, always, even when it wasn't
easy, so it wasn't her idea to leave, but she thought she'd
better get out and try to find a life for herself. She'd never
once said she didn't love him.

Allistair had taught his children to swim. He took them on
his back, telling them to clasp their hands around his neck.

"It'll be all right," he told them. "Just let yourself
float."

Sometimes the water was too cold. But Allistair persisted, while Verna watched from a distance, sitting on
the beach with her white bathing cap, her bathing suit
with the frilly skirt. Occasionally she came in, and swam
right past them with strong, easy strokes.

"The Milky Way," he said to Garnet, watching her go.
Out of the corner of his eye he could keep an eye on Neil,
Spike, and Evelyn having a water fight near the shore.
"And you're a little star floating all by yourself."

"I don't want to be all by myself," Garnet told him. "I
want to be with you."

"Well, then, we're together. There are stars like that.
Binary stars, I think they are. We'll be two stars together.
We'll go around and around and around."

He swam in circles until Garnet started to laugh wildly, joyously. He howled with laughter.

All the children left home, so that only Verna and Allistair were left. Once he found Verna after work, sitting in the kitchen, where she'd sat half the day. She was going down to Boston, she told him, turning. There was a puffiness under her eyes. She was going on Wednesday and she could take the bus. She'd stay with Lily MacIntyre. He put his hand over hers but she pulled it away. Then she turned her head so she was looking into the light, which didn't seem to trouble her. She'd been thinking about it for a long while.

But what if Garnet wasn't in Boston any more? What if he'd moved? It had been a year and a half since Neil had seen him. Anything could have happened. Though she had pushed out a chair for him, Allistair kept standing, gazing in the same direction out the kitchen window, at the pear tree that he should have pruned long ago. She made a little noise and covered her face with her hands. He put his hand on her head, then both hands, taking out her clip and combing his fingers through her hair, saying that maybe it would be a good thing if she went. Then he bent and kissed her head.

When Allistair was born his grandfather planted an apple tree. Its apples were always small and hard. But in spring it bloomed with pinkish white flowers that fell on the grass in little drifts. He could see it from his bedroom window if he leaned over the desk and looked out. Once, late at night, he watched a woman picking a few blossoms from it. At first he could only see her white neck and arms. His parents were having a party and he could hear Lauchie MacVicar playing the piano while someone else sang "Down by the Sally Gardens." Afterwards Allistair's father came outside, moving clumsily towards the tree. He talked quietly to the woman so that Allistair could only catch a word or two. "Louise, I can't—I just can't." His father walked away and then came back. He seemed loosely put together, as if he didn't have bones at all. He put up his hand as if he were going to touch the woman's face, but then he dropped it and touched her arm instead, at the crook of her elbow.

A day and a half later they found his father's body at Pomquet, on a stretch of white sand, but it was some time before they found the clothes piled up neatly on a flat rock, the watch lying on top.

One evening after Verna had gone to Boston, Allistair drove out to Pomquet. He hadn't been there in years. It was a warm evening and he could have walked on the beach. Instead, he stayed where he was on the boardwalk. The waves drew in, then out. One man strolled along the shore, bending now and then over the stones. The tides never went out very far, so there were no dramatic changes. To the left was the farm on the hill, with its broad field stretching down to the shore. There was nothing to show that anything had ever happened here, that anything of any significance ever washed up. He gazed at the water, pondering the horizon. It would be cold even at this time of year. He thought of his father, naked, his hair around his face, his body loose, rolling over like a seal, as a wave carried him in. It was not his father's body, but Garnet's. Then it disappeared and there was nothing but ocean and some gulls screaming over bits of litter in the dunes.

Allistair had always had good luck, as his grandmother had told him. He'd had everything he wanted. The sun, going down, touched the moving water. The man who had been walking along the shore was retracing his steps. But his good luck wasn't something he could give away. The man walked up and over a ridge of sand through the feathers of dune grass. He stooped and picked up a soda can, pocketed it, and continued past Allistair up the boardwalk. There was nothing he could do for Garnet. Nothing Verna could do. He made his way back along the silvery boards, past the poison ivy and the wild roses. But he couldn't just stand by and watch. He came to the end of the boardwalk and looked back. There was nothing except spruce trees and the slightly uneven boards, narrowing in the distance.

TANTRAMAR

"Where did you ever read that?" asked Robin, pushing against the driver's seat to stretch her back.

"I don't know. *National Geographic*," said Evelyn.

"*National Geographic!*" laughed Robin. "I don't think so."

"Well, I read it somewhere. Something about how if it gets really hard, there's a chance the cartilage could break."

"Is there cartilage in it?"

"Sure."

"But break right in two? You were worried that Kevin Hadley's penis might break in two?"

"Well, I'd never seen anything like it," said Evelyn. "I mean, he was just lying there on the grass with this thing sticking straight up in the air. I was amazed he could keep it up like that."

"So what did you do?"

"Well, I just got up and left him there, and then I took off all the way down the Brierly Brook road."

"With Kevin behind you?"

"No. The Margesons' black Lab."

"And Kevin still lying there," laughed Robin. "Broken in two."

By the side of the road, a teenager jolted up and down on an all-terrain vehicle across a verge of field. There was a flash of yellow T-shirt behind a screen of spruce trees. They passed a trailer park and something flashed in a window. A woman opened the door of one of the trailers and shook a mat, snapping it. Then some poplars obscured her and for a mile or two there was nothing but trees.

"Brian Prosper once told me I was frigid," said Robin.

"Because you wouldn't have sex with him?"

"Well, he smelled a bit."

"He smelled!"

"I don't know what it was," said Robin. "It wasn't BO as far as I could make out. It smelled like mildew."

"Oh, God, I can't stand it," Evelyn laughed. "The poor guy had mildew."

"I mean, I fully intended to go ahead with things that night. It was the prom and everything. But when it came right down to it I just chickened out. I had to wait four more years. And then when it happened I thought, Well, so what's the big deal?"

"That's what I thought." Evelyn grinned. "With Tony Koerner. He had a wonky eye." She glanced out the window at a restaurant with a giant-sized lobster trap on the roof. A plastic claw stuck out of the trap. In front

was a large, neatly lettered sign: HOT FOOD. MICROWAVE
IN USE. "Anyway, it was just the once with him," she
mused.

"Probably just as well."

"How'd we end up with those guys?"

"God only knows."

The first time Phonse put his hand between her legs,
gently, and rubbed the inside of her thigh, she could feel
her skin tingling. He stroked her body affectionately all
over, along the hollow place in her hip, around her
breasts, behind her buttocks. He had tender hands. She
couldn't remember ever being touched like that before.
Not by Duncan, in all the time they'd been married.
Phonse could lure her with his hands alone, letting his
lazy fingers move over her skin.

"The first time Neil and I slept together, he sent roses
the next day," said Robin.

"Oh, you're kidding."

"No," Robin said.

"When they don't know what to say, they send flowers."

"He sent me flowers a couple of times that summer,"
said Robin. She took one hand off the wheel and combed
her hair behind her ear.

Evelyn had taken some of the photographs the day
Robin and Neil were married. One showed Neil beside
Robin as they posed in front of the cake. He had a look
on his face as though he were slightly mystified by all the
fuss, as if he'd just woken up. Maybe it was because he'd

taken his glasses off for the photograph. Then he and
Robin held the knife together and tried to cut the cake,
but she was laughing, so the next photograph showed her
face, with a wispy strand of blonde hair in her eyes,
mouth wide open, while Neil looked down, guiding her
hand, concentrating on slicing a neat piece of cake. Only
part of his head was visible in that photograph, his hand
poised over Robin's.

"We caught Neil once with Barbara Gooley." Evelyn
was smiling. "Behind the barn. He was French-kissing her."

"Barbara Gooley?"

"He must have been about sixteen," said Evelyn. "Barbara was older than he was and she always wore those
house dresses with her brother's sweater over top. That
beige sweater with the green moose on the back. Spike
and I had this idea of pouring water over their heads,
except we had to get up on the roof of the barn without
spilling the water and Spike was killing himself laughing,
so he wasn't any help."

"So you did it?"

"I missed. Maybe I got the back of Neil's neck wet, but
that was all."

They passed two cyclists stopped on the side of the
road. The woman stared vacantly ahead of her, holding
her bicycle with one hand, while the man bent down to
massage her calf muscles. He was all in black, which
made him look dangerous, like a terrorist.

"It seems funny to think we were so obsessed with each

other," Robin said absently. "Or that I'd wind up with Neil. I mean, it could have been almost anyone."

Whenever Phonse was making love to Evelyn, breathing hard, she'd close her eyes and see Duncan for a moment. It would irritate her, the way other lovers crowded into her head. As if they had a right to be there. She'd open her eyes and see Phonse's face, twisted with effort, and feel comforted. It wasn't that she loved Phonse, because she wasn't sure she did, even though she'd told him that once or twice. She didn't really consider love to be the thing that drew her to him. They wanted each other. They hadn't stopped wanting each other.

"Greg was the first," Robin was saying. "I was crazy about him. I couldn't imagine anyone else."

"Then he turned out to be a jerk. Or what?"

"Sometimes I think, well, what's the point?" said Robin. "Sometimes I think that."

Evelyn and Phonse had been over at Robin and Neil's for dinner a month before. Luke hadn't gone because he'd gotten a part-time job packing groceries at Sobey's and he was out most evenings. Phonse didn't really want to go. Once he got there, though, he was happy enough. He even put a new washer on the tap in the kitchen sink when he saw it was dripping. He and Neil went into the living room, talking about entertainment units, while Evelyn watched Robin chop up some vegetables on a board. Robin made neat, quick movements with the knife, never lifting the blade completely off the board. Then she swept all the celery and green pepper into the wooden salad bowl.

"They've got nice ones for sale at Sears," Phonse was saying. "Mahogany look."

"Well, I don't know if that's quite what Robin had in mind," Neil replied. "She wants something that looks antique, an armoire sort of thing."

Robin put a sweet red pepper on the board and Evelyn watched as it fell into perfect slices under the knife. She'd offered to help, but Robin had said no, she'd got everything under control. So Evelyn sat holding her glass of white wine, watching.

"I've made that kind of thing before," said Phonse.

"I imagine it takes a lot of work," said Neil.

"Not really. You can knock those things together inside of a day."

Robin paused, listening. She rested the heel of her hand on the side of the counter.

"Well, we've got a cabinetmaker in Halifax working on this," Neil said. "He's going to make it out of cherry. He can do it without nails, just pegs."

"No nails," Phonse said.

"He drew up a design for us. It'll change, of course, but he's got the right idea. Lots of beautiful mortise-and-tenon joints. I'll show you."

They went down the hall to the study.

"Shit," said Robin. "Why does Neil do that?"

"What?" said Evelyn.

"That thing he does to people. I hate it." Her face was flushed. She twisted her hair back into an elastic to keep it out of her eyes. "I swear, Evie," she said. "If things don't change."

"I've never seen anyone so taken with someone as Phonse is with you," Robin said.

"He's good to me," said Evelyn. "And I'm good to him." She was looking at the bumper sticker on the car in front: HIGHLAND DANCERS LOVE A FLING.

"He'd do anything for you. He'd cut off his right hand if you asked him," Robin went on.

"Why would I ask him to cut off his right hand?"

Evelyn had met Phonse at the mall when he'd been selling lobsters from the back of his truck. She'd seen him before. He was stooped a little to one side with scoliosis and his hands were large and red. They made her think of raw meat. Yet his face was wide and pleasant, his eyes hazel. She found herself smiling at him and the next thing she knew he was driving her to the Ultramar station to pick up her car. She had no idea what to say to him, so she said nothing. But when she got out of the truck, Phonse fished out a couple of lobsters for her, put them in a large plastic bag, and knotted the bag with a flip and a twist. She thanked him, and all the way home the lobsters seemed to be fighting to get out of the bag. All her life she'd hated eating lobster. When she got home she didn't want to touch them, so Luke went out to the car and brought them in. He had to drop them in the boiling water, too, because she didn't have the heart.

They were coming to Amherst and now the land was wide open, less crowded with trees. They passed a farm where a man was fixing a For Sale sign in the windshield of a blue truck. A boy on his bicycle popped a wheelie. They went by a yellow house, then a small pink one, in which a blind rolled up suddenly in an upstairs window.

"I don't know if I've ever really been in love," said Robin.

"Sure you have."

"When I was growing up there was an old couple who lived beside us," said Robin. "She wanted me to call her Auntie O. Her husband Marshall was always doing things like leaving the water running in the bathtub. Once she ran over to our place in the middle of winter, just in her slip and cardigan, because Marshall had started a fire in the wastebasket. And then he died all of a sudden and we went over to the house after the funeral. She clung to my father's hand, crying, asking what would she do, whatever would she do. I could see how much she loved him, that skinny little man with the liver spots on his hands, how much she missed him."

Evelyn watched a man kicking at the door of his van on the side of the road.

"That was grief," she said. "More than anything."

Once they passed Amherst they could see the Tantramar marshland. On one side of the road past the railway tracks, far off, was a shimmer, a glimpse of the Chignecto, and on the other side were dense grasses that looked as if they'd been combed over hummocks, this way and that, like unruly hair. Evelyn imagined the Acadians building their dikes, as her father had told her, with nothing but wattles of criss-crossed trees, logs, and mud to hold back the water. It would have seeped in anyway. She could feel it. It seemed to her that there was nothing substantial here; not the road, not the railway tracks, not the CBC radio towers. But the wind and tides were forces to be reckoned with, pushing and pulling.

"I always thought it held things together," Robin was saying. "Being married."

"People believe in it."

"On the whole I think it's a good thing." Robin gazed at the radio towers, each one stiff and separate. "As long as there's love in it."

They were silent. Robin had her eyes fixed on the road and the fur of marsh grass beyond it, sucking on a knuckle, and Evelyn thought how strange it was, the way the land ended, diminishing into air, or water. She couldn't quite tell.

SCORCH MARK

Phonse gave Evelyn a present the first night he stayed over. It was a candleholder shaped like a crescent moon. Duncan would never have given her anything like it.

"Go ahead and light it," he said, giving her a candle and some matches. "I wanted to get you a heart with mirrors in it, but they didn't have any more."

"I like this one."

He unbuttoned her shirt.

"Look at you," he said. "You beautiful woman."

"Oh, I am not."

"I'd like to take a picture of you like this. Here, lie back." She lay back and he slipped his hand inside her unbuttoned shirt. "Just like this."

"Not my thighs, all right?"

"Oh, that's the best part," he said, taking off his shirt and lying down beside her. "Can't leave them out."

"Well, now," she said, considering. "I'd like to take a picture of you, too."

"Hmm."

"Your chest. Your gut."

"My great body," he said, grinning.

"Mmm," she said, running her hand over his chest. "I love your body." She licked her thumb and forefinger, reached over, and put the candle out.

There were things about being married to Duncan that Evelyn kept recalling. Except that it wasn't a marriage any more, it was a broken marriage.

There was the day she nearly killed someone just after she went to the doctor's. On the way out of the parking lot, the car barely warmed up, she collided with J.D. MacEwen on his old bicycle. He rode right into her path, flew off the bicycle, and landed against the windshield, where she could see the picture of Peggy's Cove on the sweatshirt under his half-opened parka. A gloved hand was pressed against the glass. Then he slid off the hood and stood in front of the car, shaking his head. When she got out he jumped on his bicycle and rode away, the pompon on his black-and-white-striped toque bobbing up and down. She called after him but he didn't hear her.

When Duncan came home from work that night she told him there was a dent in the hood of the car. He went outside with a flashlight even though it was nineteen below, and when he came back in he told her there were two dents and a few scratches. They'd have to get it repaired as soon as possible. He put the flashlight into the broom closet and broke a lace as he yanked off a boot.

"I'm pregnant," she said.

"What?"

"I'm going to have a baby."

"You're sure?"

"No," she said, rinsing a glass in the sink.

He walked over to a kitchen chair with one boot on and the other in his hand. He sat down and looked at her. "You mean you might be pregnant."

"Yes. I'm just waiting to hear from the doctor."

"Why didn't you say that?"

"I thought you'd be happy," she said.

"I'm happy." He unlaced the other boot and pulled it off. "First you tell me you had an accident today and then I find out there's a couple of thousand dollars' worth of damage to the car and then you tell me that you think you might be pregnant. It's not easy to keep up."

"I knew you'd be happy about it," she said, and put the glass, still dripping wet, into the cupboard.

The first Christmas Phonse spent with Evelyn there was no snow. It rained for three days before Christmas and then it turned cold. There was ice everywhere: on the driveways, sidewalks, roads. Duncan came to pick up Luke on Christmas Day and he slipped and fell on the ice walking to the back door. It put him in a bad mood.

"Where's Luke?" he asked, coming in the door and glancing at Phonse.

"He's not here," said Evelyn. "He's still out with Brad Wheeler playing street hockey. They went to the Heights."

"I told him four o'clock sharp."

"He'll be back."

"Well, it's not as if he didn't know. He's going to screw up everything. My mother's not going to want supper spoiled because—"

"Have a seat, Duncan," said Evelyn.

"No thanks," he said.

"This is Phonse."

"I know," said Duncan. "Hello."

"Hello," said Phonse.

"Listen, I think I'll take a spin to the Heights and see if they're there," said Duncan. "I'll come back if I can't find them."

He didn't find them. They could hear his car skidding in the driveway when he came back.

"Where the hell is that kid?" he asked when he came in.

"I don't know," said Evelyn. "Take your coat off."

"What, you think I'm a guest or something? You've already got a guest. I used to be your husband, not some sort of guest."

Evelyn turned and went into the kitchen.

He followed her, without taking his boots off. "I used to be your husband," he said, louder.

"I heard you." She bent down to open the stove and baste the small turkey.

"Until you ran out on me," he said.

Phonse came to the kitchen door.

"She ran out on me," said Duncan, turning to Phonse.

"Duncan," said Evelyn warningly, closing the oven door and moving over to Phonse. She took off the oven mitts and tossed them on the counter.

"She took Luke. Now he forgets that I'm his father. He goes off and —"

"Maybe you should go, Duncan," said Evelyn.

"Hell, no," he said. "You invited me in. You said, 'Take your coat off.' Here, I'll take my coat off. You wanted me to make myself at home?" He grabbed the oven mitts and opened the oven. "Fine, I'll make myself at home." He took out the roasting pan and carried it around the kitchen counter to the dining-room table, where he set it down with a bang. He must have known it would leave a white scorch mark. "There," he said. "There."

Evelyn looked at him through the coloured glass baubles that hung over the counter. One of them swung a little.

"Dad?" called Luke from the front door. "Dad?" He came into the kitchen and saw his father, still wearing the red oven mitts. "What's going on?"

"Nothing," said Evelyn. She burst into tears and ran upstairs.

What Evelyn remembered most vividly was Luke's birth.

After fourteen hours she was still only eight centimetres dilated. So the doctor induced her, feeding greenish liquid into her bloodstream through an IV. No one asked her.

The doctor vanished. Then the contractions were so painful she didn't think she could stand it. She wanted to scream obscenities at the nurse or Duncan, whose hand hovered above her forehead, clutching a white washcloth. She didn't want him to touch her with the washcloth.

"Don't," she told him breathlessly.

"It's all right." He wiped her forehead with the washcloth. "It'll make you feel better."

She turned her head away, gripping rails of the bed against the force of the next contraction. It was like being hit by a truck. Maybe it would kill her. Vaguely, she could make out what Duncan was saying to the nurse. Something about the first big storm of the season and what it was going to do to the roads. The nurse's name was Raylene. She wanted to get home to Frankville in one piece but at this rate she didn't know when she'd get there. God only knew. Just before Hallowe'en there was a woman from Port Hawkesbury who went right off the road at Dagger Woods. That was the end of her. And she had the sweetest little eighteen-month-old who kept asking where her mommy had gone.

Evelyn yelped.

"There now, the baby's crowning," said Raylene. "All right dear, breathe. Fine, breathe. And breathe. Now push hard. Get mad. That's it."

Evelyn pushed hard, grunting loudly with the effort.

"Forceps, I think," said the doctor, who had reappeared. "This one doesn't seem to want to come down."

Evelyn felt something hard and cold.

"Now we'll get it," said the doctor.

"It won't be long now, dear," Raylene said, moving around the bed. "Oh, here it comes. Now don't push until I say. Breathe, breathe, breathe, all right, now get good and mad. Push!"

She pushed.

"Push! Come on! Push!"

Evelyn could see a little spangling of stars in front of her closed eyes, but she kept pushing as hard as she could.

"All right now, settle down and relax," said Raylene.

Evelyn tried to relax.

"But that wasn't the end of it," Raylene was saying in an undertone to Duncan. "After the accident, Bob started going on benders and he just went all to hell. Oh, here she goes again. Yes, she'll do it this time. Breathe, breathe, breathe, and now bear down hard. Push!"

"We've got it," said the doctor.

Something slid out between Evelyn's legs and Raylene caught it in her gloved hands.

"It's a boy, dear," said Raylene. "A little boy. He's some cute."

After Duncan left with Luke that Christmas, Evelyn lay down on the bed upstairs. She couldn't stop crying.

"Evie," said Phonse. He sat beside her on the bed.

"Go away," she said, her voice muffled.

He put his hand soothingly on her back.

"How could he do that?" she cried.

"I don't know," said Phonse.

"I hate him," she sobbed. "Oh, I hate him."

"It's all right," said Phonse.

"No, it's not all right," she said, turning over and wiping her nose. "It's not. I don't want to live with anyone. You or Duncan or anyone. I just want Luke in this house. With me."

"Okay," said Phonse. He rubbed the top of his hand with the palm of the other.

"I don't need anyone," she said.

"I know that," he said. He got up from the bed and stood looking out the window at the headlights of a passing car. "I'm not Duncan, you know," he said.

"I don't need anyone," she said again.

"He's got me angry, too," said Phonse. "But if you want me to go, I'll go."

"I want you to go."

Even with the pillow over her head she could hear him start up his truck and back out of the driveway.

When Raylene nestled the baby in Evelyn's arms, wrapped in a length of flannelette, she couldn't quite believe it. She laid him against her chest, looking at him, examining the marks on the side of his face where they'd used forceps. Afterwards, when they took her down the hall in a wheelchair, with Raylene propelling the IV stand alongside, she didn't want to give him up when they came to the nursery. Raylene said that she had to get some rest now and they'd bring her the baby later. She was given hot tea, sweetened with sugar, which she sipped while Duncan sat on the bed, stroking her hand.

"What should we name him?" asked Duncan.

"Let's wait for a bit," said Evelyn.

"Well, I'd like to name him Luke, after my father. If it's all right with you."

Evelyn sipped the tea. It soothed her. She could see white flakes of snow drifting past the window. She took another sip of tea.

"I'm pretty worn out," said Duncan. "I think I'll go home for a sleep and come back later. Okay?"

"Can you ask them to bring him in here before you go?" she asked.

"You need to sleep," he said.

"I just want to see him."

He went away and came back with a cart in which the baby lay, snugly wrapped, asleep.

"I'll put him over here," he said.

"No, put him right here in bed. I want to look at him."

After Duncan left, Evelyn lay close to her baby. Her son. And outside the window the snow still fell. Hundreds of bits of paper. It fell more thickly, whirling and flying up, then down. Her eyes closed and she drifted into sleep.

Evelyn thought about Phonse after she sent him away. She thought about his ugly nose, his brown eyes, his

large hands. His hands were like animals, she'd told him,
with all that hair growing on them. He'd laughed, turning them over. She missed him standing in the kitchen
making his chowder, tasting it with a spoon. The creamy
taste. His boots by the door. His flannel shirt with the
tear over the pocket that he told her he was going to
mend. The little paperweight he'd given her with a tiny
schooner sailing on a wild blue sea. She'd put the paperweight away in a locked drawer. She'd put the crescent-
shaped candleholder under the bed. Once she put it
beside her bed and lit the candle, watching the thin
flame. It hissed when she put it out. Then she put it in
the locked drawer along with the paperweight. It was
time to get over these things. She could get along just
fine.

When Duncan came back to see her the day after Luke
was born, he sat on her bed and gazed at her. The baby
was at her breast and she was trying to get him to suckle.

"I love you," he said tenderly.

"I love you, too." She didn't look at him.

"I'm a father. I can't believe it."

There was something wrong with the way the baby was
latched onto her nipple. She shifted position. "Aaah!"
she said sharply.

"What?" asked Duncan.

"It hurts. I don't think I'm doing this right. There isn't
any milk yet anyway."

"It'll come," he said. "You just have to get used to it."

She glanced at him.

"You two are beautiful," he said.

She knew she didn't look beautiful. Her hair was a mess, for one thing. Her lips were chapped. There were blue shadows under her eyes.

"Well, I have to get to work today," he said. "I'll come by at noon and see how you're getting along."

And then he left them alone.

"I just called to see how you're doing," said Evelyn, twisting the phone cord in one hand. She couldn't gather up the courage to say she'd missed him.

"I'm okay," said Phonse.

She picked up a pencil and doodled on the notepad.

"How are you?" he asked.

"Good."

"How's Luke?"

"Good." She drew a triangle. "Duncan called. He said he was sorry."

"Well, at least he did that much."

Inside the pencilled triangle she drew a box.

"You wouldn't want to come over, would you?" she asked, putting a star inside the box. Then she crossed out the triangle, the box, and the star with pencil marks that were heavy and dark, firmly obliterating the doodles.

"Sure."

She rested her head against the wall. "Do you want to come for supper, then?"

"All right."

Evelyn and Phonse had begun living together in May. They'd been living together for a few months when Luke told Evelyn that his girlfriend's parents were splitting up. He was sitting at the kitchen table with one leg up on the chair across from him, drinking a can of cherry cola.

"Tara's really pissed at them," he said.

"Well, I guess she has a right to feel that way," Evelyn said.

"Yeah," he said, "she does. It screws you up."

Evelyn was looking out the window at the green lawn where Phonse was shearing the edges with an electric trimmer. She turned around and leaned against the counter.

"Does it?"

"I don't know." He fingered the hole in the top of the can.

She spoke as evenly as possible. "I had to go. I couldn't stay."

"Yeah, well," he said, getting up from the table and firing the cherry cola can into the garbage. "You didn't ask me."

It was a relief when Duncan left them alone in the hospital room. Evelyn wanted to cuddle the baby close and talk to him, but she didn't want to do it in front of Duncan.

"Sweetie," she whispered to the baby. "My sweetie." She touched the top of his head delicately, running her fingers over the veins, over the soft fontanelle. His ear was minute, fine as a sculpture. She touched it lightly. His mouth quivered a little as he sucked at her breast. She could feel it deep in her body, pulling at her. Stronger than anything she'd ever felt before. She had no words for it, but she knew it would pull at her every day for the rest of her life.

WAVE PHYSICS

A Siberian husky was in a truck in front of them, wind ruffling its fur. There were dark patches around its clear, almost white eyes. Then the truck turned and jerked along a dirt road, making the dog's head shake. The dog had uncanny eyes, thought Robin. *Uncanny.* Neil had taught her the exact meaning of that word. Strange, otherworldly, mysterious. Not quite the opposite of *canny*, which meant something closer to shrewd, or calculating.

Neil, the expert. Strep throat, allergic reactions, stomach cancer. He knew exactly what to do. The little girl who'd been knocked off her bicycle might have a brain haemorrhage. He thought it best to have a CAT scan done in Halifax. Robin moved out to pass a station wagon at the bottom of a hill and then drew back into her lane. It wasn't a good thing to take chances, Neil told her. Too much was at stake. And reputation was everything. But they hadn't thought about things like that at one time in their lives, she reminded him. There was a time when they'd taken chances. He'd been the one to say he couldn't live without her. She'd hesitated, not wanting to change anything. She'd liked the rented farmhouse in Pomquet where they were living, even though the toilet was unpredictable and something was nesting in the roof. Neil wanted a real house, though. A marriage. He'd had girlfriends before but never anything like he had with Robin. They had great sex together, he said. He loved her body. And he read about Chinese techniques. The waterfall. Halfway to the sky. Calling the tiger. He said he could gauge the time required for relaxation and excitation. He was always right. He had self-control. She didn't.

What had her father said to her about love? Something about the way it changed. But her parents had split up, so what did her father know, when it came right down to it? Her mother went off, taking Robin, leaving her father behind. He stood at the window, hand raised. Love. What did anyone know? The repetitive nature of it. Over the next hill and the next and the next. Sometimes it gave out. Like that car stuck on blocks in the grass over there. Things lying about. Remnants. Parts.

She put a hand up to her eye. She kept the other hand on the wheel, but it still made a slight yawing motion.

"Robin?" asked Evelyn.

"What?"

"You all right?"

She'd thought a lot about love when she'd first gone to the cottage in Maine nine years before. Opening the car door, she saw the poppies in the neighbour's garden that extended from the back door of the cottage all the way to the road. There were full-blown red poppies, crimson poppies, poppies without petals, poppies that had not entirely opened. She was tired from the trip and her legs felt stiff, but the poppies blazed. Someone had worked to make these flowers grow, stepped back and admired them, perhaps leaning on a hoe.

"Look at the garden," she said to Neil.

He glanced at the flowers as he pulled his golf clubs out of the trunk.

"Nice," he said.

She took her suitcase to the door and set it down. It was locked and Neil would have to sort through the keys in the shed. She went across the path to the top of the steps. It was low tide, and far off across the wide strand was the sea, blue and glinting. Even at this distance she could hear it falling against the sand. The sound of breathing. *Shuwwhhh. Sss. Shuwwhhh.* A woman passed nearby in a pink bathing suit with a frill at the back, reading a book as she went. Robin took off her sandals and went down the steps, crossing in front of an elderly man poking in the sand with his cane. He nodded to her. Looking for shells maybe. Starfish. There were ridges in the sand and little pools of water that were warm when she stepped in them. The pools opened in thin rivulets running down to the ocean over the damp sand. She walked down to the water and let the waves come up to her feet, washing over them in thin veils. Children on air mattresses braced themselves against the waves, trying to paddle over them to get out far enough to ride them back. A boy was rolled under by a wave and he surfaced yelling.

She turned back and saw Neil at the top of the steps with Allistair. And there was Evelyn with Luke, who ran down the steps to the beach, flying across the sand. He jigged, he wheeled, he trotted down to the edge of the water. Robin sighed. She would have to go and help unload the car, get things organized, take Verna shopping for groceries. She didn't want to. For a moment she turned away from them and had an urge to run down the beach as far as Fortune's Rocks, where the beach curved and ended, though she could hardly see it because of the soft mist at that end. It occurred to her that Neil would walk down there with her, holding her hand, whether she wanted him to or not.

The light striped the road where it came through the trees. It annoyed Robin. Light. Dark. Light. Dark. What did she remember of it? The Belgian lace on her dress. Freesia and baby's breath in the bouquet. The long speech that one of the uncles from Cape Breton had made. Posing for the pictures. People saying how beautiful she was, what a lovely bride. As if all she was supposed to do was stand still and try to look beautiful, beside Neil. Bride-and-groom dolls.

Verna's calm, pleasant face watching her, as Robin had turned and gone down the steps with Neil. Married. The organist was playing the recessional too quickly and an elderly woman, one of Neil's great-aunts, caught Robin's hand as she passed. She could see the boughs of the pine trees through the open doors of the cathedral, but the great-aunt clung to her hand. A white face, almost transparent. Wanting something.

The time they'd been at the cottage years before, Luke asked Neil about waves. Neil, Spike, and Allistair were talking about sprinkler systems, and Verna and Evelyn had gotten up to do the dishes. It irked Robin. She yanked at a tea towel that was hanging over the handle of a drawer and began drying a casserole dish. Luke was still at the table finishing his ice cream and raspberries. Dawdling, Evelyn said. Staring out the window.

"What makes waves?" Luke asked, tapping his spoon against his cheek as he looked at Neil.

"Well, the wind for one thing. But it's all physics," said Neil. "Gravitational force pulls the water into shore where the depth is decreased, so it gets compressed into—"

"The moon pulls the water," said Spike. "In other words."

"How can the moon pull the water?" asked Luke.

"Well," said Spike, glancing at Evelyn, "it's kind of like when your mom pulls you along in a wagon."

"She doesn't pull me in a wagon. I ride my bike."

"There are such things as rogue waves," Allistair said, looking out at the beach from the window. "Higher than apartment buildings. I read about a fellow on a boat who saw one over a hundred feet high. *Reader's Digest*, I think it was. A wonder he lived to tell the tale."

"Have you ever seen one?" asked Luke.

"No," said Allistair, smiling. "I don't want to."

Neil and Robin went for a walk on the beach when the dishes were done. He put his arm around her, sliding it under her sweater.

"Don't," she said.

He took his arm away. "What's with you?"

"Nothing."

They walked on past a man trying to fix his steps, a castle that some children had made, and a tree without leaves poking up out of the sand dunes. Little coloured things hung from strings tied to its branches. A plastic bucket. Half a frisbee. An aluminum pie plate. They turned in the wind.

"You get so pissed off at little things," said Neil. "And then you won't tell me what's bugging you."

"It's not just little things," said Robin. She felt irritable. She wanted to be unkind to him.

"Well, all kinds of things," he said.

A yellow Lab raced along the beach towards them,

ears flapping. It circled around their legs, sniffing, and then made off back to a bald man.

"Physics," said Robin. "Why'd you tell him that? Luke doesn't understand physics."

"What'd you want me to say?"

"I don't know. Not that."

"I could have told him about velocity and amplitude."

"Oh God," said Robin, stopping.

"What?"

"Why do you do that?"

She went on and he stayed where he was. After a moment he caught up to her.

"Robin."

She bent over a stretch of gravelly sand, searching for sand dollars. "What?"

"What's wrong?" he asked.

"Nothing's wrong."

"Can't we just go for a walk together?"

"I thought that's what we were doing."

They went on past the public beach at Fortune's Rocks as far as the private beach at the end and then they turned around. From there they could look back around the arc of the bay, though it was impossible to see where they'd started.

Robin first met Neil when he was at medical school in Hanover, New Hampshire. She was studying communications. She met him in the hospital cafeteria where her friend Melissa went to meet doctors. Melissa met Neil first, when she spilled her soup by the cash and he helped her clean it up. He sat with them for lunch. After a while it was just Robin and Neil who met for lunch, when his schedule allowed. She was thinking of quitting communications, but he made her see how silly it would be, especially when she wasn't really trained for anything else. He said she couldn't depend on her parents. But she didn't depend on her parents. Her father had died and left her the house in Hanover; her mother had left long before. She'd gone to Arizona to live with Jerrold, her chiropractor.

"You live all by yourself?" asked Neil.

"I don't mind," she said. "I make stuff in my spare time."

"Crafts?"

"Well, not really crafts. I'm an artist."

"So you do it as a hobby?"

Her father had taught her how to draw when she was a child. At that stage in his life he taught art to high school students, but on weekends he still did a little sketching of his own. He drew in order to observe the natural world in greater detail, as he told her. Robin thought that it was because he didn't like to be at home, where he'd be asked to do chores. His lessons were always well meant, but somehow he'd want her to draw exactly as he himself drew: quickly, precisely, with notes on the weather or the

light in tiny printed letters. Once they looked at an elm
tree together, and he pointed out the slightly asymmetri-
cal crown, the intertwining branches that diminished
into small, fingering branches. She was aware of the tree's
intricacies but it was still impossible to draw. She sat with
her pencil hovering over a smooth sheet of blank paper
without knowing how to start. He helped her get started
by drawing a swift line to represent the trunk and then he
went back to his own drawing. She stared at the one
miraculous line, put her sketchpad to one side, and took
out the sandwiches that should have been saved until
lunch. He continued drawing, unperturbed, the tip of his
tongue showing at the side of his mouth. She wandered
across to the brook with the sandwich, sitting below the
bank where he couldn't see her and skipping stones over
the water. He could draw if he wanted. He couldn't make
her do it.

Robin asked Neil over for dinner and made him ginger-
glazed chicken. He brought wine. He washed romaine for
the salad, spun it dry, and sliced up the celery exactingly,
as if he were slicing open livers or kidneys. Then he
uncorked the wine and poured two glasses, toasting her
before he drank. She was conscious that her arms and legs
were bare and that her dress was a little short. Maybe it
was a provocative dress. She turned and began dicing carrots on the counter, asking him questions. Why did he
decide to go into medicine in the first place? She tossed

the carrots into a steamer in a saucepan and flicked on
the burner. The ginger-glazed chicken was darker than it
should have been. Did he like rowing? She kept him talking all through dinner. At dessert he asked for another
slice of her chocolate cheesecake because it was the best
thing he'd ever tasted. She told him it was easy to make if
the cream cheese was soft enough. He was smiling at her.
After a moment he reached over and ran his fingers along
her arm, slowly.

When the roses came the next day she had nothing to
put them in, so she cut down the long stems and put
them in a milk pitcher. No one had ever sent her roses
before. She found herself fingering a petal, soft as the
palm of a child's hand.

She hadn't done what she thought she'd do. She went to
university simply because it was a sensible thing to do.
Better than twiddling her thumbs. In the mirror, she
could see a car with its trunk open, bobbing up and down.
A stupid thing to do. When the car passed, there was
nothing in the trunk. No reason for it to be open like
that. People did all kinds of stupid things.

Once, long ago, she'd known she was capable of something more. That time she'd gotten lost when her mother
had taken her to Durham on a shopping trip. She'd gone
into the ladies' room and cried. In the three-way mirror,
which was a gaudy, gold-edged splendour, the anguish in
her face was exaggerated. She could see not one self, but

hundreds, all standing one behind the other. She stopped crying. She moved her right hand and the thousand selves in identical blue-smocked dresses raised their right hands. She shook her head and her braids flipped up, as did thousands of other beribboned braids. She swayed gracefully from side to side and the selves swayed with her, a snake of girls. It struck her that she had enormous power, newly discovered magic. So little was required of her. The movement of her head, her hand. That was all.

On the card with the roses, Neil had written one word: *Love.*

Where was she going? She drove cautiously past a boy driving a tractor on the shoulder. She had no idea. It all looked the same to her, even though the land had broadened out into farmland and the houses were larger. It could have been anywhere. She didn't care. It was clear that she couldn't just go on with life as it had been. They'd get a divorce, she thought, and for a moment things fell into place. Precisely cut as that lawn over there with the delphiniums rising up like spears out of the garden. That's what would happen. A child scrambled up a tree, hung from a branch, and jumped down. The fields beyond the house stretched far away, in gentle undulations. Soft and blue in the distance. She could be lulled into thinking all of it went on forever. But it didn't.

THE MEMORY THEATRE

Robin's father, Larry, was an irritable old man who suffered from diabetes. He was an artist, but now he was
nearly blind. His sight became worse for a while, then
better, then worse again. Since Robin had moved out of
her mother's place and gone back to New Hampshire,
she'd been living in Larry's basement in exchange for
cooking meals and reading to him a few hours each day. It
worked out to her benefit. She planned to make a lot of
money bartending at Gary's Great Steaks and then go to
France in the fall.

She had no idea she'd like it, reading and watching
him paste his little bits of coloured paper or newsprint
onto pieces of stiff white paper. He'd ask her where he
was putting a bit of blue that he wanted in the lower left
corner and she'd tell him to move it to the right, so he
would skate it farther right with the glue leaving a milky
track. Then he'd cover the glue with a piece of gum wrapper. He sold his work in New York. People compared him

to Kurt Schwitters, the German Dada artist. But he wasn't
Kurt Schwitters and he didn't care what Kurt Schwitters
had done. He was going to die soon. He didn't have time
to do all the things he wanted to do. Somewhere along
the way, time had been wasted.

Robin didn't always go down to her apartment after she
came in from work. Occasionally she'd go up to Larry's
studio, knowing he'd be asleep. His framed collages were
stacked against the walls. One had swaths of gouache
colour over an article about setting a table, and another,
scraped and torn, revealed an image of a man diving into
a house. There was a series of photographs of the Statue
of Liberty sinking lower and lower in the water. She liked
the playfulness of it. Besides the collages, there were
small constructions on the floor. A wire house with wire
people. A wooden bowl lined with nails. A perfect repro-
duction of a skull with a handle on one side. Studded
with tiny mirrors on the inside.

She went to the work table and picked up a piece of
brilliant red paper. She ripped it experimentally and
glued it onto a sheet of white paper. It was an interesting
shape, an isosceles triangle. She glued on a piece of green,
a string, a bit of foil. Humming a blues song, she put
down a piece of purple velvet, discarded it, and kept
humming.

"Hmmm, hmmm, I feel so good, hmmm, hmmm,
whenever I see you. Hmmmm."

She held up the finished collage, studying it.

Robin was reading to Larry from a battered paperback that she'd picked up at Mr. Boone's Book Bargains for fifty cents. It was a book of love letters.

"'Honey, you're my angel, my real angel man. I dreamed I saw you at the Stop and Hop under the strobe light. Honey man, I wish I could sit in your lap and you could—'"

"Stop," Larry said, tearing a piece from a *Life* magazine cover. "Read something else."

"Why?" she asked. "Aren't you the slightest bit interested in other people?"

"I don't need to hear about their goddamn love lives."

"Why not?"

"It's poking in where you're not wanted. I wouldn't like it."

"Because you're afraid someone would find out too much?"

"What's to find out?" he asked, and went back to putting a piece of orange felt on the left side of his collage. He worked at it for a while, his tongue just visible at the corner of his mouth. "Anyway, it was a long time ago."

"But you loved her."

He snorted. "She left."

Robin fingered the pages of the book. "I've got a lover. His name's Greg."

"That's good."

"I haven't seen him for eight months but he's still very committed to me. He's in Belize."

"Dealing drugs?"

"Working for Children's World International."

"In bed with someone different every night of the week."

"No, he's not like that. He's very—well, it's just not something he'd do."

"Ah," said Larry, pasting on a bit of gold doily, "then it's obviously love."

She didn't like him. As she was walking to work one May evening it occurred to her that Larry was an irascible old bugger. She could easily come to hate him. Under a canopy of white pear blossoms she reached up to break off a snowy flower. What did he know about anything? A boy on a mountain bike made a wide arc around her. She'd stepped off the curb without looking, thinking of Greg, who hadn't written in a few weeks, except to say that he and a woman called Trina had started raising funds for a rural education project. Trina was a Vajrayana Buddhist and he'd never met anyone quite like her. She played the mandolin.

"Shit," said Robin, picking the silky petals off the pear blossom and letting them drift from her fingers. They were tiny curls of white, like earlobes, or eyelids, closed.

She was reading a new book Larry had chosen, one she didn't much like. There was a faint smell of urine in the room and she wrinkled her nose.

"'Guilio Camillo's invention appears to have been greatly influenced by the cabalist tradition, and it owes a debt to the Ars memorativa treatises . . .'"

"Why are you stopping?"

"It's boring."

"Keep going," he said sharply. He tried to pour himself some water from the jug, but it spilled on the table. Robin mopped it up.

She sighed, continuing where she'd left off. "There's a footnote here, from a letter written in 1532. 'The theatre is wondrous large, and indeed, the author of the work, one Julius Camillus, entered into it and I followed hard upon his heels. I stood in awe of this edifice of wisdom. The construction, which I do take the liberty of describing, is of wood, coloured with many images of the antique gods—'"

"Don't read so fast."

She made a face and continued, more slowly, in a monotone.

"'It is very like a small amphitheatre, excepting that it is not large enough to admit more than two people, and where it mounts on ascending grades, it is full of ornamented boxes or cabinets, which may be removed. At certain intervals are seven pillars, Solomon's Seven Pillars of Wisdom. I stood fixed, gazing with amazement as Master Camillus did elaborate to me his theatre of the memory.'"

"Ah, it's fantastic," said Larry. He stood up from the

table, knocking his empty plastic glass to the floor. Picking up his cane, he began to limp to the bathroom again, the fifth time that afternoon. When he came back he spoke decisively.

"I'll need your help," he said.

"For what?"

"I'm going to make a memory theatre."

Robin explained that the deal had been she'd read to him, which she didn't mind doing, but she wasn't just going to fritter away her time making models of some old theatre. She wasn't an artist. He ripped up a page of *The New Yorker* as she talked, tearing it into tiny pieces. He lifted his hands, filled with the papers, and let the bits fall through his fingers onto the table.

"What are you doing?"

"Making something."

"No, you're not."

"All these little papers," he said, "replete with meanings. This is what I do. I take things, make them into something else. Most people think it's unimportant." He grunted. "Maybe so."

She watched the papers, some falling to the floor, some still in the air, like snow.

"Your mother thought it was a waste of time," he said.

"Did she?"

"Oh yes, though she never said as much."

Robin bent to pick up the scattered bits of paper.

"I need your help," he said.

They began work on a small model of the memory theatre. It didn't look like much to Robin. It resembled a large birdhouse. And Larry could never see what he was doing, so he'd put a sticky bit of wood onto a section that was already finished. She'd have to guide his hand as it hesitated in the air. It was like working with a three-year-old.

"Did you always do stuff like this?" she asked. "I mean, when you were little."

He'd gotten some of the glue on his T-shirt. A dribble of glue along his thumb. "When I had rheumatic fever my aunt Mary gave me a set of watercolour paints."

"So what did you paint?"

"Oh, just blobs of colour. But I thought, This is red, this rich colour is red. And this is green, this swirl, this leafy dark colour is green. And yellow." He put down a bit of wood. "I was dabbling and I heard Aunt Mary's voice in the garden and I thought, her voice just then, when she was talking about the size of the tea roses, that was yellow. Bright yellow."

Robin wiped the glue from his thumb with a tissue.

"What about my voice?" she asked. "What colour would you say it is?"

"Mmm," he mused. "Sort of a lavender, maybe bluish. Mauve. It changes."

"And what about your own voice?" she said, animated, enjoying herself.

"Well, that's a different thing altogether. I think the colour's gone out of it."

One morning before lunch, Robin saw a silvery blue Renault pull into the driveway. She was making herself toast, staring out the basement window. The Renault drew up so one of the tires was on the grass, and a woman emerged, catching the hem of her long navy skirt as she shut the car door. Then she opened it, made a clucking noise over the grease on her skirt, and slammed it shut. A tall woman, with short grey hair. She carried a cake box. As she walked towards the front steps, her face and neck vanished, then the gold buttons of her white blouse. Pale legs spidered with blue veins, a pair of sandals. She rang the doorbell. The sandals went down a step. Up a step. The doorbell rang again. Robin could hear the tapping of Larry's cane and keys falling off a table.

"Hello, Larry."

"My Lord, Karina, I never thought you'd—"

The sandals disappeared.

Robin sat down at the kitchen table. The toast on the plate was cold and she pushed it away. After a few minutes, she got up and began to scrub the sink vigorously with a bleach cleanser. Then she washed her hands and went up the stairs, keeping close to the wall so the floorboards wouldn't creak. A cardboard box from Joelle's

Bakery was on the counter in the kitchen, blue and silver ribbons cascading over its sides. She could see them on the sofa in the living room. The woman was taking off her father's thick glasses. He blinked. His face was the colour of yellowed paper. The woman leaned over and embraced him and he seemed bewildered. Then he put his hands up to her face, touching it. He clutched at her shoulders and kissed her mouth greedily.

Robin backed away, going quickly along the hall and descending the stairs. A strong smell of bleach. She sat down on the red kitchen chair with a rip in the vinyl seat and put her hands flat on the table to stop them from trembling.

She riffled through some bits of paper on the work table. One or two had fallen into the half-finished model of the memory theatre. She fished one out: "Your lovel—" She looked at another: "—ing for a chance to—" She put them back. Larry was coming down the hall, his cane mapping the way on the hardwood floor.

"You're here." He was unsteady on the threshold. "Reading what I've written?"

"I couldn't—you tore everything up."

"Serves you right. Anyway, those were old letters."

"You still love her."

He moved over to a chair, nearly tripping on the rug, and sat down heavily.

"Who?"

"Karina, or whoever she is."

"Ah. I doubt if she'll come back. I explained what happens to a diabetic. Things like excessive thirst, screwed-up bladder, blindness, utter dependency."

"You still love her," Robin repeated stupidly.

He looked straight at her face, as if he could see it clearly. "Of course I do."

"And I suppose you and she were carrying on even before Mother decided to leave."

"No. I loved your mother. We were different people altogether, but I loved her." He bent forward, about to rise. "'There is a purity and a sweetness in all things, a silence.' Do you know who said that?"

Robin didn't look at him.

"Thomas Merton," he went on. "A Trappist monk. I have no idea if he was in love with anyone, though I suspect he was, but he said it perfectly. What can anyone say about love? Nothing, really. It's a little thing you think about, and keep thinking about until you can't stand it any more, yet you want to hang on to it at all costs. Then after a while you don't talk about it. You let go of what you thought you had to have. It's not the same thing at all when that happens."

Greg finally sent a letter. On the envelope was a stamp with a picture of a creamy beach, a golden palm. It was time they both moved on to other things, he wrote. He'd felt this for a long time. Robin would always be important in his life, but he'd found something special with Trina. When he came back to New Hampshire, Trina would be coming to live with him.

Robin picked up the nearest thing at hand, which happened to be a small blue teapot. She flung it against the wall, where it smashed, satisfyingly, into little blue shards.

"Fuck you."

Larry was drinking Scotch, which he knew he shouldn't be drinking. Robin had a glass of Chardonnay.

"No, no," he was saying, "it goes back well before Plato to an Egyptian called Hermes Trismegistus. He wrote the *Corpus Hermeticum*, a sacred book of wisdom, which was translated into Latin just in time to make it fashionable during the Renaissance. New Age stuff. Trismegistus gave an account of Creation, except that in his case man is created like God, with the same creative power."

"But what does this have to do with Camillo's memory theatre?"

"Well, Camillo was fashioning a little world with his memory theatre, using occult concepts of Creation. It was overlaid with Christianity, but there was this other subversive notion behind it, that men were gods. He included everything from the terrestrial to the celestial. The elements, the emotions, the planets, the angels. It was filled with inscriptions, images, little drawers filled with messages."

"It still sounds like a kind of filing cabinet."

"Oh, but you're missing the point." Larry made a circular motion with his glass and drank the last of it. "The memory theatre is the Mind of Man inspired by the Mind of God. Camillo could walk around this theatre he'd created and be inside the Divine Mind."

"It's a nice idea."

"Mmmn. That's what the king of France thought. Though it's anyone's guess whether his memory improved after he saw it."

Robin put down her glass on the table.

"You have to see it as a vision of the world as it could be, with all the possibilities for creativity," he said. "I don't necessarily see it as a construct, myself."

"How do you see it?"

"Without a frame. I see the mind, infinitely configured, one thought and another and another and another. Like a galaxy, like many galaxies. That's how I see it. The whole thing is beguiling, divine, endless."

In the end, Larry hired a night nurse. She changed his sheets when he soaked them at night. She gave him insulin injections. Her name was Mandy, and on Robin's nights off from bartending they watched Johnny Carson. Mandy liked to knit baby blankets and she was knitting one in soft yellow with scalloped edges for her one-month-old niece.

"You're a lot like your dad," pronounced Mandy.

"I don't know."

"My Al, now, he's got a gift for cars. He can take them apart and put them back together faster than a wet dog can shake. But me—I can't tell a piston from a carburetor." She yanked at the wool. "What I say is, if you've got the gift for something, you've got to go ahead and do it."

Robin continued to add to the memory theatre, on and off, for a couple of years, even after Larry was confined to his bed. She'd run her hand over the side of the amphitheatre, the little dowels that represented Solomon's Seven Pillars of Wisdom, the tiny images she had painted of the angels. Once she mentioned to Larry that she was still working on it and he asked her why. He said she didn't need to work on it any more.

But the little amphitheatre cradled something, a delicate wooden husk of all the hours they'd spent making it. The drawers were not expertly crafted, the frame was a little warped. She lifted the whole thing up in the air, tentatively. She put it down. It was all she would have left of him.

"You're afraid," he said to her.

The light was streaming across his bed. She took his thin hand in hers. Whenever she saw him now, his hands were useless, flat on the covers or under the sheet, maybe crossed over his chest. She couldn't stand to look at them.

"No."

"There's no reason to be."

She made a little sound; not a grunt, not a cry.

"I love you," he said. His hand moved against her palm. "You know that."

She bent her head down, right down on the quilt, so it touched his shoulder. She felt his hand on her head, stroking her hair.

Once Robin saw Greg in a hardware store. He'd been living at Tuttle's Crossing, twenty miles away, ever since Trina had gone back to Seattle. He had a package of Christmas lights under one arm. He picked up a bell covered with silver sparkles, put it down, and moved along the aisle. Then he put the Christmas lights back on a shelf. He was slightly thicker around the waist than she remembered. After Trina left, he'd written Robin a note. Couldn't they meet for a coffee or something, just to talk? There was a picture of a sleeping grey cat on the front of the notecard, and it was almost a pity to crumple it up.

Robin left the store, carefully crossing the icy parking lot. She sat in the car as the last of the afternoon sunlight gilded the windows of the Episcopalian church. There were two elm trees by the gas station, which would be cut down in the spring. They spread out generously, like vaulting in a cathedral, ending in a tracery of smaller branches against the cold, rosy sky. She remembered what her father had said about silence. She remembered his hands moving across the collages, searching, his blind hands touching Karina's face with abandon, finding her again.

After Robin's father died she sat at the work table for an hour or two each day, fiddling with bits of paper. What could she do? She didn't have any great ideas, unlike Larry, who used to talk a blue streak about all the things he wanted to do. He'd been famous, which irked him. And now Chicago wanted to do a retrospective and the dealers in New York had told Robin that his collages were a virtual gold mine. It didn't mean anything. She missed him. They were more alike than she'd realized. If she could just sustain him somehow, retain what she remembered. She pushed back her chair and walked to the window to look at the light on the snow, the mauve-grey shadows of a blue spruce on a lip of pure white drift. No, she was bound to lose something. He would drift away in bits, like his little scraps of paper. A fine dusting of ashes.

She began wrapping some twine around a dowel, knotted it, put the dowel on the table between her hands. The veins stood out faintly blue under her skin. She turned her hands over. Once her father had taken her hands and laid them out flat on the dining-room table, perhaps to see if she'd washed them properly. But he just studied them. Then he told her that hands were beautiful, very beautiful. And the space between hands, too, he went on, and paused, holding up her hands, was also beautiful. Did she see what he meant?

Robin held up her hands in front of the window with the tips of her fingers barely touching. It was a remarkable shape, a construct, a theatre; each finger a supple bridge, spanning an enclosed space. She turned them this way and that, considering the light on her fingernails, on her knuckles. Gradually she moved her fingers apart, observing the way the light informed each hummock, each line on her palms, crossing over tinier lines, lines that she couldn't see, that went on and on crossing and recrossing, infinitely.

CHICKEN

Spike leaned against the car, sipping his coffee, which tasted like perfume. A lemon scent wafted from the adjacent car where a girl was putting on a pair of earrings. Her boyfriend craned his neck back as he finished a drink, crumpled up the can, and got in beside her.

"I don't know why you freak about a little thing like that," said the boyfriend.

Spike looked down at his coffee cup. "Flip your lid," it said in red letters. "Win a million."

"Fuck off," said the girl.

"It's not like you own me."

Spike glanced over and saw the girl sitting with her tanned arms folded across her chest. She couldn't have been more than fifteen, already resolute, tough-minded.

"So what if I got loaded?" he said to her.

"Just fucking go, okay?"

The boy jerked the key in the ignition and revved the car. Then he took off noisily, narrowly missing a tractor trailer on the highway. Verna watched them as she followed Allistair out of the coffee shop.

"Almost got themselves killed," she said.

Spike finished his coffee, looked on the underside of the lid to see if he'd won anything, and tossed the cup in the garbage. His father was having trouble with the seat belt and Spike went around to help him retract and pull it forward again. He could see his father's skull through his thinning hair. He was getting old. Spike shut the door carefully and walked around to the driver's side. He hadn't been paying attention and suddenly his father was old.

Spike had once been in love with Janelle MacEachern. They went steady for a while, until Janelle seemed to lose interest. She was older than he was by two years, which accounted for some of her charm. By the time he was eighteen and she was twenty, she'd been married, had a child, and gotten divorced. She still had the same great body, the same dark hair and white teeth. He thought he'd give it another try.

A couple of nights before Christmas he got together with Bill Dykstra. They had a couple of drinks and Bill told him he was going down to Bangor to see his girlfriend. Bill worked in Port Hawkesbury at the mill, so he had money to do things. They had another drink. The rum was smooth and warm going down their throats. Spike began thinking about Janelle and how it would be nice to give her something for Christmas, so he and Bill went to the drugstore where he finally bought her a little portable electrolysis machine, because he saw a dark-haired model on the cover of the box plucking her eyebrows. Her face reminded him of Janelle. Then he bought some wrapping paper along with a bag of bows and they went over to the lounge at the Ceilidh Inn to wrap it. They had another drink. The waitress had a pair of nail scissors and she cut the paper for them, telling them that things were slack and she didn't like being without anything to do. Her name was Jackie. She went away and when she came back with the tape Bill put his arm around her waist, saying what a great gal she was, wasn't she a great gal? He asked her to sit on his knee while she wrapped it up. She wrapped it, bending over the table. Then Bill got the bag of bows and put a few on and then a few more for good measure. Spike had another drink and asked if he could borrow the truck, and Bill slapped the keys down on the table, smiling. Jackie stood next to Bill and he seemed to be rubbing her buttocks.

It changed from rain to freezing rain as Spike drove over to Janelle's basement apartment on Hawthorne Street. There were two cars in the driveway already so he drove the truck onto the lawn, out of the way. Janelle was in her bathrobe when he knocked on the basement door.

"What?" she asked.

"I wanted to bring you something," he said, stepping inside.

"Don't wake the baby."

They were in the kitchen, which was also the living room. He didn't know whether he should sit on the brown couch or the old yellow velvet chair with the broken leg.

"Have a seat," she said. "Want some coffee?"

He sat down on the couch and turned the present in his hands. "I guess so."

"How've you been?" he asked.

"All right." She stood with her back to him, unscrewing the lid of the instant coffee.

"Don't see much of you now."

"I don't have a lot of time to myself."

He was touched by the slight stoop of her shoulders, by her bare feet on the linoleum floor. He put down the present and went over to her, gathering her into his arms.

"Don't," she said, freeing herself.

"Why?"

"You're pissed to the gills."

"Janelle."

"What do you want? A guy like you. If you want to get laid, go somewhere else."

"I didn't come because I wanted to get laid."

"Bullshit," she said quietly and started to cry.

He picked up a cup of coffee and gave it to her.

"I like milk in it," she said.

He put milk in it. Then he drank his, looking at the way her hair fell over her shoulders. He wanted to touch her hair. There was nothing for him to say, so he gave her the present. She put down her coffee cup and took off the eight bows and the wrapping paper, turning the box around in her hands.

"Thanks." She put it on the counter.

"Well, I guess I'll be going," he said.

He didn't want to go. Even when she'd said good night and closed the door, he could still imagine kissing her hair, her mouth, the creamy part of her neck where the bathrobe had loosened. But she was right. He scraped the ice off the windshield, wondering why he'd parked the truck on the grass. He hadn't thought about what he'd say to her. He hadn't thought about her baby, about waking anyone up. All he'd been thinking about was the way her skin would feel when he was lying beside her.

They were passing Moncton, without ever seeing anything of it, except for a few motels. The road ran along a ridge and down a green, gradual slope. In the mirror, Spike could see his mother nodding sleepily in the back seat. Occasionally her head would jerk up and then slowly begin to fall again, her chin nearly touching her shoulder.

In the front seat, Allistair stared at the road as if it hypnotized him. He might have been gazing at the trailer in front of them with the I ♥ CINCINNATI sticker on the back. It was hard to say what he saw. When Spike was young he'd sometimes asked him questions, like the meaning of circumference, or the length of time humans had been on the earth. At times like that his father would fix him with his penetrating eyes. Then he'd wrinkle his forehead as if in pain. Circumference was the boundary of a circle, as in the circumference of the earth. As for humans, they might have been on the earth for a million years, three million years. Who really knew for certain?

"Did you get that book I sent you?" asked Spike.

"Hmm?"

"That book about trends. You know, business, technology, all that stuff."

"Yes. Sure. Money is a conversation," said Allistair. "The future is hidden in the present. Seemed pretty straightforward to me." He kept gazing ahead. "Meister Eckhart, now. You know about him?"

"No."

"Les Duggan loaned me a book last winter."

"Uh-huh." Spike's father usually read things like *Burt Greene's Easy Composting* or *Famous Shipwrecks of Nova Scotia.*

"I was reading some of it the other day. It was something like, 'Let a man decide on one good way and persist in it.'"

His father had a large head, which moved up and down a little. Maybe it was a tremor.

"You've always done that," said Spike. "You've done one thing well."

"It's not about me." His father's head was still nodding slightly. "This book."

Once Spike had gone to have his tarot cards read. It hadn't been his idea. His girlfriend, Andrea, wanted to go and he'd gone with her. When Andrea paid for her reading, the woman told her that she'd do them both for thirty-five dollars, which was a deal considering that it usually cost twenty dollars per person. The woman waited, sipping her tea at the counter, while Andrea dug in her purse and produced the money.

Spike wandered over to the window, picking up a magazine as he went.

"Come on," said Andrea, tossing her head prettily.

"What?" he said.

"I paid for you, too."

So he had to go. He sat back in the chair with his arms folded while Andrea had her cards read. The woman was talking about the propitious nature of the cards. He watched her, thinking that she didn't look like a fortune teller. She had frosted hair, nicely cut, and small, even teeth. She wore a beige sweater with costume pearls around her neck, which she fingered now as she told Andrea that she would marry later than usual, and that it would provide her with stability. Her husband would be good to her. And her children would give her great happiness. Andrea turned to Spike, slightly pink, and put a hand on his knee. There would be disruptions in the near future, though, the woman warned. A difficult time.

After shuffling Andrea's cards, she left them neatly stacked on the table for a moment. She closed her eyes as if she were praying. Then she laid out Spike's cards and considered them, the fingertips of her hands touching.

"With the Queen of Pentacles in this position, it's obvious that money comes easily to you," she said. "A great deal of money. And people like you. They're drawn to you because you're warm and generous. Life is good to you, on the whole." He realized she had large brown eyes. "But you are in need of a mentor."

"The cards say I need a mentor?"

"Well, they don't spell it out, but it seems clear that you do."

"How did you get that?"

"This card, in particular. The number of cups. And then the swords in this card beside it. Everything is at cross-purposes. You must do something to restore the balance or you will perpetuate the cycle."

"That doesn't seem to match up with what you said before." He could feel the warm pressure of Andrea's leg against his under the table.

"I said you've got a nice life," she said. "That's all."

"What's the name of that girl you brought home last Christmas?" asked his father.

"Andrea." Spike was trying to pass a truck in which a sofa, a washer, and an upended table were piled precariously in the back, covered by a plastic tarpaulin that was flapping in the wind.

"Yes, that's the one."

Spike saw his chance and pulled out to overtake the truck. "Now she's with some lawyer called Warren."

"You mean to say you've bought yourself a big house and you're going to live in it all alone?"

"For the time being."

"That's no way to live."

"Then how should I live?"

"I don't know," said his father irritably. "Most people have families."

"I'd like a family. I just can't find the right person to live with."

"*Fiffhh*," said his father, punching at his pillow and putting it behind his head. "It's not as hard as all that. You're just afraid of it."

On Spike's sixth birthday Leslie MacKenzie told him that she'd pull down her underpants if he'd pull down his. They were up in the oak tree in the backyard, sitting on the platform that he and Neil had made. The platform was to be part of a tree house, but they hadn't done any more work on it. Leslie blew on a party favour that rolled out and touched his face and then made a shrill sound as it recoiled.

"You first," said Spike.

"No."

"It was your idea."

"*So.*"

They sat at the edge of the platform, dangling their feet over the edge. The other children had gone home, but Evelyn and Garnet were sitting on the back stoop somewhere below them, blowing bubbles.

"I bet your dicky is shorter than my brother's," said Leslie. "He's making his longer by rolling it over his finger. Then he pulls it."

"Why'd you do that?" Evelyn squealed from the back stoop. "I'm not playing with you." The screen door banged.

"So, come on," said Leslie.

Spike stared down at his sneakers. "Girls don't have anything at all."

"Yes, they do," said Leslie, taking a candy out of her party bag and popping it into her mouth. "But I'm not going to show you until you show me first."

Spike lay down flat on his back, looking up into the leaves. Some of them were pale, almost golden, with the sun coming through, and others were bunched together in darker clusters. Leslie leaned over and he looked at her upside-down face, at her sticky mouth where her eyes should have been. The mouth moved and he watched it, fascinated.

"You're just chicken," she said.

He rolled over and scrambled down the tree.

The sky was pale blue, softened with warmth, and even the barns in the distance seemed to waver in the haze, insubstantial and colourless. Spike's hands were heavy on the wheel and he felt a little annoyed that both his parents were asleep.

He did want a family. He even wanted to get married. But Lisa, whom he'd known for a few months, didn't want to get married. She hardly paid attention to what he said sometimes. The last time she'd stayed over she gave him a quick kiss in the kitchen, a piece of toast in one hand, leaving crumbs on his cheek. She'd asked him to tell her something funny but he couldn't think of anything to say. He watched a cardinal poking for seeds in the bird feeder. He said he loved her. And she told him to think again, or something like that, something like who did he think he was kidding.

He lifted one hand off the wheel, opening and closing his fingers. It was as if she thought he was somehow limited. They all thought that. He passed two trailers quickly on the slope of an incline. The road was empty in front of him except for an oncoming jeep that passed in a flash of green. His father made a little gurgling sound and then settled into slow, rasping snores again. Spike accelerated and the needle on the speedometer moved to the right. If he wanted, he could go on to Vancouver, or maybe even California. For a moment or two, as he opened up speed on the empty stretch, he felt light-headed, almost weightless. He wasn't afraid of anything.

"You married?" Rick asked.

"No," said Spike.

"Got any plans?"

"Not right at the moment," said Spike. Rick had taken over his computer, as well as his desk and leather chair, while he had to sit by the window, trying to work on a laptop.

"It's not so bad," said Rick. "Tying the knot."

Spike had to clear one of the spreadsheet entries because he was distracted.

"I used to like to fool around a bit," Rick said. His fingers moved quickly over the keyboard, making little tapping sounds. "But not after I met Keri."

Spike looked out the window. There was nothing to see except slanting flecks of snow, sometimes criss-crossing when the wind let up, then whipping down again. There was a vague, grey shape of a building in the distance and little humps in the parking lot half-covered in snow. A plume of white sprayed against the window and left a pattern of icy marks.

"Virus," said Rick, swivelling in the chair.

"What?"

"Looks like one of those viruses that attack the hard drive. If it's the one I think it is— 'Jam Donut' —you'll have to reload everything."

"Everything?" Spike asked, gazing at the ugly mottled flesh of Rick's face. Hands. The skin looked melted and patched together. And his features seemed slightly askew, which made him look stupid.

"Yup."

The first time Spike got laid was with Alice Blaney. It should have been Janelle. But Alice was built and had a nice face, except her blonde hair was stringy. People said she was a slut. It didn't make much difference to Spike. She'd been with most of his friends already and they put him up to it. He and Alice drove out to Malignant Cove in his dad's car and sat for a while looking out at the ocean. It was summer and the sky was wide open, even as it darkened. Spike put one hand under Alice's skirt but got stuck with her pantyhose. She pulled them off and he put his head between her legs.

"Can't you do better than that?" she asked.

"What?"

"Don'tcha know how to fuck?" she said.

"So," Rick said, after he'd been working for the best part of two hours. "You ever fallen for someone, hook, line, and sinker?"

"I guess. A long time ago."

He took a disk out of the computer and put it carefully into its case. Then he turned the computer off and on again, rebooting it to see if everything was working properly. "There, that's the job done. Should be ready to roll."

"It's all done?"

"Mmhmm. I'd say it's A-okay now. I better get myself out of here."

"Well, thanks a lot," said Spike. "Listen, I'd like to buy you a drink or something."

"Sure. Whenever. All I drink is soda water."

"Just something quick before you go."

"Now?"

"Well, it's as good a time as any."

They went by his office so he could get his coat and put on his big white moon boots. Spike glanced around, his eyes resting on a framed photograph of a healthy-looking woman with sandy hair, who was smiling and putting her hand up as if to stop the person taking the picture. She was tanned, her body trim. She didn't look older than twenty-five.

"That's Keri?" he asked.

"Yup," said Rick. He stood up and put on his coat. "Funny, you know, she's not exactly who I had in mind."

"Who'd you have in mind?"

He closed his office and stumped along the hall beside Spike. "Well, I dunno know if I was looking. Last thing I ever thought was that someone'd fall for me."

The snow had changed to freezing rain outside. They walked side by side without talking, bending their heads to keep it out of their faces. When they got to the pub, Spike ordered drinks while Rick called home.

"Decent place," Rick said, coming over to the table. He sat down and looked around the room, his gaze resting on the cheery fire blazing in the fireplace.

"It's all right," said Spike.

The waiter slapped down a pair of coasters and put their drinks squarely on them.

Rick was still staring at the fire. Spike looked at it, too. They sat like that for a while, just looking at the flames that were bluish, almost transparent, tipped with yellow gold. The logs were only pressed sawdust, wrapped to look like real logs.

"I can't even light a match any more," said Rick. "Scared, I guess."

Spike glanced at his hands, disfigured like his face.

"When my car caught fire I got fried," he said. "I couldn't get out the door, so I had to dive out the window. Burns over fifty percent of my body. Full-thickness burns. My face isn't as bad as the rest, but I've got a chest and back and arms that look like grilled cheese."

"God."

"Keri, she used to come to the hospital every chance

she could get. But I lost those months altogether, so I had
no idea she was there. There's a lot that I don't know:
how swollen I got, like a balloon. How they had to cut
away the burned skin, how they sheathed me in cadaver
skin. It could have been a coat, y'know, somebody else's
coat. I didn't know any of that until later. But, Christ,
what I woke up to was horrible. They just wanted to give
me back my life, but I didn't think I wanted it if it was
going to be like that. It was like medieval torture. All
those bandages. You feel like you're going to be wrapped
in silvadine-soaked gauze for the rest of your life. But
then they have to get rid of the cadaver skin and take
your own skin and cut it off and put it where you need it.
They use a machine—a Zimmer dermatome thing—like
a meat slicer. That's how I thought of it. Most of that
time I think I lived on morphine and Versed. I didn't care
about anything else, except the pain. Ever feel like that?"

"I've only ever burned my hand on the stove."

"I felt like—well, I'd rather have been dead than feel
that."

Jeff Hicks lived with his brother, Dennis, in a ramshackle
house in Ballantyne's Cove. Sometimes their father lived
there when he wasn't driving trucks out of Halifax. They
had a party once and Spike took Janelle, who was mad at
him for some reason and didn't say a word all the way out
in the car. The only sounds were the tires on the wet road
and the slapping wipers. When they got there she sat on

a chair in the kitchen, her legs crossed so almost nothing
of her green miniskirt showed because it was all bunched
up at the top of her thighs. Spike leaned against the
counter with Joey Gunn, drinking. Jeff wanted to show
them a car he'd been working on, but since it was raining
nobody made a move to go and look at it except Janelle.
Dennis loaned her his huge rubber boots and laughed
when she put them on, slapping the flat of his hand
against his thigh. Then he gave her a garbage bag she
could hold up over her head.

Jeff and Janelle took a while out there, and just when
Spike was thinking he'd go and have a look they came
back inside. Janelle's mouth was bright red, as if she'd just
smeared lipstick on it, and he could make out the outline
of her brassiere through her damp blouse. Her hair was so
dark and shiny it seemed there were blue highlights in it.
She sat down in the chair and Jeff crouched down beside
her where he could talk to her from time to time. Spike
couldn't hear what they were saying. The cases of beer
were stacked on the kitchen floor and Sandy Noseworthy
was by the fridge, ready to get out a beer for anybody who
wanted one, so they didn't need to move. Dennis was
telling about the time he'd seen a bear by the road and
nearly pissed his pants. It was a real live bear, he told
them. Dwight LeBlanc said Dennis was probably dead
drunk at the time. It could have been a dog or something
like that. But Dennis shook his head. He kept saying he'd
been scared shitless, scared shitless. Spike looked over at

Janelle and saw that Jeff had his hand on her leg. He was moving it up and down.

Spike put his beer down on the counter and went out the front door. The rain had stopped but the driveway was all muddy, like brown glue. He pissed into it. Then he walked down to where he'd left the car and each time he lifted his boots he could hear a *sloop, sloop.* He got in the car and sat there, looking out at the dark space beyond the slope of hill where the ocean was, though he couldn't see it. He must have fallen asleep in the car. When he woke up he had pins and needles in his feet and he was cold right through. Jeff's truck was the only one left in the yard besides Spike's but the kitchen light was still on in the house and he went back up to take a look, sliding on the mud as he went. He fell down and his whole left side was covered, even his face. When he went inside, Dennis was still in the kitchen, sitting on the floor with his legs sprawled out in front of him as if someone had kicked him there. His socks were red and there was a hole in one of them. He was awake but he looked at Spike as if he wasn't there.

"Seen Janelle?" Spike asked.

"Yeah," he said. He had piggy eyes, Spike thought, and his face was puffy.

"She get a ride with someone?"

"No."

"Well, so where is she?"

He jerked his thumb upstairs. "You can go see, if you like," he said.

Spike went outside, trying to figure out which window was Jeff's. It was an old house with lots of windows. One had a board over it. He started banging on the clapboard siding and shouting for them to come out but there was nothing to show that they'd heard him. His hand was bleeding and after a while he went back to the car and drove home.

"I read somewhere about blind people," Rick was saying. "I read that they see different things, if you can talk about it as seeing. One guy saw everything as grey, or at least he called it grey, and this other woman, she could make out light and dark." He stared into his glass as if he expected to find something. Then he drank the last of the soda quickly. "It was like that in the hospital. Everything felt sort of washed-out. Keri read me things, all kinds of stuff, but mostly about gardening because she knew I liked it. Once she was reading about hedges, about flowering quince, mock orange, boxwood. She was trying to say the Latin name for flowering quince, japonica something, and got it wrong. I thought what a nice voice she had, and even when she went away I thought about it."

"You were getting better."

"I dunno." He picked up his drink again, though he'd already finished it. He set it down. "You'll want to get back to the office soon to finish your work."

"It'll get done," Spike said. "So you were married at this point?"

"Nope. You're thinking why she'd ever get married to me."

"Well, no."

"I said that to her, I said she should look around. That got her pissed. She called me a self-centred bastard. That I couldn't see further than the nose on my own face." Rick laughed. "The thing was I couldn't. See further, I mean." He smoothed the back of his hand with his fingers. "I was so goddamn afraid she'd leave me."

"That's how I was with Janelle," Spike said. "But things happened and we split up. Next thing I knew she was married to another guy and she had a baby. I saw her a few times around town and I even went over to her place one night after she'd left Jeff, but she didn't want to see me. And then I saw her last summer when I was home."

"Must have been weird."

"It was. I hadn't seen her for seventeen, eighteen years. She told me all about what she was doing, about a business she had selling jewellery. And I fixed the windshield wiper on her truck for her."

Rick moved his empty glass on its coaster around in a circle. "It's strange."

"What is?"

"We get all these chances."

Spike saw her before she saw him. She was getting out of her truck. He waited until she paused, with a little shock of recognition. He gave her a hug. There were lines around her eyes and her mouth, but her face was the same. The way she smiled was the same. She said, "By God, if it isn't the Spike himself."

She asked what he was doing, had he settled down yet? Did he have a bunch of kids? She kept talking and he just looked at her, shaking his head. Why didn't he have a bunch of kids? Then she told him about her jewellery business, that she'd earned herself a new car a couple of years before and she'd traded it in for a pickup, except now the windshield wiper was stuck or something. Did he know how to fix things like that? She said it was good to see him. She'd tell Pat she'd seen him. She went out with him sometimes now. Did he remember Pat McIntyre? The skinny kid who'd tried to break the windows in the school in grade five. Never did manage to break any of them. And she laughed so Spike could see her front tooth, the one that was crooked. Pat wasn't skinny any more. He had to watch it, drinking beer, because of his gut. Spike asked about her son, Colin, but she clammed up at that. They talked a little more and he tried to think of something else to say, just so she would stay a little longer, but he couldn't think of anything at all.

"My parents fell for each other just like *that*," said Spike, snapping his fingers. "And then they got married right away. They were just kids."

"Funny about parents," Rick said. "I have this black-and-white picture of my parents in a boat. My dad is fishing and my mother is smiling idiotically at him. He has this doting look on his face. I'd look at that picture and think it was perfect. But they didn't have this great marriage or anything."

They each ordered another drink when the waiter came around.

"It wasn't always easy to tell with mine," Spike said. "I mean, it seemed all right. But my little brother was kind of a handful."

"I never remember seeing my dad fishing," Rick went on. "He never taught me, anyway. And last winter he died in Florida."

"That's too bad."

"Yeah, there's always stuff I want to tell him. Even now." Spike looked down at his hands.

"There are things you have to tell people. Or *pifff, zip,* they're gone."

The fire was almost out now but they sat, inert, gazing at it as the waiter set down their drinks.

The time Spike saw Janelle outside Sobey's Garden Centre she talked a mile a minute and kept pulling on her necklace. She was thinner than he remembered. But her hair hung over her shoulders, blue-black. She didn't look at him when she mentioned Pat. Spike could have reached out and touched her face, she was so close. She asked him to fix the windshield wiper, but he could see she'd need a new one. It didn't make much difference what he did to it. He wiped his hands on his jeans. Her son, Colin, how was he doing? She looked at him in a puzzled kind of way. She wasn't pulling on that necklace of hers any more as if she wanted to break it. He was good. He was out on his own. She glanced at Spike and then she looked down at the pavement. After a moment she said something else, in a little twisted voice, so he wasn't sure he caught it. He didn't have any idea, did he? She looked up and her eyes were wet. She said that maybe it was time he knew. Everybody knew, she said, except Colin. He'd always thought Jeff Hicks was his dad. But Jeff Hicks wasn't Colin's dad.

Spike looked at her without saying a word. She said if only Spike had said something back then, anything, she wouldn't have gone and married Jeff. Spike was trying hard to breathe. She stood looking at him for a bit longer, waiting for him to say something, and after a while they said goodbye and she got into the truck and drove away.

The waiter was wiping up tables. They were the last ones in the pub but neither of them made a move to leave.

"I have a son," Spike said. "I never knew about it until last summer. He's about nineteen now."

Rick whistled lightly. "You're kidding."

"I wouldn't mind getting to know him a bit."

The waiter wiped their table, lifting the glasses between his thumb and forefinger so they clinked as he took them away.

"But he might hate me or something," Spike said.

"He might not."

He glanced at the window, covered with a half-curtain on a brass rail, suddenly aware that the sound of freezing rain flicking against the glass had stopped. A sanding truck went by with its yellow lights blinking. It was quiet again after the truck had gone and they could hear the waiter standing at the sink, rinsing the glasses. The water came out in little bursts. *Pfft. Pfft. Pfft.*

EVENING

Spike leaned back and stretched his neck. It was hot in the late afternoon, even in the air-conditioned car. They were in St. Stephen, New Brunswick, home of Ganong chocolates. Gateway to the U.S.A. Paradise Vacationland. He pulled into the Bell Motel. Above the office door were two gold bells tied with a blue ribbon. Gateway to Borderland. Limbo.

"The girls must have been delayed somewhere." Verna got out of the car and scanned the road. "They wouldn't have taken a wrong turn, would they?"

"They won't be long," said Allistair.

Spike and Allistair went inside the office and Verna wiped her face with a hanky, then took a compact out of her black purse and powdered her nose and forehead. At a car dealership across the road, light glanced off a car door as a man opened it. She watched him talk to a young woman, making an expansive movement with his hands. Verna shifted her gaze back to the road. Maybe they'd had an accident. Or something worse. An old pickup truck passed, sparks flowering around the trailing muffler each time it clanked on the pavement. She'd heard of women being left naked in the woods with their throats slit. A couple of motorcyclists went by, one driven by a woman wearing a black helmet, hair streaming from it like a banner. Several men with beards drove behind her. Verna moved around the car, closer to the office. Perhaps they'd been kidnapped by some deranged character. Tortured slowly, by degrees.

Spike and Allistair came out of the office laughing.

"I'll get the bags," said Spike, opening the trunk. "Mom, you all right?"

Verna thought she saw a blue car behind a van. Yes, there it was, turning in to the motel. She walked towards Robin's car and then paused as if she'd forgotten something, slumped to her knees, and collapsed on the pavement. Spike dropped the bags as he and Allistair ran to her side.

"Mom!" cried Evelyn, throwing open the car door. "Mom!"

Verna struggled to her feet, allowing Spike to support her on one side and Allistair on the other. "I'm fine," she said. "I'm just fine. It was a dizzy spell."

"It could be heat exhaustion," said Robin. "We should get her lying down."

Verna wouldn't allow them to help her to her room. She wouldn't let anyone check her pulse. She sat down heavily on a chair in the motel room, her purse on her lap, and Allistair got her a glass of water. That was all she needed. She'd have an early night and be fit as a fiddle.

The others checked in at the office and then drifted back to Evelyn and Robin's room. Spike slung his overnight bag on a table and Evelyn lay down on one of the beds.

Robin sat on the edge of Evelyn's bed and turned on the television.

Evelyn watched Miss Piggy bounce on a horse. "Do you think she'll be all right?"

"She just fainted. She'll be okay." Spike sat down in a chair and leaned back with his arms behind his head.

"Maybe we should have taken her to the hospital," said Evelyn.

Miss Piggy fell off the horse shrieking and Robin turned off the television.

"It could have been the first sign of a heart attack or something," Evelyn went on.

"She's not about to die." Spike got up, felt for his wallet. "Let's get something to eat."

"Well, a lot you'd care."

He picked up his bag as he went to the door. "Give me a break, Evelyn."

The room was ugly and dim now the door was open. Robin got up. "Evie, come on."

"No, not right now."

Robin caught up with Spike as he was going into the Red Hen Restaurant. She told him not to worry, she'd get something later. Kicking a half-open potato chip bag on the sidewalk, she went on down the street. Someone unloading a truck across the road whistled, a long drawn-out wolf whistle. If Evelyn wasn't coming, she didn't want to eat dinner with Spike. Maybe she didn't want to eat with any of them.

She found herself going into a McDonald's half a block farther, sitting down at one of the picnic tables outside and ordering a cheeseburger she didn't really want. A heavy man and his daughter sat down at the table next to hers, and a milkshake was knocked to the ground. The child whined at her father for another one as the soft pink liquid oozed over the patio stones. A teenage boy came almost immediately with a wet cloth to clean it up. His ears were neatly shaped, close to his head, and his neck was tanned. He went inside and came back out with a bucket and brush to scrub the patio stones clean. Robin felt a little rush of sympathy for him. He stood up and caught her eye.

"Finished, ma'am?" he asked politely.

"Oh, with the tray? Yes, fine." She handed it to him. He had a finely shaped nose and brown eyes. He bent down and picked up the bucket with his free hand.

"Messy stuff," she said.

He nodded. "On vacation?"

"Yes."

"Uh-huh." He didn't move. "Would you like coffee or something?"

"Oh, you don't have to get anything for me. Thanks."

"Sure," he said, and went inside.

She was still at the table after the man and his daughter had gone. The boy returned, this time wearing cut-offs and T-shirt, and he brought two cups of coffee, cream, and a few packets of sugar. He put one coffee on the table, along with the cream and sugar.

"Looked like you wanted some," he said.

"Well, that's good of you," said Robin, digging in her wallet for change. "Thanks."

"It's on me."

"Oh, well, thank you." She poured in the cream, though she usually didn't use it, and one packet of sugar. The coffee tasted rich and sweet.

"I'm off work now," he said. He was still standing, his cup on top of the garbage can.

"Are you?"

"Uh-huh."

Robin looked down at her coffee, which was an insipid beige colour. She set it down and made a gesture. "Have a seat."

"I'm okay standing," he said, and smiled again.

"So you live here?" asked Robin.

"Yup. With my dad. My mother lives in Calais. I work here days and I got another job there in the off-hours," he said, jerking his thumb in the direction of the border. "Body shop. Jason's on tonight, though."

"Must keep you busy." He was like her; he had one foot in each country.

"Not much else t'do. Fishing, maybe."

"I couldn't catch a fish to save my life," said Robin.

"Not much to it." He put his coffee cup in the garbage. "What do you do?"

"I work at a hospital doing PR. I'm the one who's supposed to make everything look good. But I think I'd rather work at home," she said, surprised she was telling him. "I'd like to have a workshop of my own, a sort of studio, you know?"

"You could work when you want to," he agreed, sitting down at the table. "Clear out when you felt like it."

"Mmm," she said. He had thick brown hair with glints of red in it. She imagined that his tan was even all over his body, perhaps from lying out naked on the days when he went fishing.

She looked at the coffee in her cup, at the cold, brownish liquid with a scum over the top.

"There's a game on at the ballpark," he said.

"Is there?"

"Yeah, no big deal or anything."

He couldn't have been more than eighteen, if that. She was twice his age.

"You're going?"

"You can come, too, if you like. Just as easy to walk as drive."

"Well," she said uncertainly. "I'd like a walk."

She was careful, all the way there, not to brush against him.

Verna was lying on the bed, gazing at the ceiling. She could hear Allistair brushing his teeth in the bathroom, then spitting into the sink. There was a crack on the ceiling. There were two cracks. And in the nubbly brown curtain over the blind at the window was a long tear, as if someone had gone at it with a knife. There was no telling. In places like these, there was no telling. Allistair came out of the bathroom, wiping his face with a towel.

"How are you now?" he asked.

"Fine. I don't think there's any real need for me to lie here like this, twiddling my thumbs."

"Do you have a book?"

"I'm not crazy about it." She showed him the cover, a knife drenched in blood, stuck into a pink satin garment. "Looks ghoulish, doesn't it?"

"Well," he said, examining it, "no trouble about the plot. It's all there."

"A murder in the first chapter. Then the second. And people hopping in and out of bed when they're not getting murdered."

"At least it's active. How about television, then?"

"Muppets," she said. "Wrestling. Some people dancing to country and western. They go round and round in circles."

He took her glass to the bathroom where she could hear him filling it. He came back, putting the glass and an aspirin on the bedside table.

"You take this while I get us something to eat."

"Can't we just order something in, like Chinese food?"

"You don't like Chinese food."

"Well, a pizza, then."

"I'll just be gone a minute, Vern. I'll get some juice and things."

He left. She put her hand over her heart but there was no constricted feeling, no shortness of breath, no more dizziness. Robin was probably right. It was just heat exhaustion. She closed her eyes and pictured a lake, a brilliant greenish blue lake. There was a photograph that hung by her bureau mirror at home. Lake Louise. She'd always wanted to go to Lake Louise. Breathing deeply, she told herself to calm down. Concentrate on a quiet place. But she couldn't concentrate. What if Garnet didn't come? She'd written him after he'd sent the postcard, giving the dates and a map, and asked him to come. He probably wouldn't come. She sighed, thinking of the time she'd gone to Boston and not been able to find him. It had been disappointing. But if he didn't come, no one would be any the wiser. At least she hadn't gotten Allistair's hopes up. She sat up and drank a little water, popping the aspirin into her mouth at the same time. But maybe she should tell Allistair anyway. Picking up the remote control, she flicked it at the television. It didn't come on even when she went over to it and pressed a button. She gave it a bang on top with the flat of her hand. Nothing happened. She went back and sat on the bed, staring at the television's blank face, and burst into tears.

Evelyn came out of the room to find the air was warmer
and heavier. She swung the key in her hand: a red plastic
woman with a gold number ten engraved on her skirt.
She went to the car and took out the cooler and two zip-
pered bags. Her father was crossing the street, stooped
and thin at this distance. What if one of them died? Her
father. Her mother. How would one cope without the
other? They were two sides of the same coin.

Did they need her? All Evelyn's life she felt like she'd
tried not to upset them, not to make things harder.
Things were bad enough with Garnet. But there was no
way around it when she'd left her marriage. As though
she'd taken a hammer to glass, things had gone off in all
directions. It hurt her parents. She was not the person
they thought she was.

Taking the bags back to number ten, she dropped hers
on one bed, Robin's on the other. She folded down the
bedspread, found a long red hair on a pillow, and plucked
it off. After a long shower, she sat on the bed, clad in a
towel, combing her unruly hair. Her thighs were too big,
she thought, like her rump. Phonse liked her that way. But
she wanted to be slim and careless about her body, like
Robin, with that blonde braid she was always tossing over
her shoulder. She got up and dressed without bothering to
look in the mirror.

She went to her parents' room and knocked. She
rapped hard again on the door and her mother opened it,
blinking at the light.

"Evie," she said, smiling.

"You all right? Your eyes are red."

"I was just having a lie-down. Maybe I rubbed them when I got up."

"But you're all right?"

"Yes. Now you go on and get yourself something to eat. Your father will be right back."

Her mother had taken off her thick-soled shoes. Her feet seemed tiny in her sockettes.

"I can't get you anything?"

"There's nothing I need, dear."

Evelyn found Spike finishing up his chicken wings at the Red Hen.

"Have some," said Spike, offering his plate.

Evelyn ate coleslaw from a tiny paper container. "I was tired when we got in. That's all."

"It's been a long day. You were worried." Spike pushed a little piece of chicken on his plate with his knife. "What the hell happened to Neil? Why didn't he come?"

"He's being a shit. He said he had all kinds of day surgery booked this week. I don't believe it for a minute. He's got a thing going with Carolee Levangie."

"He's a jerk." Spike put the knife down on his plate. It made a little metallic sound against the china. "I got a call from Garnet. He's coming. Or at least he said he'd try to come."

"You're kidding! Is he bringing that woman he's with?"

"No, I don't think so. He just got a job and wasn't sure he'd get time off."

"What kind of job?"

"He didn't say. He didn't say much, really."

"Well, what if he doesn't come? That's the sort of thing he'd do. He only thinks of himself."

Robin enjoyed the warmth of the evening sun on her back as she walked. She didn't have to talk much, except for the odd comment once in a while. The boy's name was Kyle. He played baseball himself when he got a chance and he used to play hockey in the winter but there wasn't time now. When they got to the ballpark, he dusted off the bleacher for her and asked if she wanted anything, like an orange soda or something. She didn't. Her bare leg touched his as they sat down. It was risky, she thought. She knew almost nothing about him.

It was the fourth inning, he told her, but the guy up to bat didn't stand a chance. The pitcher, now, he wasn't bad. Robin looked at the pitcher, who spat. The first batter struck out and the next one chewed nervously on the inside of his cheek, waiting for the ball. He hit a fly ball and Robin could hear the *thwack* as it landed in the outfielder's glove.

"Shit," said Kyle. He had moved forward and pressed his leg absently against Robin. She leaned a little closer. "You okay?" he asked, putting his arm around her.

She nodded.

"We can go anytime," he said. "Just give a shout."

"All right," she said. It was pleasant with his arm around her, his body close to hers. She looked beyond the baseball field to the tiny houses in rows beyond and the remote green hills far off. But the field in front of her was touched with evening light and each of the baseball players cast long shadows. The man next to her was eating salt and vinegar potato chips and the tangy smell made her feel oddly happy. There was nothing else in the world she wanted.

"Christ," said Evelyn. She was standing like a flamingo with one foot drawn up. "My sandal—I knew I wouldn't get very far if we walked."

They went into a dark pub, where the stench of beer made Evelyn wrinkle her nose.

"Why you wear things like this is beyond me." They sat down and Spike pulled out some dental floss to fix the sandal buckle. "They're ugly."

"I like them. Anyway, I don't criticize your stuff."

"My stuff's well made." He put the sandal down. "I'm getting a beer. You want one?"

"All right," said Evelyn. "Maybe one of those ice ones. But only if you're buying."

She sat back in her chair. On a tiny dance floor was a single chair with a broken back. Some plastic mistletoe was tacked to the ceiling. A black helmet lay on a table between a large man with a beard and a woman with long, wild hair.

Spike came back and set two glasses of draft down on the table. "No ice beer."

"This'll do," said Evelyn.

A skinny little man came in, bought a beer, and sat in a corner, staring at Evelyn. He stood up and sat down again. "Honey," he cried. "I love you, love you, love you. Honey, honey, honey."

"We can go if you like," said Kyle. "They're going to lose this game in a big way. Even Cormier can't save them."

"All right," said Robin.

"We can just go back and get my car. Drive around a bit."

They walked out of the ballpark. A gull flew up noisily in the sky.

"You've got nice hair," he said. "Real nice."

"Maybe I should let it out of the braid."

"It's all right like that."

He had a little red car he'd done some work on. One of the doors was rust-coloured.

"You ever seen St. Andrews-by-the-Sea? Big spread there. A hotel," he said. "We could go have a look."

"Sure."

They went east along the highway, passing the Bell Motel as they went, retracing the same route they'd driven that day, before turning down a side road to the ocean.

"You know I'm married," Robin declared suddenly.

"Yeah," he said. "You've got a ring."

She twisted the ring on her finger. Then she leaned back, her eyes half-closed, but she could still see his arm, his hand on the wheel. He reached over and gently put one hand at the nape of her neck, rubbing it briefly.

"Maybe he *is* fiddling around with that woman," said Verna. "Carolee someone, I think."

Allistair had fixed the television and now he was sitting on the edge of his bed with his back to her, flicking through the channels.

"I don't want to know," he said, turning off the television. "If he is or if he isn't."

"Well, it was you yourself said that Robin was moody. Maybe that's the reason."

"Verna."

"What?"

But he wouldn't say. Verna studied the sweater pattern. "I don't like it either," she murmured.

He went into the bathroom, where he stood for a moment with his hands on the edge of the sink, thinking. After a moment he came back out, undressed methodically, and put on his old striped pyjamas that Verna had mended so many times. They were soft and comfortable. He turned down the sheets and got into bed. Neil. When he picked up his book the bookmark fell out. What the hell was Neil up to? It was wrong. That's what it was. He got out of bed and went to the bathroom again. He brushed his teeth thoughtfully, drew back his lips in a grimace to examine them, and padded back to bed. It made him think of Verna and Colwell. What didn't happen. What could have happened. He didn't like to dwell on these things. They became real. He'd never said anything about Colwell to Verna, but it wasn't as if he didn't know.

Verna glanced at him. He'd read a bit, put the book on his chest, pick it up, and read a bit more. She finished purling a row and went on to the next. He just didn't want to face up to things. She put down the knitting, staring at a framed print of purple willow trees above the television. Allistair slumped down a little on the pillows and put the book on his chest. She didn't like it when he didn't talk to her. She felt it keenly. Maybe Neil wasn't seeing anyone. That Carolee girl was nothing special. Why would it ever cross Neil's mind? She stuffed the knitting into the flowered bag. But she shouldn't have said anything to Allistair. She went to the bathroom, washing her face and patting night cream on it. Then she went back to bed, picked up her novel. Allistair was snoring now, a rattly inhalation, a breathy exhalation. If he didn't wake up, she'd take the book and try to slip out one of the pillows without waking him. She opened her book: "Johanna gazed at him, thinking a curious thought, one that couldn't be stopped from floating leisurely into her mind. How strange it was that this man might turn out to be someone else. But she set the thought aside. She trusted him."

"You don't really know Phonse, though, do you?" Evelyn said. She picked up her glass, the third beer she'd had that evening, and drank.

"It's your life." Spike wiped his mouth.

"And you never liked Duncan, did you?" said Evelyn. "You really never liked him."

"It wasn't that I didn't like him, it was—"

"At least Duncan was straightforward," said Evelyn. "You could talk to him and know what he was on about. Unlike you, for instance."

"Me?" said Spike.

"Anyway, I could tell you never liked him," said Evelyn.

There was a rosy glow in the sky as Robin looked out the window. There were curious rock formations out in the bay, like heads, or upside-down jugs, and sometimes there were one or two spruce trees on top of them. The water was silky, entirely calm. She reached out her hand and touched Kyle's thigh at the fringe of his cut-offs, and then moved her hand forward, gliding it along his skin. After a while she took it away and folded her arms. But he reached over, pulled at her hand, and returned it to where it had been.

When they got there, Robin paid for the suite at the Algonquin Hotel. It was the only one they could get because of the bus tours. Kyle held her hand in the elevator and in the corridor he put his arm around her. Once they got inside the room they took off their clothes

quickly, without speaking. Kyle put his hands on Robin's
waist and looked at her. She looked back.

"Christ," he said softly.

"What?"

"You."

It was still light outside when Verna went over to the
window and looked out the window, twisting up the
ancient blind. It was nine o'clock. Only Evelyn had come
by to see her. She must be getting old, wanting to know
what the young were up to. She let the blind fall into
place and it clacked lightly against the glass. The curtain
bloused out and fell back. Old woman. That's what she
was. She crept back into bed, wrapping her arms around
herself. She'd had a nasty dream the night before. Great
sheets of flame at the windows of the house. Dark smoke.
When she woke, terrified, she prodded Allistair, who had
only grunted in his sleep. She'd gotten up and checked
the stove, the iron, the washing machine, and dryer.
Opened things up, closed them. The night had worn her
out, followed by the long day in the car. Now people
passed the window and she caught a snatch of conversation.

"What, they stapled the skin together?"

"After they did his bypass, that's what they did."

She wouldn't be able to sleep well. Perhaps it was the
fact that they were on a journey. It was disquieting, moving from one place to another. And there was something

about this place, this motel, that she couldn't put her finger on. Something had happened to them. They weren't together. They'd all drifted apart. It made her feel as though they hadn't gone anywhere at all.

"What, you mean hanging should be brought back?" asked Evelyn.

"Ev, some of these guys murder kids. I'd like to see them lit up like firecrackers."

"You never used to talk like this before. You're like a different person."

"I just don't believe all that save-the-world crap. I would never have gone to Indonesia."

"What was wrong with going to Indonesia?"

"Nothing. You taught school, got yourself a boyfriend. It was your very own personal experience."

"And that about wraps it up," said Evelyn. She banged her empty glass on the table.

"Well, I don't know. I wasn't there, was I?"

"Oh, you prick," she hissed. "You think everyone else is stupid, don't you? No one can make money like you. No one has a dick like you."

"Evelyn!"

"Don't *Evelyn* me."

"You're drunk."

"Well, so are you. You're just like Garnet." She glared at him. "We're just one big happy *family*."

S N A K E S K I N

Evelyn sat sullenly. Spike finished his drink. At the bar a man was laughing with his head thrown back, his arm around a woman in a black halter top. His hand was rubbing the flesh of her stomach as if he were kneading it. The woman smiled at him, hooking her fingers into his belt loops and tugging him away from the bar until he sat down heavily on a chair and pulled her into his lap.

"You can be a real pain in the ass," said Spike.

"So can you."

Evelyn couldn't talk to him. She couldn't talk to the rest of them. Her mother. Her father.

What had happened to them all?

One Hallowe'en when she was young she'd gone out with Spike and Garnet. She'd wanted to go out with Leslie Mackenzie, but Leslie had made plans with Carol Ann MacGillivray, so Evelyn had to go out with her brothers.

She was dressed as a bride, in a gown that her mother had found at Beatty's Good Quality Used Clothing. It was white and spangled all over with sequins, but the fitted bodice was too big, so she'd stuffed socks into it and covered it with a section of white tablecloth that she'd found in the ragbag. Her mother gave her a veil that had been a crinoline once, so it stuck out in all directions. But Evelyn was satisfied. In the bathroom vanity she found some Sultry Crimson lipstick, smearing it a little on her upper lip, instead of making two perfect wings the way her mother did, first on one side of her top lip and then on the other. When she was finished she put a tissue between her lips and smacked them lightly, leaving an imprint.

Garnet was covered in a flannel sheet with two blackened eye holes. And Spike was Count Dracula, his face whitened with paint and his mouth distorted by plastic fangs.

"Okay?" said Spike. "If you're not ready, we're going without you."

"Yup," she answered, picking up the edge of the gown so she could put on her rubber boots.

"You look dumb," Garnet told her.

"Shut up."

"Wait, you kids," called their mother. "I want a picture before you go out." They trooped back into the kitchen and waited while she fished through the string drawer to find a flashbulb. "There, get a little closer," she said, motioning with the side of her hand. "Stand in front,

Garnet. Good. Now, just a moment while I focus it.
Spike, take that piece of gum out of your mouth and
don't go putting it under the table. Okay, everyone, look
a little lively."

"Say, 'Peter, Peter, pumpkin eater,'" said their father,
who had come into the kitchen, smiling as he leaned
against the counter.

"Peter, Peter, pumpkin eater."

There was a flash of blue light and they stood blinking
for a moment.

"Bingo," said their father.

Evelyn got herself a Scotch and water at the bar.

"That's a pretty stupid thing to do," said Spike. "Mix-
ing beer and Scotch."

"No, it's not," she said, bumping the chair as she sat
down.

"You don't have the stomach for it."

"How do you know?"

"You do stupid things like that all the time."

"I do not."

"For instance, you wind up with the wrong men. And
now you've got this thing about men. All men."

"I don't have a *thing* about it. I'd say you've got a *thing*
about women."

"What do you mean?"

"They're good for a screw. That's how you see it."

"That's how I see it?"

"Well, look at Alice Blaney. I remember that."

"You're kidding. Nothing much happened with Alice Blaney."

"Oh, come on. That's all she talked about for weeks. How you two were going steady, that you'd given her your ring."

"And you listened to her?"

"Why wouldn't I? But it wasn't just Alice. It was Tammy Jane Pushie and Florence Archibald and then Janelle. It was unbelievable the things that went on between you and Janelle."

"Shut up, Evelyn."

She sat back in her chair, her hands slack over the armrests. She might have been smiling.

The leaves were thick and wet on the sidewalk, and made a soft noise as the children tramped through them. Evelyn's dress was already damp at the hem, and muddy in one place where Garnet had stepped on it. Spike soaped the windows of Mr. Hennessey's Oldsmobile because he'd only given them one black licorice pipe each, but the Marchands made up for it with candy apples with a glossy red glaze, handed out from a tray in Mrs. Marchand's kitchen. Evelyn walked very slowly licking hers, letting the boys get ahead of her. She saw Garnet sneak behind a bush.

"Woooouuuu," shrieked Garnet, jumping out.

"You really think you're going to scare me?" asked Evelyn. "You don't even look like a ghost."

"Well, you look like a retard," he hooted, the stripes on his flannelette sheet fluttering out behind him as he ran to catch up with Spike.

She hated them. She hated them both.

"Janelle was just like Alice when it came right down to it," said Evelyn.

"Christ, if you think you can—"

"Oh, hit a nerve, did I?"

"You're worse than Garnet when you're drunk."

"Am I?"

"Yes."

"How?"

"You talk about people. I don't remember Garnet ever doing that."

"So."

"And you think you have the right to say what you want."

"I do not."

"Yes, you do. You have no idea about someone like Alice. Or Janelle. You don't know a thing."

"I know what I see."

"You see what you want to see."

Spike didn't know what she saw, Evelyn thought. He had no idea.

They went up Hawthorne Street as far as the Brierly Brook road and by that time Evelyn wanted to turn back.

But there were two or three more houses that Spike and Garnet wanted to visit so she followed behind them, afraid to go back along Hawthorne Street by herself because she might run into the Fougère kids.

"Come on, Evie," called Spike. They were waiting for her. "Here, I'll hold your pillowcase for you if it's too heavy."

"No," said Evelyn firmly. She knew he'd take it from her.

"Go up to that house, Evie," he said.

"Yeah, do it," said Garnet.

"No," she said.

"I'll give you my peanut butter cups if you do," wheedled Spike.

Evelyn looked at the house. There was a long driveway up to it and a dim light at the side door. There was no jack-o'-lantern.

"No," she repeated.

"And my candy apple," said Spike.

Evelyn considered. She kicked at a scattering of leaves on the sidewalk.

"You'll wait right here?" she asked.

"What do you take us for?" said Spike.

"Scout's Honour?"

"Scout's Honour."

She walked up the driveway, looking back every once in a while to make sure they were still there. For a moment she stopped when she heard a low moaning coming from the bushes that lined one side of the driveway, but it was only a cat and she went on, slowly, the skirt of the dress dragging on the ground. At last she came to the little porch, climbed the steps, and rang the doorbell, listening to the shrill little noise it made inside the house.

"What?" shouted a man's voice. "Who's there?"

She could hear the sound of something crashing to the floor. She backed away.

"What'd you want?" A man stood at the screen door. His belly, in its undershirt, nearly touched the screen mesh and his bare foot protruded past the door frame, holding it open a couple of inches. Evelyn stared at his foot, paralysed. "Oh, yeah, wait here a minute," he said, and vanished into the gloom of the room. He reappeared with one round white mint, like a pebble in his hand. "Here."

Evelyn took it. She ran the length of the driveway stumbling on her dress.

"At least I don't delude myself," said Evelyn.

"Ha." Spike was leaning back in his chair so its front legs were raised off the floor.

"You really piss me off."

"I know."

"I can't talk to you. You're a—"

"Oh, right, here it comes. I'm a thick-headed jerk who only thinks about himself."

"Yes," she said, "exactly."

"There you are, Evelyn. Case in point," he said, rising from his chair. "You see what you want to see." He put down a few dollars on the table. "That's for your taxi, and this," he said, taking a card from his pocket, "is the name of the motel, in case you forget."

"Just piss off," she said.

He left.

She didn't really want the Scotch and water after all. She'd had enough. What was it about Spike? Why did they always argue? He made her feel like she was a kid. That's what it was. And she wasn't a kid.

She hadn't fought with Neil when they were growing up because he'd never had anything to do with her. And she hadn't fought much with Garnet. He'd looked up to her. Well, until he dropped her. He'd dropped them all. She couldn't imagine him coming back into their lives. Some kind of tornado in the distance, a grey funnel getting closer, closer, ripping up everything and setting it down all wrong. That's what he'd do to them.

Maybe all this time Evelyn had just wanted a sister. She was alone among them. That was what *unique* meant, in the end. She wasn't exactly the kind of daughter her parents wanted, she wasn't the kind of sister her brothers wanted. She was alone.

When she got to the end of the driveway, Spike and Garnet were nowhere to be seen. Two kids with monster masks brushed past her.

"That's Blaney's," said one. "I'm not going up there."

"He'd fry you up and eat you for breakfast," said the other.

Evelyn ran down the sidewalk, still hampered by the dress. She ran all the way down Hawthorne Street, hardly seeing a thing. Old man Blaney. All she could think of was a man's shadowy face in the half-light of the porch, his huge, shambling body, his yellow toes with the curved, uncut nails. It must have been that she'd wakened him, and that was why he'd stood there, blinking, at the door. But she hadn't been able to move or speak, even as he handed her the mint and pulled back his lips over his teeth in a sort of grin. *Peter, Peter, pumpkin eater.*

The tablecloth flapped loosely like a bib and she flung it on the ground as she ran, breaking through clusters of children. Clowns, tramps, a boy with a plastic axe. She'd pound Spike's and Garnet's brains out. But she didn't see them, and by the time she reached the house her dress was nearly at her waist and dragging on the ground. She ripped it off and left it behind her, along with the veil. It lay on the ground like a snakeskin, and the veil snared itself in the raised branches of the pear tree before ripping free.

N I G H T

Evelyn walked along a side street in St. Stephen, occasionally bruising her feet. She'd taken off both sandals after she left the bar, because of the broken one that Spike hadn't really fixed. The sky was indigo, except in the west where the blue was still faintly tinged with pink. A bat dipped overhead as she stood in front of a grey house with a For Sale sign on the lawn. She was a little drunk. She looked at the pulled curtains, glanced up and down the street, and then walked up the driveway to the shed at the back. The blinds had been pulled in the kitchen, too. She sat down on the grass. Someone had kept up the garden, which was filled with snapdragons, begonias, impatiens, and pansies; clusters of colour surrounded by heaps of balsam wood chips. From where she was lying she could reach out and touch the flowers. She picked a pansy, a purple flower with a yellow centre. It was velvet-soft as the ear of an animal and she smoothed the petals between her fingers.

Once Garnet and Evelyn had broken into Doc Welsh's house on the Brierly Brook road when he was visiting relatives in Vermont. There was no one around, no one to see what they were up to. Garnet had been inside it once before. He'd been inside a lot of places, he told her, but he never took anything. He'd been inside the Dubrovnys', the MacGillivrays', the MacDonalds', the Sewells'. He counted them off on his fingers as he sat on the Welshes' kitchen windowsill with one leg hanging out. He knew how to get into just about any place in town.

"What do you do once you get in?" Evelyn asked.

"Just look around," he said.

"But what if you get caught?"

"I never have."

He told her that all the doors in Belly Schulein's house had to be widened because he couldn't get through them. Joe Aucoin's kids kept a pet skunk. In the New Christian Reformed minister's wife's top right-hand drawer there were seven pairs of black lace panties, and each pair was embroidered in red with the days of the week. Behind the furnace was a stack of *Playboy* magazines.

"Ever seen them at it?" Evelyn asked, climbing up on the overturned garbage can. She reached up to the kitchen window.

"Not yet," he said, dropping down out of sight. "I've only seen her undressing."

She crawled through the window and scrambled down

onto the counter.

"What's the matter?" he asked.

"Nothing."

"The best place I ever saw," he said, "was this little shack by the train tracks. It's not far from here."

"Will you take me?"

"Sure," he said. "Sometime."

Evelyn sat up, feeling a little dizzy. Someone was roaring up the street on a motorcycle. Plucking a blade of grass, she pulled it taut between her two thumbs and blew lightly through it. *Wiuuueee.* She got up slowly and brushed off the grass. Then she saw the dog in the driveway; a yellow-ish white dog that barked snappishly until a man whistled from the porch of a house across the street and the dog ran swiftly to him. They went inside and the screen door shut with a small severe sound. *Click.* She began walking in a careful line along the sidewalk under the bluish lozenges of streetlights, from one island of light to the next.

Garnet showed Evelyn the small study in Doc Welsh's house. There were flat glass-topped cases of butterflies, piled one on top of the other; small ceramic containers filled with an ashy, sandy substance; an envelope of dead flies; animal skulls; rocks; the shed skin of a snake; a box of dirty plastic combs; several stamp albums; newspapers; old records in a box. Everything was labelled. "*The Tartan,* 1923–1930." "Weasel skull, found in McCafferty's ravine, 1957." "Topographical maps of Cape Breton."

"Here," he said. "Look at this."

On one of the shelves near the desk stood a little object on a stand. It looked like a dark, shrivelled apple, but when Evelyn looked closer she realized it was a little shrunken head. It had eyes, a nose, a mouth. And it had hair.

"Oh, gross," she said.

"It's real, you know."

"Real?"

"It's from South America. See?" He showed her the label: "Jivaro shrunken head. Upper Pastaza River, Ecuador." He turned it around. "But I don't know how they did it. I mean, they had to get rid of the skull, so—"

"That's disgusting."

He laughed and put it up close to her face, so that she could see the little ridges of leathery skin, the strange, blind eyes. She turned and fled.

Evelyn turned around at the sound of a noisy car. It was full of teenage boys, one with his head out the window and his lips puckered and extended towards her. "Cunt," he said, and the others laughed.

The car moved away, several heads leaning out the window.

"Pussy, pussy gangbang," called one.

"Roll her over, lay her flat," yelled another.

The car progressed slowly along the street and turned at the corner. Evelyn stood absolutely still by some bushes at the corner of a lawn. Was it safe to keep going? She pulled free of a lilac branch that had caught in her shirt. She waited.

Garnet never showed Evelyn the place by the train tracks. He never took her on another of his "trips." Sometimes he went with Guy McEwen, but mostly he went on his own and no one really knew what he was up to, except Evelyn.

But she wanted to see the shack, so one afternoon she went by herself. At the building supply sheds near the water tower she turned and went through the bush, past the signs that read No Dumping and No Hunting. There were tire tracks for a while, ending in flourishes and skids, and then a track that descended to the river through the spruce and birch trees. Briefly, she saw a pileated woodpecker, with a fantastic red brush on his head. When she came to the shack it was padlocked, and the one small window in the back was covered on the inside with cardboard. She jiggled the rotten window frame and after a while bits of putty fell out, loosening the glass. She tried to push out the pane, but she had to bang it hard with her fist until the glass broke. Her hand bled, but not as much as she'd expected. She picked out the pieces in her skin and removed the shards from the frame. Then she pushed the cardboard aside, put her hand in, and unlocked the window, pushing up the sash.

The shack was full of things. There were two televisions,

one with its screen smashed, a hi-fi, radios, bicycles, two chairs, an overturned crate with a metal cash box on it, and empty rum bottles on the floor. *Playboy* magazines. A chalk drawing of a face with horns on one of the walls, and under it the word "Guy." This had been crossed out and beneath it, "You cocksucker," along with a sketch of an oversized penis and testicles. The testicles looked like balloons, and the penis was a huge carrot. There was a dartboard next to it and some of the darts had landed on the sketch of the penis. Things were hanging from nails on the wall beside the window: a couple of watches, a necklace with a pendant heart, a silver bracelet with tiny charms. The bracelet was within reach. Evelyn could see a fish, a pirate hat, and a cuckoo clock, a charm that said "Elizabeth" in tiny letters, an old-fashioned bicycle, and a miniature cradle with a silvery baby. But it wasn't the bracelet that interested her so much as the object suspended from the ceiling of the shack, a strange blackened object that swung a little in the air. A shrunken head.

She couldn't get the cardboard back in place, but she put the window sash down with its edges of broken glass, leaving a smear of blood from her hand on the frame.

She still had the pansy in her pocket. It was a little crushed and wilted, and she couldn't smell any fragrance as she held it to her nose. She was sobering up as she walked. In some houses there was a blue flicker of television light, and in one living room a man in a dressing gown was patting a baby's back as he paced around the couch while a woman leaned against the doorway, holding a plate in one hand. A fork moved to her mouth. The man began to sway from side to side and then to dance, his mouth opening and closing as if he were singing. The woman smiled.

When she came to the intersection of Rose and Queen, she wasn't sure which way to go. Her feet were dirty and her sandals dangled from one hand. She was a little bewildered. Where was she, anyway?

When Doc Welsh came to their house, Evelyn asked him if he'd mind waiting in the hall while she went to find her mother. He took off his hat and waited. From the top of the stairs where she crouched in the shadows Evelyn could see him examining the wallpaper. He seemed fascinated by the green woman swinging on the green swing, pushed by the green man. The top of his head was bald and the skin was shiny, as if it had been rubbed with polish. It could have been a large bird's egg. Then her mother came into the hall, apologizing, one hand still clad in a red-and-white oven mitt. She called him Cameron because she knew him from church. He said he'd come about Garnet, and then with a motion of his hand as if he were the host, Doc Welsh ushered her into the living room and closed the door behind him.

Even when Evelyn went downstairs and stood by the door she couldn't hear what they were saying. She retreated back up the stairs and after a while her mother came out, rubbing the side of her forehead with her fingertips.

"Of course, the alternative is worse," Doc Welsh was saying. "That's not something we'd want."

"No," said her mother distractedly, "we'll handle it."

At the gas station an attendant drew a rough map on a piece of paper towel. "Could always take a taxi," he grinned as he went out the door.

"Thanks," she said, taking the piece of paper towel in her hands. There were several lines on it in blue pen. He'd marked the motel with an X and circled it. She examined it, not wanting to turn around, thinking she'd see the faces of the boys pressed to the window, their noses and lips flattened grotesquely against the glass, as if they weren't part of them at all but something else, like white grubs.

After Evelyn had broken into the shack and bloodied her hand, she climbed up the hill in a different direction, glancing behind her as she went. If she was right, she'd come out on the Brierly Brook road somewhere just above Doc Welsh's place. The spruce wood was thick, though, and the hill much steeper than she'd expected, and she slipped several times trying to get to the top. But when she reached it there was a path through the woods, which she thought might lead to the road. Instead, she came out at Doc Welsh's driveway, near his car. He was bending over the hood, waxing it patiently, a container of wax in one hand and a cloth in the other. Evelyn froze. Far off, the woodpecker began to drill against a tree trunk. Evelyn had no idea what to do. Then Doc Welsh looked up, straight at her, studying the streaks of dirt on her clothes, her bloodied hand.

"It wasn't me," she blurted out. "It was Garnet."

Evelyn breathed in the rich, sweetish smell of gas as she went outside to the pay phone, where she took out the card Spike had given her and studied it, swaying a little, before dialling a taxi. She wasn't taking any chances. She'd had too much to drink for one thing, and she felt a little nauseous. When the taxi came she walked across the lit area and into the darkness where it was waiting.

"Hey, cunt," said a soft voice.

It was impossible to know whether the voice was real or imagined. It was a soothing, quiet voice, just loud enough for her to hear. She opened the door of the taxi and got in without looking around. The driver hadn't spoken. His hand was on the car roof where he was drumming his fingers.

"Where to?" he asked.

She glanced out the window but there was no one there. Only a velvety darkness, as if the warm air had the weight of a thick curtain.

"The Bell Motel, please."

The shrunken head was returned to Doc Welsh. The

MacIntyres' television set miraculously reappeared without its picture tube. Beth Crawley's charm bracelet was discovered one night in the Crawleys' doghouse, along with her mother's pendant necklace.

One evening Evelyn heard fire engines roaring up Hawthorne Street. She had an idea where they were going, because there was a smudge of smoke expanding and darkening in the sky near the water tower. The next day she found the shack burned to the ground. Nothing was left but dirt and ashes, blackened boards, a grill, an open cash box, and bits of glass scattered here and there. She found a dart, which she picked up and put in her pocket. As she was turning to leave, she found some red letters painted on the bole of a tree. A message from Garnet: CUNT.

Evelyn got the key from the motel office and went to the room. In the bathroom she realized she was still holding the map the gas station attendant had drawn, rolled into a little ball. She ran a bath and took off her clothes. It was possible she was still half-afraid of Garnet, after all this time. She turned off the water and got into the bath, scrubbing hard at the soles of her feet.

After the bath, she towelled herself dry. Then she sat down abruptly on the bathroom floor. She listened to cars passing on the highway. Trucks gearing down as they came into town. A woman was calling for someone named Len in the parking lot. She called again.

"God, Len, what's keeping you?"

"Keep your voice down, Maureen. Just give me a minute."

After Doc Welsh left, Evelyn went downstairs to help her mother finish getting supper ready. She set the table, drained the vegetables, and called the others to come to the table. Her mother didn't say a word, even when she burnt her thumb. When the others came into the kitchen, she set the pot roast down on the wooden coaster in the centre of the table. Her face was pinched. They sat down in silence and Neil gave Spike a kick under the table as Evelyn said grace. Then their mother went around the table to dole out overcooked carrots and broccoli from the saucepan, her serving spoon making a hard little sound each time it touched the plates.

When she came to Garnet, she stood with the serving spoon raised.

"So, young man," she said.

She gave him a helping of vegetables. Then she sat down in her place, shaking out her napkin, without looking at any of them.

When their father came home he had a talk with Garnet, in the kitchen, with the doors closed. Upstairs in her bedroom, Evelyn tried to concentrate on the habits of the hummingbird: "Some three hundred species of hummingbirds belonging to the family Trochilidae inhabit the southern areas of the Americas as far as Tierra del Fuego."

She doodled on a scrap of paper, drawing a bird and embellishing it with stars and flowers. Pushing back her chair, she picked up the transistor radio and lay on her bed fiddling with the knob, trying to tune it to the station in Charlottetown. She heard Garnet coming up the stairs, slowly, not two at a time. He put his head in at her door and it was all she could see of him, except for his fingers gripping the edge of the door. His face was white, twisted with anger.

"It was you, wasn't it," he said.

She went out of the bathroom, put on her nightgown, and lay on the bed, but it didn't do any good. It just made her feel nauseous. She got a magazine out of her bag and went back to the bathroom, where she sat on the floor again. The magazine was full of recipes for New York fudge cake, orange-and-pineapple chicken, poppy seed buns. There was an article about Aruba with photographs of turquoise water and perfect golden sand. A woman in an orange bikini, tanned and oiled, leaned against a palm tree. Evelyn slapped the magazine shut. It didn't matter what she looked at, she could still see the white shape of a face in a car window, mouthing words, but it seemed as if something had collapsed it, so that it was smaller than it should have been.

BED

Robin contemplated the young body of the boy who had just made love to her. Kyle's eyes were closed. His skin was dark against the sheet. After a moment he reached over and put his arm around her.

"You okay?" he asked.

"Fine."

She looked at the ceiling and twisted a strand of hair around her finger.

"What?" he asked.

"Well, I don't know. I should feel terrible right now, but I don't."

"When was the last time you had sex?"

"I don't know."

"See?"

"Well, it's nice, but you can live without it."

"Sure you can. But it makes a difference," he said, propping himself up on one elbow and looking at her. "Doesn't it?"

She kept twirling the strand of hair. "Well, yes."

He put his hand over the fingers twisting her hair. She looked at him.

"We had sex," she said firmly. "It's not love or anything."

The last time she and Neil tried to have sex, five or six months ago, they both decided they weren't really into it. He sighed and rolled over to his side of the bed. After a while he fell asleep and she went into the bathroom. She shrugged the bathrobe off her shoulders and looked at her body in the mirror. She turned around so she could see herself from behind. Then she turned around to face herself and looked at her breasts, appraising them.

It wasn't her fault.

"I thought I'd talk about things with my husband," she said. "I had this idea that people did that when they got married."

She turned to look at Kyle.

"It's not like we didn't talk," she went on. "We talked a lot at first."

"But not now."

"We talk about who's going to take the car in for rust-proofing." She put her arms above her head and stretched. "It makes for real conversation."

He ran his hand over her breasts.

"You can talk to me." He kissed her shoulder. He kissed her lips. She kissed him back.

"Don't you think it's sort of funny that I'm in bed with someone I don't know, talking about my husband?"

"No."

"Why?"

"You like me." He put his leg over hers.

She smiled.

Neil was sitting at the breakfast table a few months after they were married, looking at the toast on his plate. "Burnt," he said. "I always burn it. Is that toaster set wrong or something?"

"I don't know," said Robin. "Mine's okay."

He picked it up and began buttering it.

"I've been thinking about kids," he said.

"Do you always put the butter on like that?"

"What? I like butter." He licked his finger. "Anyway, I've been thinking about it."

"You want to wait a while. I know, you've said that."

"No, it's—" He put down the toast.

"What?"

"I don't know if I want kids."

She looked at him. "You don't know?"

"Well, I don't know if I do."

She got up and took her plate over to the counter. She stood with her back to him. "I want kids."

"I know you do."

She turned around. "If I want kids and you don't, then we've got a problem."

"Well, that's why I think we should talk about this."

"No," she said, tears welling up in her eyes. "I don't want to."

"We'd better go," Robin said, sitting at the edge of the bed and taking a comb out of her purse. She parted her hair and began braiding.

"How do you do that so fast?"

"What?"

"Your hair."

"I can do it in my sleep."

"It's nice," he said admiringly.

"It's just hair." She finished braiding it, fastened the elastic around it, and turned around to face him. "When I was little, I used to think I could have hair like a mermaid. You know, all this long floating hair."

"Why don't you just wear it loose?"

"I don't know. Habit."

He stroked her arm.

"What?" she said.

"Let's not go yet."

Neil came up to the bedroom to find Robin after they'd quarrelled during breakfast.

"It's a beautiful day out there."

"I know."

"Listen, I think if you want kids, then maybe we should have them."

"I don't want to have children you don't want."

"I'd get used to it."

"You'd get used to it?"

"I don't want to argue, Robin."

"Neither do I." She picked a tiny white feather out of the duvet and let it drift to the floor. "Let's not talk about it, then."

"All right," he said. "That's okay by me."

"I thought that's what you'd say." She picked at another feather.

"I said if you wanted kids, we'd have kids."

"So what'll we do, snap our fingers?"

"There," said Robin. She'd put on her sundress.

Kyle sat on the bed looking at her.

"You're different."

"It's the dress," she laughed.

"No, it's not that." He pulled on his clothes. "I guess you're ready to go."

"Yes."

"Just come here for a minute."

"Why?" She came close to him.

"Just because," he said, lifting the dress and kissing her stomach. "Maybe I'll never see you again."

"I know. But people do it."

"Have you ever done this?"

"No. Have you?"

"Not with someone who's married. Not in a hotel room." He lay back on the bed. "I'll miss you. I bet you'll miss me, too."

She was looking straight ahead. "My father had an affair. My mother did, too."

He shifted position so he could look at her.

"And my husband," she mused. "Everyone. Me included."

Robin was up late the night before she went to the cottage because she'd left her packing until the last minute. Neil was already in bed with the pillow over his head to keep out the light.

"Aaah!" she yelped, stubbing her toe on the bureau.

"Couldn't you do that in the hall?" His voice was muffled.

He rolled over, grunting. She put the stack of T-shirts and her flowered bathing suit in the bag. An old navy sweatshirt. She tossed in the beach sandals. Then she sat down on the chair and regarded his lumpy form under the duvet.

"I know why you're not coming," she said. She hardly trusted herself. What would she say next?

"I told you why I can't."

"You don't want to come." She wanted to slap him.

He couldn't hear her. He'd wrapped the pillow tightly around his head.

She got up and turned out the light. It had been more than a week since she'd slept in their bed, but he hadn't asked her why, as if he knew she'd learned something about him. Her eyes got used to the dark and she could see faint lights on the ceiling. He turned over and unwrapped the pillow from his head.

"I'll miss you," he said. Then he covered his head again.

He couldn't hear what she said. She could say anything she wanted. "I won't miss you," she said quietly, experimenting. There was no response from under his pillow. "You can go ahead and do whatever you want. And I'll do whatever I want."

She stood at the threshold. Nothing. They'd never really argued much. It might have been better if they had. She imagined herself tossing things out of her bag, calling him names, pounding his chest with her fists. No. Her anger might take her to the edge of a cliff. It might take her right over it. She didn't know, so for now she'd just hold on. The idea of talking about Carolee, about Neil with Carolee, was beyond her. She picked up the bag and put it in the guest bedroom. It would be an early start the next day; she wouldn't be expected to say goodbye.

Neither Kyle nor Robin said much on the way back. Robin imagined all the things she couldn't see in the darkness. The black ocean, the islands like bent knuckles. Sea of loss. It was difficult to make out anything on the road ahead, except what was visible in the milky glow of the headlights. Kyle flicked on the high beams and the road was suddenly illuminated for a greater distance. But the darkness was all around them.

"What are you thinking?" he asked.

"Oh, not much."

The headlights of an oncoming car blinded them for a moment as it came around a curve.

"They used to hang people for adultery. And they stoned them. Imagine being stoned."

"It's different now."

"Yes," she said. "It doesn't matter. That's the thing. It just doesn't matter."

He didn't say anything.

"What is it?" she asked.

"Don't do that."

"What?"

"It was a good thing. Don't spoil it."

They were silent for a while. He reached over and took her hand in his. It was a firm hand, comforting to hold.

"You'll be all right," he said.

KAYAKING

Robin and Neil lived in a large house on the waterfront in Seabright. It was built of stone, in a place where houses were usually built of wood, and it had a wide front entrance and a lawn that rolled, unimpeded, down to the water. There was a screen of trees on each side, but Neil had had quite a lot of the scruffier ones removed. Alder would be everywhere, he said, if it got a toehold. There weren't many other places along the dirt road that led to the point, except for a summer establishment with house-keeping cottages and a tiny yacht club that wasn't really a yacht club, just a couple of docks.

It gave them privacy. It gave them so much privacy that once Robin had screamed at the top of her lungs in the garden just to see if anyone would hear. No one did, except the birds. She went back to weeding the garden, which Neil had rototilled, so that it was a huge patch, filled with tiny sprouts of all kinds of vegetables they would probably never get around to eating: broccoli, cabbages, spring onions, squash, cucumber, zucchini. She had to cover them with newspapers every night. She worried about leaving it when she went to Maine. Being in the garden, coddling and pampering it, helped her think only of things that were in the soil. She didn't have to think of what she'd found in the driveway a few weeks ago. A new car, parked next to her sensible blue one. Neil had bought a little sportscar over the Internet. He hadn't said anything about it. And there it was: a little yellow convertible. A Miata, Neil told her, when she came to look at it. He separated the syllables with pleasure. Wasn't it great? He'd slid his hand along its side, describing all its features. Leather seats, cruise control, state-of-the-art sound system. She didn't want to hear about its features. She turned on her heel and went into the house, slamming the front door and surprising the cat, which jumped down from the top of the antique grandfather clock.

It was just one of many things that had driven her crazy about Neil lately, Robin thought. Spending upwards of thirty thousand dollars out of the blue like that on something they didn't need. But it was more than that. It was the kind of car a man bought when he wanted to impress women. It was a teenager's dream car.

The car led her to suspect things. She'd never thought she would go through Neil's drawers, that she would check the return addresses on his letters, and even, surreptitiously, his credit card bill. If she looked scrupulously enough, she would find something. She did. It was around midnight some weeks after that; she'd gotten up for a glass of water. On the counter was Neil's wallet. His keys on the familiar key chain: a miniature golf ball with a little club. There was one key with a red star sticker marked C. This wasn't Neil's key. Whose was it? She usually didn't pay attention to keys, and often dropped old ones into the drawer with coupons, string, and tape. C. Carolee. Her friend? No. C probably stood for cabinet, closet. Not Carolee.

There was a vivid flash in Robin's mind: the party they'd given last August. Neil giving Carolee a drink on the screened porch. A margarita, with a rim of sugar around the glass. Neil knew how to do things like that all of a sudden.

"Just the way I like it," she said, glancing up at him, her long brown legs neatly crossed at the ankles.

"I know," Neil murmured.

Robin had caught that and at the time she hadn't paid any attention. *Just the way I like it.*

A few days afterwards, she phoned Verna to invite her kayaking. She could have called Sharla, who was closer than Carolee. But Sharla ran a bed and breakfast with her husband and it was impossible for her to get away from it in the summer. And there was comfort being with Verna. Verna had gone kayaking once or twice before, with a little apprehension, saying that she'd get stuck if the thing rolled over. But it was a good day for it, a clear Saturday in June, just days before they were to leave for Maine. There was

only a whiff of wind on the harbour. And Robin checked
the weather reports on the computer. A light west wind,
ten to fifteen knots, shifting southerly by evening. Verna
would be fine, and Robin would be right beside her.

So Verna had come. Robin had slipped the red sea
kayaks into the water, adjusted the foot pedals, tucked a
thermos and plastic bag with sandwiches in the space
behind her seat, and they'd slipped into the harbour.
They stayed close together in the shallow water. The eel-
grass moved under them as they went, like thick hair.

"Put your rudder up," said Robin. "It'll get caught."

"Oh," said Verna. "Right. This cord, I think." The rudder came up with a *fwlap*.

They went on together in silence, only the paddles
making sound as they scooped the water. It was easy to
cover distances, but the trees and barns, the intermit-
tently visible road, the occasional orange buoys, all
seemed to be moving while they were standing still. They
were floating, disembodied, lifted off the face of the earth.

"Beautiful." Verna handled the paddle the way someone might dig with a snow shovel. She was pink with the
effort. "I was busy packing for the cottage. But now I'm
glad I came."

It was absolutely tranquil. It had been a harsh winter
and then there had been rain after that, but today everything was lush and green. Verna put her paddle down.

"I could do this forever," said Robin dreamily. "Never
go back to the house."

"Never?"

"Sometimes it all seems difficult. You know? Everything."

"A change is as good as a rest," said Verna. "You could
do your art for a while."

Robin could make out a bald eagle on a dead tree near
the water. "I've been thinking about doing that." She
pointed at the eagle, which appeared to have spotted them.
It glared in their direction with its yellow eyes. They paddled apart for a while and then came back together. The
water was rippled like bunched-up fabric where the wind
skimmed over it. Further on, it was smooth and glassy.

"I can't paddle the way you do," said Verna. "It looks so
easy when you do it."

"Just keep your paddle lower between strokes. It's not
so much work."

"Ah, there." Verna tried a couple of strokes, circled
around, and came up beside Robin. She was a little
breathless. "You know, there was a time I wanted everything in my life to change. I sent poor Allistair packing."

"Did you?"

"Oh, I was being silly. Our neighbour caught my eye
and I caught his eye. That was all, but it was more in my
mind, and there was a time I thought I couldn't bear it."

"So you separated—"

"Well, no, not really. I didn't tell Allistair, but something was up and he knew it. He left. Neither of us
thought it through. And I heard the car going out the

driveway. I went running to the door to tell him I was being a fool. But he'd gone. And I sat down on the stairs and cried and cried. I felt terrible. Just terrible. I don't care which side of the door you're on, when something like that happens it's the worst thing in the world."

Robin's parents got married in the middle of an April snowstorm in New York City. A freak snowstorm. Her mother didn't have a wedding dress, but she had a bouquet of lilies. They didn't have any photographs, except for the ones a friend took a few days later, in Connecticut, when the sun was shining. They were sitting on the grass. There was nothing to show that there had been a snowstorm a few days before. Her mother's hair looked silver in the black-and-white photograph because the sun was on it. Her arm was linked through Robin's father's. He was smiling at her, or at something just beyond her, so his face was turned a little away from the camera.

The day they got married they walked down the middle of Broadway, which was covered in snow. Nothing was moving along it, not even taxis. They scattered the lilies. They threw snowballs in Central Park. Her mother said they'd never had so much fun. It didn't matter that they didn't have a honeymoon, she said, because they had that wonderful day just being silly. Robin tried to imagine her mother being silly. She tried to imagine her throwing snowballs in Central Park. She tried to imagine her mother in love with her father.

Robin asked her father once about his wedding day. He remembered eating cold mushroom soup after the snowstorm when the power was out, and the way the sun melted everything the next day, so the whole city was swimming in puddles. But he hadn't wanted to get married. He loved Robin's mother, but he thought it would change if they got married.

"I don't think I'm the sort of person anyone should have married," he told Robin.

"Why?"

"Oh, I think about myself too much."

But Robin's mother wanted to get married. Afterwards she got pregnant right away and Robin's father got a job teaching in Hanover, New Hampshire, because her mother said they couldn't live on art alone. Her father gave up doing his own work for years, except for sketches.

They had Robin. And they had each other.

Robin was afraid she might start to cry. She looked away from Verna, who was concentrating on getting her rudder back into the water. "How long did it last—what you felt about your neighbour?"

"Oh, my dear. Every time I saw him. But after a while I didn't feel it any more. I could just see him for who he was. As for separating, Allistair came back the next day. I never knew where he went, but he might have vanished. Sometimes I think being married, staying married, is a bit of a miracle. You must know that. I think it might just be the hardest thing we do."

Robin let herself drift, not paddling. She could just make out—now that they'd passed the dead tree where they'd seen the bald eagle—a nest the size of a giant's purse, half-hidden in the trees by the water. "So why do we do it in the first place?"

But Verna was a little ahead of her and seemed not to have heard.

Her mother had sent a card in which a cheque was enclosed for Robin's wedding dress. It was a pink card with a picture of a bouquet of roses held by two slender white hands, with a diamond on the finger of one of the hands. Inside the card was a poem:

When a Man asks his Sweetheart
to be his own dear Wife,
It is the Day when first begins
a magical new Life.
Love welds two Hearts so tenderly
and forges them as One,
The golden Ring that shimmers like
the rising of the Sun,
And the Vows that are spoken
between a Loving Pair
Joins them close Together 'til
they reach Heaven's Stair.

The cheque was for two thousand dollars. Her mother wanted her to have a lovely dress, and if the money wasn't enough, Robin could let her know and she would send more. Robin found out later that her mother had sent another cheque to Verna and Allistair to help defray the cost of the wedding, which Allistair never deposited.

Robin bought a dress in Halifax a few months before the wedding. It had been made in France and the fine lace with its scrolled flowers and leaves came from Belgium. And didn't it just fit her perfectly, the saleswoman said. She had extremely red fingernails that looked like drops of blood when she put her hands around Robin's waist. Such a tiny waist Robin had. She was the kind of girl who could be in magazines. She really could do very well for herself in magazines.

Robin turned around in front of the mirror. It was the kind of dress she'd dreamed about as a child. White, frilly, extravagant. It fitted perfectly, as the saleswoman said. The gown fell to the floor like the translucent petals of a flower. The tips of her sandals showed underneath. The saleswoman arranged her hands in front, as if Robin were holding flowers.

"You could have a bouquet of pink roses, with baby's breath and ivy. It'd be perfect."

"I don't think I want roses," Robin said.

"Oh well, you could get away with anything," said the woman, her hands smoothing the lace. "A dress like this."

She was right. It was the dress.

The same night that she'd gone down for a glass of water and found the unfamiliar key, Robin had a rash impulse. She acted on it without thinking, picking up the phone, dialling a number. It rang once, twice, three times. Her heart was pounding. On the fourth ring, Carolee answered.

"Hey." The voice was slurry; she'd just woken up. "I knew you'd be calling—the number came up on call display."

Robin held the receiver away from her.

"Neil?" There was a tinny urgency to the voice, even at arm's length.

Robin put the receiver back on its cradle.

She dropped onto a chair as if someone had kicked her in the stomach. Carolee. She was quite numb. Neil. She lifted up her arms to see if they still worked. They went up, they came down, but it seemed that they were on all wrong. As if they'd been put on backwards. And her legs, too. She stood up. She'd put two and two. What was wrong with her? Her feet felt as though they were not her own at all. Two and two together. Carolee and Neil. She put her hand up to her face. Her arms, her feet, her face. Everything was wrong. Her arms were wet, her face was bare, her feet were taking her backwards through the house, all through the dark house and up the stairs. Two and two. What was she to do with herself? She curled up on the chaise longue in the guest bedroom and got up hours before Neil.

When she saw him in the morning, she didn't do anything. She could have. It occurred to her that she could have taken the set of knives off the knife magnet on the wall near the stove. She supposed she could have thrown them at him, one at a time. His arms and legs wide against the basement door, pinned by his collar, sleeves, pantlegs. But it seemed like too much of an effort. It was hard enough to make toast and sit in a chair without speaking to him. That wasn't unusual, so he didn't know anything was different.

Robin finished her chicken salad sandwich, got up, and stretched her legs. She went to the end of the little beach and stood, gazing out at the water. Then she returned. "We'd better go back, I think. The tide's going out and it'll be shallower."

Verna helped her shift the boats into the water and then sloshed into it up to her knees. She almost capsized it, trying to get in. "Oh," she cried, laughing. "I'd better do it on land. What am I thinking of? An old gal like me, trying to fit into this thing. It's the size of a shoebox." She kept laughing as Robin helped her pull it up on the shingle, where she got into it again. She wiped her face. Robin pushed her boat off the sand.

"There we are," Verna said. "Thank you."

Robin was about to give her the paddle, but Verna put her hand on Robin's wrist. "Neil's not an easy man. I know that. Garnet was a black sheep, but Neil's—"

The water was cold around Robin's ankles. "Neil's what?"

"He keeps things hidden. The rest of them I know, I understand. Evie is always straining at the bit as if she's got something to prove. Spike just goes along and the world seems easy, but I know he comes up against things. And Garnet always had a way of exploding. He was the one who had such trouble fitting in." She sighed, taking the paddle from Robin. She put it down abruptly across the boat and it startled them both with the hollow noise. "But Neil fit in and kept everything hidden. As if he were afraid."

"Afraid?"

"Afraid that people would find cracks in him. And, really, there are cracks in everyone."

They could see jellyfish as they paddled back. They were purplish, with long strands trailing like transparent strings behind them. How odd they were, thought Robin. And how strange things seemed from this point of view. The carpet of silvery water, the green, rolling hills, a flash of sun on a car going along the road, the weightlessness of the world. She scooped the water with the paddle, and it dripped a spangle of drops below. She pulled hard through the water, then realized she was quite a distance ahead of Verna and turned around smoothly. A heron lifted up, flapping awkwardly: a prehistoric creature. A pterodactyl, thought Robin.

There was a crack in Robin so wide it let the moonlight in when she stood in the kitchen that night. A crack in Neil. A crack in their marriage.

Robin breathed deeply, but the flowers trembled in her hands. Evelyn began to walk down the aisle. Robin began to move forward. Evie walked slowly, almost too slowly, Robin thought. The aisle of the cathedral went on forever, and there at the end of it was the priest. Neil was looking at her. Spike. The gilded body of Jesus, suspended on the crucifix. Robin fixed her eyes on the flowers in Evelyn's hair as she moved forward. She didn't look up at the pillars lavishly decorated with gold, but glanced down at her white satin shoes moving over the red diamonds in the dark-yellow linoleum floor. She could hear the occasional flutter of whispers.

The light blazed yellow and rose through the stained-glass windows as they came to the end of the aisle and Evelyn went to one side. Neil and Spike smiled. The priest smiled. Even the golden Jesus seemed to smile.

Later, outside the church, the sun blazed as Aunt Min kissed her on the cheek, Uncle Frank gave her a hug, and a boy threw confetti in a pastel-coloured cloud over her head. She had to brush it off her eyelashes. Neil laughed and talked to people, holding her hand the whole time. Squeezing it a little. Two children raced down the grassy slope in front of the cathedral, one pink, one yellow. Hair ribbons flying.

"So," Evelyn said. "Feel any different?"

But Robin didn't feel any different. Neil kissed her ear and led her down the steps to the limousine that was waiting at the curb. "You're gorgeous," he said. The driver opened the door for her and she got in carefully, gathering up the skirt of the gown. Everyone was clustered around the limousine, watching them go. Neil got in and they waved as they drove off. He put his arm around her and kissed her again.

"I love you," he said. "I love you. D'you love me a bit?"

"I love you, you idiot," she laughed. "Of course I do."

Now they were within sight of the house, which sat on the hill as if it had grown out of it. What an attractive house it was, thought Robin, as if it wasn't hers at all. The screened porch, the flower garden, the path down the slope. And as she and Verna, side by side, drew closer, she felt a sickening feeling. It was her house as well as Neil's. It was hard to think about the fact that he'd loved her, she'd loved him.

"There now," said Verna as they pulled up on the thin stretch of beach. The kayaks ground against broken shells and stones on the shore. "Isn't it good to be on dry land again?"

BARBECUED RIBS

Spike headed down to the pier at the end of King Street, empty except for a few teenagers huddled together smoking something. The scent was pungent and slightly bitter. The kids watched him, but he strode past them and sat at the far end, looking out over the water. He wouldn't have minded smoking a little of it himself. The lights on the American side were shivering white lines on the black water, but a powerboat disturbed the reflection, making it jump and scatter on the waves. Evelyn annoyed him. She had a way of being difficult, deliberately setting him up for a fight even if he wasn't really interested. He didn't care about these things one way or the other. Another smaller boat wrinkled the water as it passed.

The kids were laughing and hooting among themselves as one of them started to dance, his hair flaring up when he whirled and then fell giggling on the boards. He got up again and fell down. Then one of the girls pulled him close and put his head in her lap. She had long hair parted in the centre that fell straight down over the boy's head like a curtain.

In Spike's pocket were a few small stones, a tooth-pick, a safety pin. He tossed the stones over the edge of the pier one by one, listening to the faint sound they made as they splashed into the water. He rubbed the toothpick clean and began picking his teeth thought-fully. What would it be like if Garnet came back? He was a loose cannon. After a while Spike stood up care-fully, waiting to get his balance because he was a little bit drunk, and then he walked to the other end of the pier. The kids watched him. He crossed the street and went past the pool hall where the faint green lights showed the tables and people standing beside them, rub-bing chalk on the tips of their cues and bending down to eye the balls. He'd taken care of Garnet in a way Neil never had. Neil couldn't even talk about Garnet any more. But to have Garnet in the middle of things again, in the middle of the family. Anything could happen. There'd be no way of stopping it.

Just past Mattie's Lucky Stop Billiards and Arcade was a fast-food restaurant, brilliantly lit, making the people behind the counter look pale. A boy was cleaning the front of the counter, moving his hand in slow circles, and a girl with bleached hair was standing behind it, staring, one hand at the side of her face. Her mouth was half-opened. When Spike went in, she smoothed her hands down the sides of her uniform and put on her gloves.

The boy finished with the counter and began cleaning the mirrored wall behind the counter, where Spike saw himself reflected. There were pouches under his eyes, and his hair looked sparser than it had been that morning. The girl asked him again what he wanted. He looked at the shredded lettuce, the transparent half-circles of onion, the olives, and the bland white cheese, each in a metal compartment. Maybe he'd like a ham and cheese, or barbecued ribs, she prompted. She was smiling, her plastic-gloved hand poised over the bread. He nodded and asked for the barbecued ribs.

"How'd you like that, sir? On white or whole wheat?"

"White, I guess. No, whole wheat."

"Lettuce, onions, tomatoes?" She looked a little like Alice Blaney.

"The works," he said.

"You can sit down, sir, and I'll bring it to you."

"Yes," he said. "That'd be fine." He put some money on the counter and went to sit by the darkened window. The submarine sandwich, when it came, was still warm from the microwave.

"Thanks."

She smiled at him, shoving hair off her forehead with her wrist. "No problem."

Somewhere far off came the clamour of a siren and he turned to the window, where he could see the reflection of the girl. The siren wailed and then stopped abruptly, but Spike kept staring out into the dark.

"They were fucked by the second inning," the boy was saying.

"What about Wayne Cormier?" asked the girl. "He's good."

"It didn't matter," said the boy. "They were fucked."

The last time he'd seen Alice Blaney was at her brother's funeral. She was with her father and a few uncles, and they all sat at the front of the cathedral with their heads bowed, not looking at the coffin. It was a steely blue, shiny as the hood of a truck that had just been waxed. Inside it, lying against the white satin, was Pete Blaney, whose body had never lain against anything so beautiful before. When Spike had seen him during the visitation at the MacEwen Funeral Home, he knew it was supposed to be Pete, but looked more like a good imitation. Almost perfect. Even the little hairs in his nostrils.

Father MacInnis talked about the brevity and beauty of Peter's life and Spike stared at the red diamonds in the linoleum. He could feel the back of his neck prickle thinking of Pete lying against the satin. Pete and Sean had come by a couple of days before to get him to go to Heatherton with them, but Spike's mother had washed both pairs of his jeans, which were hanging, frozen, on the line. Spike was wearing a pair of his father's long johns. Sean told him to come anyway, his head stuck out the passenger window, but Spike laughed and waved at them as they pulled out of the driveway. On the way back from Heatherton Pete was killed when they hit a moose. Sean had been taken to Halifax; he was in a coma.

Spike hadn't known what to say when he saw Alice and her father at the funeral home the day before. Old Blaney had tears in his eyes, but he was standing stiffly in his black suit. It was the first time Spike had ever seen him dressed up. And Alice was wearing a lacy black blouse and a skirt with a hem that went down a little on one side and up a little on the other. Her face was white and plain, and she didn't look at him when he shook her hand. Then he shook Old Blaney's hand.

"It looks good like that," the girl was saying, and her hand, mirrored in the window, reached out to the boy's hair. "She did a good job cutting it."

He caught her hand at the wrist before she touched it. "You'll wreck it," he said. It was parted down the centre and hung almost to his ears.

"No, I won't." She glanced over at Spike, but he was looking out the window. "It feels weird," she said, touching the shaved hair at the back of his neck.

"Huh," said the boy.

"Yeah, I think it looks good," she said again.

The boy went to get the mop in its metal pail. It was on rollers and clanked as he pulled it across the floor to the far corner of the restaurant where Spike couldn't see him. The girl watched him, thoughtfully pulling on her earlobe.

Once Pete asked him about Alice.

"D'you fuck my sister?"

Pete and Spike were behind the school gym, drinking vodka out of a bottle in a paper bag. They'd been sitting there for an hour or more even though the grass was wet.

"You mean d'your sister fuck me?"

"So did you?"

Spike stared at the hole in the toe of his left running shoe.

"I knew it," said Pete. "She might be a slut, but you're a bastard."

Pete stood up and walked away from Spike unsteadily. After a few yards, he turned and threw the bottle of vodka at the wall of the gym, where it shattered. Bits of glass flew through the air, one fragment landing in Spike's arm, like a tiny spear. He looked at the dark blood that dribbled from it.

The boy rolled the mop in its metal pail across the floor and stopped it with the side of his foot.

"I'm going out for a smoke," he said.

The girl nodded. After a while she wandered over to the window and stared out, her mouth a little open. She could have been a pretty girl, Spike thought, if she hadn't bleached her hair. He went up to the counter and asked for a coffee.

"Cream, sir?" she asked brightly. She'd plucked her

eyebrows too much and they looked like commas over her eyes.

"No, just black."

He went back to his seat. He could do something for her, maybe get her a job away from this place. Then she wouldn't have to get married to some kid who was two inches shorter than she was. Who didn't know how to mop a floor.

After Pete died, Alice didn't talk back to teachers and none of them said anything about suspending her, as they might have before. Garnet took up with her around the time Spike was seeing Janelle, but he was just a kid. Alice wouldn't bother with him for long. Sometimes they necked in the cafeteria, or against the lockers. Once they were leaning against Spike's locker and didn't move when they saw him.

"Oh, now," said Alice, smiling at him with her eyes half-closed, "look who's here."

She disengaged herself from Garnet, clutched at Spike's shoulders, and gave him a sloppy kiss. Then she moved her mouth across his cheek, leaving a wet track. "There," she said, standing back but still holding on to his shoulders. "Was it good for you?" Then she laughed—a deep, loud laugh—kicking the heel of her shoe against his locker before she took Garnet's hand and moved away.

The boy came back out, quickly brushing his hand against the girl's hip as he passed, and went back to mopping the floor. She came out from behind the counter and stood on a damp part of the floor that he'd already mopped.

"You missed a bit," she said, smiling. "Right here."

He slopped the mop towards her feet and a few stringy coils slid over her shoes.

"Yeah?"

"Yeah," she said. "And another one right here."

"You want to do it?"

"No." She stood watching him, leaning against one of the tables. "You can."

Spike got up and took his plastic tray to the garbage, dumping the paper and putting the tray on top.

"Night, sir," said the girl.

"Thanks," he said.

He crossed the street and stood looking back at the restaurant, where the boy had put his arm around the girl's waist. Her face was flushed; she was happy.

Alice Blaney dropped out of school and got married to someone from Havre Boucher. He was a carpenter and in his spare time he coached bantam hockey in town. They bought a piece of land just off the highway past Willy's Surf and Turf and built a colonial-style house with pink sheers at every window. But Spike had heard his mother say that they'd had two girls and then something happened, Lord knew what. She'd seen Alice at Sobey's with a bruise on the side of her face and her lip all swollen up like German sausage, but Alice had turned away when she'd seen her coming. His mother had even made a pork pie and taken it out to the house, where she'd had to leave it on the doorstep because no one was at home.

After a while Alice moved out of the colonial house and into a basement apartment in town with her children. There was a restraining order out against her husband. But Spike knew all this from his mother because he'd only seen Alice once or twice when he was home from university, once at the bank and another time at the Ultramar station. Both times she'd been looking down, so she hadn't seen him. Or maybe she had, but she didn't let on.

Once, years ago, Spike and Garnet had driven out to Monastery and they'd passed the colonial house, a dead Christmas tree lying at the end of the driveway, dry and brown.

Spike kicked at a soft-drink can as he walked up the street. When he got back to the motel he went straight to bed, but he couldn't sleep. He wondered if Evelyn had got back all right and he sat up, thinking he would go and check on her. But he went into the bathroom instead and washed his face. Evelyn would still be annoyed with him. He went back to bed and tried to put things out of his mind so he could sleep. But it came back to him, just the way he'd seen it when he'd been driving past Alice

Blaney's house that day with Garnet. The sky had been a uniform grey, like rinse water, and the spruce trees were sharp as knives against it. When they'd passed the house they'd seen a face at the window. Spike thought it was Alice, but it could have been one of her girls. He'd only taken his eyes off the road for a moment and maybe he hadn't seen a face at the window. Maybe he'd just imagined it.

But it must have been Alice.

He rolled over in bed and put his arm over his face.

They'd both known it was Alice. He'd just driven down the road to Monastery with Garnet sitting there stupidly beside him. They could have done something for her. And they hadn't done anything at all.

OSIRIS

Spike couldn't hear some of the things Garnet said to him on the phone because a few guys came along the hall in the dorm just then, and one of them banged a frying pan against the wall. It was something about Lawrence Welk. Spike thought of women with helmet hairdos waltzing around with men in tuxedos. Bubbles floating in the air. Then Garnet said he was going to kill himself. He said something after that but Spike couldn't hear what it was. Drown himself, maybe. There had to be easier ways, he said. He was kidding. He had that kind of humour. Spike asked him what else was on television and he said, laughing, that Lawrence Welk was the only thing he could find but that Spike should hang on for a sec, while he dropped the television out the window. Then he put down the phone, maybe on a table, and Spike heard sounds, like things being kicked out of the way and then a distant crashing. He came back to the phone and said he'd dropped it out the window. He'd looked first, to see if anyone was coming. The thing was he'd never liked Lawrence Welk. Then he hung up.

He'd been drinking. That's probably why he'd been talking about killing himself. Spike stood for a while in the alcove where the phone was, tapping his fingers on the shelf; someone passed him and went into the common room, thumping books down on the table. He stared at the orange sticker on the telephone. Ambulance, Fire, Police. If Garnet meant what he said, he'd be dead, far away in Boston, before anyone could get to him.

Garnet and Spike were at home one New Year's Eve, with instructions from their parents that Spike was to look after him, and no funny business. Evelyn was at a sleepover. Neil was out with his friends. When their parents left, Garnet got the key for the liquor cabinet that was kept in an old soap dish in the linen closet. He had rum and Spike had Irish whisky in paper cups from one of Evie's birthday parties long ago. They had blue and yellow balloons on them and handles that had to be opened. They sat in front of the television switching the channels between Lawrence Welk and somebody in Times Square. Spike had another paper cupful of whisky and Garnet had another of rum but they couldn't take any more because it'd be noticed. Not that they cared. They watched a woman in a shiny dress singing, but Garnet turned the volume down so they couldn't hear anything. Her mouth made shapes as if she were in pain. Her breasts jiggled.

Garnet started to laugh and then Spike got going and
Garnet fell on the carpet with his arms wrapped around
himself because he couldn't stop.

"If we went to Schulein's now," Spike said, "we could
be back before they come home."

There were red-and-green Christmas lights around the
windows of the Schulein house, and on the sill of the
kitchen window was a beer bottle with a couple of plastic
flowers stuck into it. There were a few people outside
standing around without coats and one guy was leaning
against the screen door, holding it open. Spike didn't feel
like going in with Garnet, but he wasn't going to stand
around outside in the cold so he left Garnet there. In the
kitchen were Billy Dykstra and Alice Blaney and Clayton,
the jerk who lived next door, and Kevin Hadley. Kevin
was with one of the Gooley sisters—Becky or Barbara—
but he couldn't tell which because the only significant difference between them was the birthmark on Barbara's
inner thigh that he'd been told about. Clayton got him a
beer that didn't go down well after the Scotch, but it didn't
matter. Spike asked him about the Ice Men, and before he
knew it Clayton was giving him a rundown on all the
games so far. When he finished a beer, Clayton would give
him another. He could feel Alice looking at him even
while Billy had himself wedged in beside her, nice and
close. After a while she went out of the room and then
Billy went out, too, and Spike had another beer.

He tried to listen to Clayton and at the same time he
was thinking that he should go and see about Garnet. He
watched Clayton's hand reaching into the fridge between
the mustard and pickles to take out a beer and heard the
siren just as his hand clasped the bottle.

"What?" Clayton said, looking at him.

"Have you seen Garnet?"

"No. Did you bring him?"

Spike pushed his way out of the kitchen, which wasn't
easy because more people had come in and they were
chanting something. Nine, eight, six. He saw Becky or
Barbara with her mouth wide open so he could see the
fillings in her molars. She tried to kiss him as he pushed
past. Five, four, three. When he got outside he couldn't
see Garnet anywhere, only Newt Dykstra taking a leak in
the snow. Spike asked him if he'd seen Garnet, but there
was a roar of "Happy New Year" from inside the house,
and Newt didn't hear him. The siren was still wailing,
coming closer, and Newt's piss made a long mark in the
snow, along with several little yellow holes that pocked it
here and there.

"Garnet?" Newt asked. "I saw him talking to somebody
in a pickup. Thibeau, maybe. I think he was asking for a
ride home."

Spike could see a flash of light between the town hall
and the insurance office as the ambulance passed, its siren
blaring. *Whuuuoooooupp. Whuup.* A man ran towards
them, waving his arms.

"It's Thibeau," he yelled.

When Spike ran to the corner at Main Street, he couldn't see what had happened at first because the ambulance was in the way, its flashing light illuminating the faces of people watching. They were flushed deep red for a moment and then they were pale again. It was Thibeau, all right. He'd driven right into the wall of MacPherson's Fashion Palace and now they were trying to prise his body out of the truck. But Spike couldn't see inside. And then one of the Mounties was shoving him back out of the way and telling him to put a lid on it.

"Hey," the Mountie was saying, "calm down." He had Spike by the arms.

"My brother's with him," Spike cried.

"No." The Mountie moved him back a couple of steps as he talked. "There was nobody with that kid."

Spike broke away from him and ran down the middle of the street, slipping on a patch of ice in front of the barber-shop. He was panting as he turned and went up the Hawthorne Street hill, and there was a sharp pain in his ribs as if they'd been ripped apart. He found Garnet at home, sitting in front of the television as if he'd never left, with a bag of chips open between his legs.

A week after Spike talked to Garnet on the phone he flew down to see him. He had a few days before his final exams started, so he put the airplane ticket on his credit card, sinking him deeper in the hole. It was just before

Easter and the flight attendant handed out chocolate eggs from a basket when she came around with magazines. The foil wrapper on Spike's was red and gold with little zigzags around the middle. He put it in his pocket.

He didn't know what he'd find when he got to Garnet's place, even though he'd talked to him on the phone the night before. He kept buzzing the doorbell until he remembered Garnet had said he kept the key under the doorstop. Then he went through the place calling Garnet's name. He wasn't there. He wasn't behind the shower curtains or under the bed. Spike looked out the window in the living room but there was nothing to see except a strip of weedy grass, a cracked sidewalk, a street. Everything, even the kitchen, was tidy. He hadn't been expecting this empty apartment with the sun streaming in. He sat down heavily on the couch and looked at the poster of Jimi Hendrix and another one of a swimming pool, done by some artist who didn't know anything about perspective. There were books stacked by the wall and more in boxes, and in the corner a pair of rabbit ears, but no television set. On the table beside him was a piece of rose quartz, a rough bit of tourmaline, a flowering chunk of amethyst. They were labelled in small precise letters. Spike turned them over one by one before putting them back on the table and then lying down, taking the chocolate egg out of its wrapper and eating it slowly. Part of him was in sunshine: half his face, one shoulder, part of his stomach, a knee. He fell asleep.

When Spike woke, Garnet was sitting on the floor across from him with his back against the wall, peeling an apple.

"I was sleeping," said Spike.

"It's all right," said Garnet, making a curl of apple peel. "Go back to sleep if you want. I just got off work so I'm going to sit here for a while."

Spike sat up on the couch and rubbed his face. It occurred to him that he should tell Garnet why he'd come. But here was Garnet calmly cutting the apple into pieces, some of which he offered to Spike, who chewed on a slice thoughtfully.

"So, you didn't find any bottles under the sink," said Garnet.

"I wasn't looking."

Garnet laughed briefly. "Neil told me I was crazy." He ate the rest of his apple and got up. "Neil's a bugger. Let's get something to eat."

He took Spike to a Chinese restaurant with red walls and little paper lanterns hanging from the ceiling. The small waitress brought them won ton soup, a colourless liquid with noodles and thin pieces of pork. Her hair was in her eyes and she didn't smile as she set down the bowls.

"I love you, Shelley," said Garnet. "Give me a smile."

She said something briefly in Chinese and went back to the kitchen.

"She loves me. She called me a bastard."

After the won ton soup they had steamed vegetables with cashew nuts, sweet-and-sour pork in a thick red sauce, and chicken balls with rice. Garnet didn't eat much but Spike had second helpings of everything, even rice.

"What happened to Cinta?" asked Spike.

"Cinta? Gone." Garnet pinched a cashew nut between his thumb and forefinger. "Finished. Now there's a marriage that fell apart. Ashes to ashes, dust to dust." He pushed his plate away and traced something on his paper place-mat. "According to this," he said, tapping it, "she was a monkey. Like me." Spike saw a wheel showing each year under its sign when he looked down at his own place-mat. Year of the Horse. Year of the Snake. Year of the Monkey. "The monkey is the most fortunate of all the signs," said Garnet. "Manic, erratic—"

"Don't get going," said Spike.

"Alcoholic—"

"Garnet!"

"Smart as hell."

They were given a small plate of fortune cookies by an emaciated waiter with yellowed teeth. Shelley had disappeared.

"I've been reading," said Garnet. "I like reading about art."

"You do?"

"Yeah."

"You should take a course or something," said Spike. "Or go to some art galleries. Neil's wife, Robin—her dad was an artist. Lawrence Freisen. You should watch for his stuff."

Garnet opened the wrapper of his fortune cookie. "I don't know." He broke the cookie and removed the slip of paper. " 'You bring good cheer to others.' " He laughed and crumpled it up. "What did you get?"

" 'Make the most of your luck.' "

Once Spike heard his parents talking about Garnet. He was in the basement, looking for his shoulder pads for hockey. When he heard voices he went and stood under the hole in the kitchen floor where the radiator used to be.

"She says Garnet's gifted," his mother was saying.

"Well, he's got a strange way of showing it, the way he acts up in class," his father responded.

"She says he does things because he gets bored. She gave him books that the grade eights are reading and he's already finished them."

"He never talks to us about any of these books."

His mother said something else but Spike couldn't hear it because a chair scraped on the floor.

"He's an odd one, Vern," said my father. "Maybe it's because—"

"Oh, now don't get started on that again."

"Well, it was my fault."

"No one's blaming you, and anyway, it's over and done with. It's as simple as that."

"No, it's not." There was a chinking sound as something was set down. His cup. Then his heavy tread across the floor, making the boards creak. "You ready for practice or not, Stephen?" he called downstairs. "Five minutes, or I'm leaving without you."

Spike took Neil's shoulder pads and put them on, lacing them up in front. Garnet. It was hard to believe. He was so weird, after all.

"See," Garnet was saying, as he put down his mug of instant coffee and turned the book around so Spike could see the picture. They'd come back to his apartment and he was showing Spike his books. "They used to wear cones of perfume on their heads that would drip down into their hair."

"Why?" asked Spike, gazing at the picture of bronzed men wearing what looked like pleated white skirts. "Unless they wanted to keep mosquitoes away."

"Deodorant," he said, closing the book and putting it into one of the boxes, which he had taken pains to label in small capital letters with the words EGYPT: DOMESTIC. There were other boxes: EGYPT: OLD KINGDOM, MEMPHIS and EGYPT: ART, AMARNA PERIOD.

"What else do you read?"

"Physics. Cosmology. You know, black holes and supernovae and stuff. I read a lot of shit, all second-hand. Philosophy. History. I got a book on electronics out of the garbage last week. But I don't read novels," he said. "I only want to know the beginning and end of novels."

Spike was lying on the couch, covered with a blanket, his head on the pillow Garnet had brought out. Garnet was sitting cross-legged against the wall in the same place he'd peeled the apple earlier, and it seemed to Spike that he'd become thinner, almost gaunt. His nose was sharp as a razor. His eyes were blue. Spike hadn't remembered how blue they were.

"I was going to kill myself," he said, "when I called you."

"But you didn't." Spike sat up, propped on his elbows.

"No." He drank some coffee. "Gave you a bit of a scare?" he said, looking at Spike with a wry smile.

"Yes." Spike figured Garnet had always done that. Maybe he enjoyed it. Maybe he just wanted to see whether Spike would come when he was in trouble.

"You're a bit like Neil," he said, scrutinizing him. "Well, no, maybe not." He moved his cup in a circle. "I was feeling a little wild when I called. I could do just about anything when I'm like that. I almost killed a guy once in a bar—I didn't mean for it to go that far. I didn't want to hurt anyone."

Spike rested his head on the pillow again and closed his eyes. After Neil had visited Garnet he'd said that he was a real nutcase and that maybe no one would have been upset if Garnet had drowned in the bathtub.

"Have you had anything to drink yet?" Spike asked, his eyes still closed.

"No, and it's been a week or so now. Longest in a while."

"What happened to the TV?"

"It's in the Dumpster. What good's a TV, anyhow?"

He took another book out and Spike felt himself drifting off, disturbed only when Garnet shifted position or turned a page. After a while Spike opened his eyes and looked at the large yellowish stain on the ceiling that resembled an umbrella.

"Would you say you're gifted?" he asked.

"What?"

"Nothing." The stain didn't really look like an umbrella. "I should be studying," said Spike. "I brought my accounting book."

Neil and Spike had a clubhouse that they'd built down by the river near the school. They'd taken apart the old tree fort and carried boards there in the wheelbarrow. It wasn't well made and the floorboards got wet when it rained. No girls were allowed. Garnet wasn't allowed. They could smoke in peace.

Spike took Garnet there once even though it was against the rules. It was early in November, and it had snowed and then rained, so the ground was cold and slippery. The roof of the clubhouse had fallen in because they hadn't used it for a while, and Garnet wanted to help him fix it, but there wasn't much they could do because they didn't have a hammer or nails.

"We could take it apart," Garnet suggested.

He tossed a board in the river and watched its slow

passage along the surface of the brown water. Then Spike threw one in. They took down the rest of the roof and the walls, breaking apart the boards and throwing them in the river. Every time a board hit the water it made a satisfying sound, like the *whack* of a beaver tail.

"Neil will be mad, won't he?" said Garnet.

"Yup."

Neil would blame Spike, and then Spike would blame Garnet. That's how it went. Spike ripped apart a comic book and stood for a moment, looking at Superman glide across the yellow cartoon sky. He showed Garnet the picture before flinging it in the water where it turned lazily around and was submerged.

"Go get 'em, Superman," yelled Garnet.

Spike's fingers were cold inside the damp gloves. He didn't care. Garnet whooped and hurled a crate into the river. Together they wrenched up the floorboards, all joined together, and pitched them in the water, too. They bobbed on the surface of the water and then floated away with the rest of the debris. Neil wouldn't find out unless Spike told him, and he wasn't going to tell him. Spike stamped his numb feet on the bank of the river to get the circulation going, thinking of Superman, his cape unfurled and hands rigidly outstretched as he sank into the murk.

They came out of the bushes and went across the field, where the light was feeble. It had grown colder, icing up the little slope from the field to the road, and Garnet kept slipping on it until Spike put an arm out to help him. Anyone could have taken apart that clubhouse. And only the two of them would ever know.

"What are you reading?" asked Spike.

"About Osiris," he said. "He was murdered by his brother, Seth."

"I didn't think gods could be murdered."

"And then he was revived by his wife, Isis."

"Oh," Spike said, still gazing upwards. "So he wasn't dead for long."

SMALL HOURS

When Robin came in she found Evelyn throwing up in the bathroom.

"Robin," said Evelyn, "is that you?"

"Yes."

Evelyn threw up again. "Oh, geez. Geez. I haven't done this since high school."

"Just sit for a minute," said Robin, wiping Evelyn's face with a washcloth and giving her a glass of water. "Feel any better?"

Evelyn sat down on a magazine on the floor, her eyes glazed. "I'm okay now."

"You sure?" asked Robin, turning on the tap in the bathtub. She stripped off her sundress and took a shower cap out of a little plastic package.

"You've been out prowling," said Evelyn.

"So have you," said Robin, putting on the shower cap and testing the water with her foot.

"What were you doing?"

"Not much," said Robin, getting in the tub. "I saw a bit of a baseball game."

"Rob, it's two o'clock."

"I know."

Evelyn gazed at the floor to steady herself, listening to Robin washing herself in the bathtub.

"I don't know why Neil's not here," said Evelyn, rubbing her eyes. "I don't know what he's thinking of."

Robin got out of the tub, dried off, and wrapped herself in a towel.

"I don't know what he's thinking of," repeated Evelyn as Robin went out of the bathroom.

Evelyn got up carefully, stood for a moment, and sat down again. She could hear Robin rummaging in her bag. She sat down and even with her eyes shut she could see the black-and-white tiles moving.

Robin returned, setting a small bag on the counter and taking out some lotion. She applied the lotion to her cheeks, forehead, and chin, smoothing it over her nose. She rubbed it in small circles over her skin. "Neil's with someone," she said.

"I know," said Evelyn.

"Right now, this very minute," said Robin, gazing at her owlish expression in the mirror. The white cream circled her eyes, making them look darker. "I can't stand it." She wiped off the lotion gently with a tissue. "I don't even want to sleep in the same room with him any more."

Evelyn got up, unsteadily, and held on to the towel rack. "What about leaving him?"

"Carolee," said Robin. "My friend Carolee, who took woodworking classes with me. Who wanted me to get a mountain bike so we could do some trails together. And weightlifting. We even went to the same gym, for God's sake."

Evelyn washed her face and patted it dry.

"Not that it matters," Robin said, leaning against the wall and running dental floss between her teeth. "It doesn't matter." She put the red string of floss in the garbage, changed into her nightgown, and went to bed.

"Get some sleep," said Evelyn, coming out of the bathroom and getting into bed. "Don't make yourself crazy."

Evelyn fell asleep almost at once, her breathing regular and subdued. Robin lay looking at the thin line of light that came through the curtain from the motel parking lot. She had just spent the better part of a night with a boy she didn't know, made love twice, and would never see him again. She'd never done anything remotely like it in her life before. It had been so easy. Maybe he'd tell his friends about it, but he didn't strike her as the kind of kid who'd talk a lot. On impulse, she'd asked him if he had a girlfriend, but he didn't, not now anyway, because this girl he'd been seeing had given him the shaft. He said he wished Robin wasn't just passing through. She didn't say anything. It was ludicrous to think of something coming of it.

She lay in bed, listening to Evelyn's breathing. Maybe he did this sort of thing a lot. Watched for nice, nubile girls. Screwed them in the little red car. And she was just someone to spend the night with, someone who had money to pay for a hotel room. She felt her face grow warm. What had possessed her?

Spike shifted in his sleep. He lay with the sheet half over his body, an arm out to one side so his hand was off the bed, cupped upwards. The fingers were long, squared at the tips, and slightly curled over the palm. The hand was completely relaxed. The face, too, was smooth, except for the lines between his brows that deepened when he frowned, and the tinier lines around his eyes, especially at the corners. His mouth hung open a little. He shifted again, this time turning over with the side of his face against the pillow, his hair dark where it had been cut carefully around his ear. As he moved his leg he caught it in the sheet, waking himself. He went to the bathroom, pissed, shook himself, and went back to bed. He fell asleep easily, but this time his hand wasn't suspended with the palm open, as if he were asking for something.

Verna was dreaming of her family eating dinner together. Garnet among them. His face a little like Spike's. From under the table he produced a glittering object, like a globe or a lawn ornament, which he gave to her with a smile. She woke with the same tightness in her chest that she'd felt earlier, just before she'd fainted. It was nerves. She breathed slowly and carefully. But the thought of Garnet soothed her because it was possible that it was a sign, and a good sign, judging by the gift in the dream. It might mean that he would come after all. The pain lessened in her chest and she breathed more freely. Was there a chance she might die before she saw him? Would her heart suddenly stop? She turned towards her husband.

"Allistair."

But he lay outstretched on the bed, face to one side. Away from her. He didn't hear her, and anyway, he would only tell her to go back to sleep. There was nothing he could do in the middle of the night. But it was always the small hours that made her anxious. The dream might mean that he was not coming. Garnet's gift not a gift at all. That was it. She felt that the darkness was heavy as a set of drawers, a sofa, a piano, on her chest. It frightened her. It was the heavy thing that she'd always pushed away and postponed. Like the idea that she could bring her family together somehow, when it was clear that they were all separate and divided. She didn't have the strength.

Robin checked her watch, turning it this way and that to see, finally going to the bathroom and switching on the light. Four forty-one. If only she had a book to keep herself from thinking about Neil. She didn't want to think about him but she couldn't help it, like an animal with something between its teeth. She sat on the toilet seat, hands covering her face. It was impossible to live with him any more. She had to shake herself free. People did it every day. They got an idea in their heads and moved right out of the place where they'd lived, slept, breathed.

The window was up in the bathroom and through it she could hear the occasional *wwwish* of a car passing, but she could also hear a snatch of birdsong. One sweet, high-pitched warble. She looked at the open window, at the whorls in the glass, at the screen which had been patched, and through the screen the world growing lighter at the beginning of the day. It distressed her. She went back to bed. It didn't do any good to cover her head with a pillow. The thought was still there, drilling into her skull.

Allistair got up and went to the bathroom early in the morning. It was five-thirty and he was up for the day. Habit. He went back to bed and picked up a book, turning on his reading light and glancing at Verna, whose face was tranquil. She could sleep anywhere. He wasn't really interested in the book, he thought as he opened it, because he couldn't keep track of the characters. There were too many of them and the book itself could have been half as many pages long. He usually chose good, straightforward books. He put the book down and tried to doze.

But then he had liked Les Dunphy's book about Eckhart. He'd liked that bit about a good builder knowing how to build a house in his mind. It was something Allistair had been able to do all his life without thinking about it. He could take what anyone gave him, like their ideas for windows, doors, porches, and make it entire in his mind in a matter of moments. When he was a child he'd drawn castles in cross-section, with trap doors leading down to dungeons. He thought everyone could do it.

Outside it began to rain, just dribbling at first and then pouring down. He shut his eyes. There would be a time when he would lie in a bed and not get up from it. His life would pass out of him and where it would vanish to, he had no idea. But, of course, Eckhart knew. God the Master Builder knew. The rain came down in torrents, beating down, sinking into the soil and bringing things up from it. He settled himself into the pillows, steepled the book on his chest, and slept.

Spike rolled over, opened his eyes, and listened to the rain. Soon he'd get up and go for a run.

Robin slept. Her hair was released from the braid, and slightly crimped lengths of it fanned out on the pillow. Her cheeks were a little flushed and her arms extended. One pillow—the one she'd put over her head—had fallen to the floor. Her breathing was slow and even and she didn't turn over or change position. She didn't hear the rain on the roof.

The rain stopped by degrees. It no longer fell out of the sky in watery sheets, making things beyond the window seem grey and formless. Water pooled and went down drains. Birds strutted on the wet asphalt, examining the worms. They perched on the white tires that rimmed the garden on one side of the parking lot. After a while the rain stopped altogether, eaves dripped, and the few trucks and cars passing on the road sprayed up water as they went.

Allistair picked up his book again, putting a hand on his stomach to stop its noise. Verna turned towards him and opened her eyes.

"What time is it?"

"Just six."

"Mmm."

She rolled over and slept again and he looked at her body, shapeless under the sheet. She might die before him, though he'd never thought about it much before. It could be her heart. His own heart seemed to move inside him as he thought of it. Maybe he'd get someone to look at her before they went anywhere today. He could think about his own death, even consider what his ashes might look like once he was cremated. Doc Welsh had once told him that the ashes were more colourful than he'd expect. Blue-and-orange bits. A real texture to it, not like ashes from a fire. But Verna. He couldn't imagine handfuls of Verna, tossed out like sand. And then nothing. What would he do? What would they all do? She was the one who held them intact, as if she knew what it was they made together, as if she could see something solid and complete arching over them.

WATERS OF IMMORTALITY

Because of his father, Allistair ran away from home when he was ten years old. He wasn't going to listen to news of the war on the radio. He had what he needed. Water in a tin canteen, maybe the same kind the soldiers used at the front. Sandwiches. Peppermints from the drawer in the front hall. Two undershirts, because his mother always said they were necessary. A pencil with the end bitten off. A black comb. A handkerchief. First he was going to Halifax and then he was going to war.

When Allistair left Verna, years later, he didn't know where to go. He stood on the front steps thinking he should go back inside and explain this, but the door was closed. It was dark and his children were in their beds. So he drove to Truro and took a room for the night, in the place near the tidal bore. There was a mustard-coloured duvet on the bed and a Bible in the drawer. In the morning he saw the muddy waste below him, where the Fundy came in, taking everything with it when it ebbed, except the shiny red muck. But in the middle of the night he couldn't see anything and he sat down on the bed with the Bible in his hands. *Asunder. Let no man.* On the wall of the room was a mural of Cape Breton, with the dark hills sloping down to blue ocean. He lay down fully clothed on the bed and slept.

On his way to war, Allistair came across blueberries just behind Aunt Dot's house. He picked a few, ate a few. It was hot as blazes so he lay down under the elm tree, thinking about what he knew of war. Willy Cramer had come back without legs or arms, just a torso and a head. He didn't come out of the house, except on nice days when they brought him out and put him on a blanket. They'd seen him, Frank and Allistair, from behind the woodpile next door, wondering what he'd stepped on to rip off all his limbs. He looked like a bundle that his mother could pick up in her arms. Like a baby.

Allistair's Uncle Lester was missing then. There was a photograph of him in the living room. Smiling. Once Allistair picked it up and ran a couple of steps, zooming it over the sofa, like a plane. But Uncle Lester didn't fly planes. Allistair put the photograph back on the table and it fell over. He propped it up again but it wouldn't stay so he just put it down with Uncle Lester looking up at him, at anyone, who came into the room. It didn't come as a surprise when they told Allistair he'd died. He thought of his uncle looking up as they shovelled dirt over him. Over his black-and-white face, his mouth, his eyes. Over the glass and the frame. Maybe he knew it was coming.

Verna had told Allistair she couldn't go on with it. Being married. He thought it had something to do with an old boyfriend of hers. Bart couldn't keep a job for longer than he could spit and turn around. Or it might have been Colwell. In the afternoons, maybe. In their own bed. He got up, turned on the light, and saw the scenic hills of the mural spread out in front of him. Vista. Her legs, her flesh, the mounds and hollows of skin. His legs, his flesh. Allistair went over to the mural, pulled back his arm, and let fly with his fist. It didn't damage the hills any. But from the room next door a sleepy, angry voice called out, "Whaaaat?" He went back to bed and turned out the light. She'd said that nothing had happened and he needn't worry on that score. But there was something she wasn't saying. Some little thing she was holding back. *What? What, Verna?* Nothing. So he left.

Allistair's father drowned at Pomquet. He could have died another way. For years Allistair pictured it. Rope, fire, electrical shock. Trampling stallions, poisoning, falling, flying. He saw his father looping through the air in a biplane, scarf blown back, tracing figures in the air. *G—O.* Then another oval. *O.* A downward stroke, an arc. *D.* And the last few letters. *B—Y—E.* The plane suddenly askew and

out of control, flames leaping from the fuselage as it plum-
meted to earth. His father's little joke. But it didn't happen
like that. Maybe he didn't die at all. And it was some other
body they'd found at Pomquet. Somewhere his father was
alive because it was a different body they put in a coffin,
earth settling on top of him, spadefuls of earth, while his
mother wept suddenly. Soundlessly. Her red mouth making
a shape. O.

This was what Lauchie MacVicar told him about it.
Allistair's father was upset because they wouldn't let him go
and fight in the war. His father's eyes weren't good enough,
for one thing. But Allistair knew his father didn't want to
go to war. He could see it in his face when they went to the
beach after church on Sundays. Once or twice his father sat
in the car while the rest of them played in the sand. He was
looking out at the ocean, as if there were something they
couldn't see. Staring. After a while he fell asleep, *The Tartan*
newspaper folded over his face until it slipped down to his
chest, exposing his wide-open mouth, slack jaw, head to
one side.

Allistair remembered the plaid of the blanket that day at
Arisaig. Yellow and blue. Clover at the edge of it. The
flies on the sandwich bag that Verna had pushed out of
the way. Her legs, the way her skin became softer, a little
fleshier on her thighs. Her hand at the back of his neck,
her mouth partly open. The pleasure of it. Rising, falling.
Her quick breaths. My. *Oh my.*

These were the things, Allistair's father lectured him, that they were losing. General knowledge. Informed knowledge. Take the horned toad. Genus Phrynosoma. Family Iguanidae. Who knew that it could spray its enemies with blood from the corners of its eyes? Who knew the nesting habits of the bald eagle? The Code Napoléon. The basis for civil law in Quebec. His father sat at the kitchen table, staring into his teacup. Empty. Who knew anything? He poured himself more tea and continued, measuring a little sugar into it. Or even, he went on, such things as hedgerows. Allistair said he didn't know of any hedgerows in Canada. But Allistair had missed the point. People didn't know how to grow hedgerows properly any more. His father moved his hands in the air, showing Allistair how they ought to grow, tangled together to form a natural fence. Home to thrushes, warblers, hedgehogs, voles. Hundreds of creatures. He dropped his hands. Or take cathedrals, he said, those great houses of the spirit. No one could build them now. There were maybe a handful of master masons in Europe who could do it. Soon they'd be dead.

He took up his cup again, though the tea was cold. They were in danger of losing everything. He drank and grimaced. To think of all that had been accumulated in knowledge. Then a gleam in his eyes. If they forgot these things, they would all be forgotten. Like

Atlantis. Cities in ruin under the sea. Fish swimming
through houses. His fingers floated through the air to
show Allistair.

The day would come.

Verna said it was a shame Allistair's father had never been
diagnosed. She thought he was manic-depressive. Ran in
families. She knew someone in Goshen like that.
Afflicted. But Allistair's father didn't seem afflicted. Frank
wasn't afflicted, or Bunny. Or Allistair. He loved his
father. His mother didn't play with them because there
wasn't any time, but sometimes his father did. Once he let
them tie him up to the chestnut tree, a kerchief over his
eyes so he couldn't see. He stayed there patiently until
Allistair's mother freed him. He made a tree house for
them and one night they went up there and lay flat on the
platform. His father and Frank and Allistair. Squeezed
together so they'd fit. Allistair thought he was going to
tell them about the stars, which were mostly obscured by
the leaves. Something about Aquarius. Sumerian constel-
lation. Pouring the waters of immortality upon the earth.
Something like that. But he didn't. He told them he was
born five years after the new century, which made him too
young to go to war. The Great War. Frank and Allistair lay
in the dark listening to him, thinking of him young. It was
a century of discontent, he told them. Century of sadness.
Frank told him they would win it, though, in the end.
What? The war, Frank assured him, now that the Ameri-

cans were in. His father made a little sound. *Whuuu.* Breathing out. Of course, he said, and if not this one, then another.

There was nothing to do in Truro. Allistair couldn't sit on the bed reading the Bible any more so he drove back to Antigonish. Thinking of what to say when Verna opened the door. But she wasn't inside. She was around at the back, pulling weeds.

"Vern?"

Not looking up.

"I don't know what I did, Vern."

"You didn't do anything," she said.

"Well, something's the matter."

"No."

"I can't do this," Allistair said.

Her hand pulling out some dock, laying it on the heap.

"Vern."

She sat on her heels looking across at the Dysons'.

"Say something."

"I can't," she said. Nose red at the tip.

He went and put his arms around her, kneeling on the heap of weeds. She sobbed while he held her in his arms and rocked her, the way he had with the children. He wasn't going anywhere.

At his father's wake, people came to Allistair and put their hands on his shoulder, on his back, on top of his head. They spoke to his mother. But they didn't know what to say to him or Frank. Bunny was sitting under the table eating a piece of frosted white cake. She was too young. Any other time his mother would have called her out of there, for heaven's sake, she was too big a girl for that nonsense. Allistair wanted to curl up under the table beside her and eat cake full of rationed sugar.

"You poor things. You poor, poor things," said Mrs. Crawley.

Allistair looked at her red lips and yellow front teeth, and then turned and ran out the door, down Church Street, and under the hedge at his aunt Dot's, flinging himself down in the field behind her house. He lay on his stomach, screaming like a stuck pig, kicking his legs and pounding his fists into the grass.

His father found Allistair under the elm tree when he ran away to war. His son's face was sunburned, pink as boiled ham. He lay down next to him, and when Allistair woke he found his father's arm around him. They lay there looking up through the greeny-light, greeny-dark leaves, way up high. They lay still and didn't say a word.

MORNING

They sat at a large round table at the Red Hen Restaurant. Allistair had bacon and eggs with toast on the side, which he was busy dipping in egg yolk. Spike had pancakes dripping with syrup, because he'd been for a seven-mile run, or at least a fifty-two-and-a-half-minute run which he estimated to be just shy of a seven miler.

"Coffee, Evie?" asked Verna.

"Uh, no thanks."

"You look a little under the weather, dear."

"She's hung over," said Spike, putting a large forkful of pancake into his mouth.

"No, I'm not."

Allistair folded some toast over a couple of pieces of bacon. He didn't have bacon very often any more, or eggs, for that matter. He wouldn't have said no to another plateful.

"Eat something," he said to Evelyn.

It always seemed to Evelyn that her father didn't talk,
he instructed. He'd taught her to play chess when she was
younger, just as his father had taught him, and even now
she could hear his voice. *Never ever make a move like that
with your queen. See? You're finished before you even get
started.*

She sipped her apple juice.

"Now we'll get some toast," said her mother.

Verna's hair was pure white and waved away from her
face. Evelyn could still see the resemblance to her wedding picture, in which she stood, a little solemnly, looking straight into the camera, her mouth dark with
lipstick, her eyebrows arched, and a wing of fair hair
showing beneath the veil. Same face. Softened and loosened with age. Only Evelyn resembled her, but she hadn't
inherited her shining hair. They were all dark, like Allistair. They had his height. They had his nose, in varying
degrees, and his eyes.

"There's Robin," said Spike.

"Morning," Allistair nodded as she sat down.

Evelyn watched. He was always gallant with Robin.
How did she manage to look so clean and polished? Her
hair was braided like a Mennonite girl's and she wore that
plain sundress. But her shoulders were brown, burnished
by the sun. Now Spike was leaning forward, telling her
something. Like a bird fluffing his plumage.

"You should put ice on it," Robin was saying.

"It always acts up on me," he said.

But Robin didn't think about how she looked, Evelyn knew. She never noticed that people brightened a little when she came into a room. The way they relaxed a little, sat back and smiled.

"Coffee," said Evelyn to herself and turned to wave at the waitress.

Robin felt like she was floating somewhere above the table, trying to attend to the bits of conversation that came and went. Puffs of cloud. She tried to concentrate, but she kept thinking of what they'd say if they knew where she'd been the night before. Straddling a hand-some boy and enjoying it, her body oiled in sweat. Her face reddened.

"Pardon?" she said to the waitress.

"Soft or hard boiled?" asked the waitress, one hand on her hip, the pencil sticking out of her pocket like a dag-ger. "Your egg?"

"Soft," said Robin. "Three minutes, please."

"Mmm," said the waitress, displeased. "Coffee now or later?"

"Now, please."

The waitress went away and came back, sloshing dark liquid in Robin's cup. A little spilled over the edge of it, making a brown puddle in the saucer.

"You don't want to go into Bangor," Allistair was say-ing to Evelyn. "You can take Route One to Topsfield and get on the interstate at Lincoln."

"It's just the turn at Topsfield, and a bit of working your way through Lincoln," said Spike.

Robin wasn't really a part of them, anyway. A big family, always big enough to include one more. Octopus. Tentacles reaching out to pull her in. Yet they'd always been good to her. They knew what was going on now, for instance. Verna knew. She'd known when they'd gone kayaking, Robin suspected. Maybe Allistair knew. If she and Neil got a divorce, they wouldn't hold it against her.

"I just came back and went to bed," Spike was saying.

Any minute now they'd turn to Robin and ask her where she'd been. She didn't know what she'd say, though it would be worse if she said nothing. But they turned their attention to Verna. Had she slept all right? How was she doing now?

"Maybe we should get you checked," said Allistair quietly. "There's a hospital here."

"I think that's a good idea," said Evelyn.

"I'm not a prize cow," said Verna. "I can speak for myself and you know I said before that I don't need any looking after."

"Verna," said Allistair soothingly, "don't fret."

Spike had finished repacking the trunk and now he sat on the damp edge of a white tire beside a garden of pink geraniums. He glanced at the flowers, reminded for a moment of his grandmother's garden. Neil lobbing a baseball at the white plastic swan, at the geraniums bursting out of its back. And who took the blame for it? *Stephen, my good man, look at these flowers. Look at them.* And Neil never saying that he'd done it. Neil, the good son. *Stephen, these are broken from stem to stern.*

He saw Robin come out of the motel room carrying a suitcase. Where had she been the night before? She stepped over a puddle, and he felt a little pang as she put her bag in the trunk, saw him, and raised a golden arm in greeting.

Neil was a stupid bugger.

Evelyn stuffed her bag in the trunk and looked at her brother, twisting a leaf between his fingers. She walked over and sat beside him, regarding the Japanese maple, its red leaves glistening, scattering droplets. It was still cool because of the early rain, but judging by the sky, which was gradually becoming hazy, it would be hotter than the day before.

"You have a way of pissing people off," she said.

"So I've been told. You do, too." He threw away the leaf. "You got home all right."

"Yes." She wasn't going to tell him anything.

They sat watching Verna and Allistair come out of their room. He put his hand on her shoulder as she spoke to him. It could be that he'd shrunk a little over the years. He was stooped now, so his back curved, and his head seemed to be flattened by that cap he wore.

"Forty years," said Evelyn. "I wonder what it feels like
to know exactly what the other person is going to say.
You'd know the answer before you even asked a question."

"I don't know," said Spike. "It wouldn't be that pre-
dictable."

Spike looked at Allistair's hand on Verna's shoulder.
His elderly hand. Her low voice, speaking to him alone. A
breath of wind lifted the red leaves of the maple again,
turning them dull side up, shiny side up.

"I wrote back to Garnet," Verna was saying to Allistair.
"After he sent that card. And he might show up at the
cottage."

"You wrote him?"

"Well, I just thought it wouldn't hurt."

"No," said Allistair. "It doesn't ever hurt, I guess."

"I wanted to tell you."

"Don't get your hopes up now." He put his hand on her
shoulder. He rubbed it a little.

"I know. I just wish he'd come. I spend so much
time—"

"Don't, Vern. There's nothing we can do."

Robin drove down King Street and over the bridge where
they waited at customs. She was going into home terri-
tory, but it now seemed strangely alien. The United
States of America. Star-spangled country of her birth.

Evelyn was silent, resting her head against the window.
Their turn. A small man with a moustache, precisely
trimmed.

"Where were you born?

"Length of visit?

"Alcohol or tobacco?"

The little nod of the head.

"Firearms?"

The lizard gaze. Flick. Flick.

Up the little hill and into Calais, a right turn on the
rain-slick road snaking above a field, past a school. Robin
thought of her body against Kyle's. Those hands on her
waist, that young mouth against her lips, pulling a little
on hers, so she could feel his teeth. She fitted to him. He
fitted to her. Perfectly. Then folding against him, quietly,
his fingers still moving up and down the length of her
body. The fingers, ghost fingers. Limbo. Now nothing, a
bare field, a gas station.

Evelyn's head ached. She put a water bottle absently to
her lips. The car was already warm and Robin was occasionally driving on the shoulder. Not paying attention.
Evelyn went back to reading the magazine, one hand
resting on a picture of a woman in an orange bikini, leaning against a palm tree.

"Shit," said Evelyn.

"What?"

"Says here that we're all becoming less fertile. In

twenty years we'll have trouble reproducing. What'll happen to Luke?"

"Pollution," said Robin. "That's what does it."

"Yes. And stress. One scientist—oh, now listen to this—this guy thinks it's shampoo."

"Shampoo?"

"And there's a theory that it's got something to do with what's happening in nature. They've found female trout with male organs."

"Maybe it's always been that way and they're just discovering it now."

"No, the female trout thing has some connection with DDT, raw sewage, PCBs."

Contamination, Evelyn thought, looking out the window at the marshes, a veil of mist lifting here and there. The end of birth, of first things. The end of everything.

She'd heard the low voices outside the motel room. But she'd been feeling nauseated, and she hadn't caught everything they'd said. Robin and someone else.

"Will you call me?"

"Maybe."

"God, I wish you didn't have to go."

Gone. The lovely, vanished things of the world.

"Garnet might be coming," said Evelyn. "But you don't know him, do you?"

"Only what I've heard."

"That can't have been good."

"No. Which makes me want to see what he's like."

"He's nuts. The stuff he put Mom and Dad through . . ."

"Maybe he's changed. You know, everyone said Neil was perfect and Spike was lucky. Garnet was a subject to avoid. I don't know. I think people are a little bit of everything: good, bad, smart, not so smart."

Allistair was driving behind a semi. It was empty, fishtailing all over the road. Devil's country, this, with marshland on both sides. Verna next to him, holding tight to the wooden handles of her knitting bag because she was worried about something. He'd been gruff with her the night before. Annoyed about Neil. He could catch the semi, if he went quickly enough. He pulled out, passed it. Clear going, with the sun coming through the trees like that. Everything green. He reached out and touched Verna's arm.

"All right?" he said.

"Mmm."

What was it that held them back? Spike wanting to find someone he could stay with. Evie messing up with Duncan, and now living with that fellow Phonse. Garnet and Cinta. Even Neil and Robin now. Each in a world apart. Unjoined. Only himself and Verna. The same words. The same little things. She picking at hangnails, he scratching his ears. But at the beginning of it, standing side by side in front of the priest. *Sacrament of love in this broken world.* Verna beside him. The rings on her finger. *God, in your mercy. Hear our prayer.*

HAILSTONES

"So I decided to run away to Halifax," said Allistair.

"But you got sidetracked stuffing yourself with blueberries," said Verna as she set the soup bowl in front of Grace MacKenzie. The dollop of sour cream on the beet soup wobbled a little after Verna set it down.

"So then what?" said Bob MacKenzie.

"Nothing," said Allistair, laughing. "I fell asleep."

Verna went back in the kitchen and opened the swinging door with her hip as she brought in two more bowls. The beet soup might not be to everyone's liking. And if they didn't eat it quickly, the main course would get cold. It was crown roast of pork with apple and cranberry sauce, along with stuffed sweet potatoes, peas, and carrot rosettes. She sat down and opened her napkin, giving it a shake before laying it over her lap.

"It's good," said Colwell.

Verna smiled.

"Delicious," said Les Duggan.

"Oh, now," she said. His nose was a little rosy because he'd had a few glasses of wine.

She had a spoonful of the rich, faintly sweet soup. She looked at Allistair, who was breaking his dinner roll into bits and sponging up the last of his soup. It was his birthday, after all. He could do as he liked with his dinner roll.

"We've got some news," said Liz Dyson. "Gaby's getting married."

"That MacLeod boy from Tatamagouche?" Verna asked.

"Well, he's a good kid," said Colwell. "He's got a little electronics business going."

"In Halifax," added Liz. "But the main thing is that he's steady."

Through the lace curtains Verna could see the faint whirl of snow outside the window. It whirled, sank, and whirled again. Not that it was anything to worry about. It wasn't a blizzard. But it worried her all the same.

Allistair's face was beaming when Verna brought in the chocolate layer cake.

"Where're the candles, Verna?" said Les.

"You can't put fifty candles on a cake," said Liz.

"Fifty," repeated Allistair. He cut the first slice and flipped it onto a plate. "Half a century." He worked his tongue across his bottom teeth as he cut the other slices and passed around the plates.

"Now," he said, "tell me if you've ever tasted better."

They were halfway through the cake when they heard the back door bang open and hit the wall.

"Goddamn it," said Garnet.

Allistair got up from the table and tossed his napkin over his half-eaten piece of chocolate cake. Verna could hear his low voice in the kitchen as he talked to Garnet.

"I haven't had too much," Garnet was saying in a loud voice. "What do you think? I took your vodka or something?"

The others were looking at their plates. They knew about Garnet. Verna stared at the perfect scrolls of icing on the cake. Dark. Shiny. She moved her fork, pushing some crumbs out of the way.

The door between the kitchen and the dining room swung open.

"Hey," said Garnet, coming in. "There's a party going on here."

Verna didn't look at him.

Allistair came in after him. "Garnet, go upstairs."

"How come? There's a party going on here. Come on and eat your birthday cake, Dad."

"Garnet."

"What?"

"You heard me."

"So?"

"Go upstairs," said Allistair again.

"No fucking way."

Verna's fork clattered on the plate as she got up. "You will not speak to your father that way."

"Who says?"

"If you speak that way to your father, you can leave this house." Verna was shaking.

"All right." He looked at her. "You want me to leave. I'll leave."

He turned and walked out of the dining room. He walked out of the house. He left the front door open so the snow blew into the front hall, a sugary coating on the floor.

Liz and Colwell were the last to go. They took their time putting on their coats.

"It was good soup," Colwell said. "Everything was good. The cake, too."

"Thank you," said Verna.

"He'll come back."

Liz gave Verna a hug before they left. It wasn't snowing much any more and Verna stood at the window by the door and watched them walk down the driveway. At the end, just as they turned into their own driveway, she saw Colwell clasp Liz's hand. She felt a sudden little pang.

Allistair switched off the lights. "Time for bed."

"Shouldn't we do something?"

"No." He started up the stairs. "Garnet'll be back when he's sober."

Verna sat up for a while in the living room, knitting. She knew that Allistair was reading upstairs, or if he'd

turned out the light he'd be looking at the ceiling, trying
not to think of Garnet walking around in the cold, in the
middle of the night.

Garnet must have come back. He must have slept for a
while and then packed his things because he was gone
the next morning long before they were up.

His bedroom was empty. Verna never imagined Garnet
would really leave. But he'd taken things from the dresser,
clothes from the closet. His bed was rumpled, with the
sheet kicked back, blankets on the floor. It was a small
room. Maybe it would have been better if they'd left him
with the other boys from the start. She ran her hand
along the top of the dresser. A plastic figure of a hockey
player. Yvan Cournoyer. A small trophy. His favourite
books: *Robinson Crusoe*, *Treasure Island*, *The Black Stal-
lion*, *Around the World in Eighty Days*. A box of Chiclets.
A red pencil crayon. A globe. She turned the globe to
Africa. China. There were tears running down her face.
She'd told him to go. And he'd gone.

She looked out the window, pulling her housecoat
around her for warmth. There was a pinkish red light in
the morning sky. It flecked the clouds with colour and
turned the snow mauve under the trees. The footprints in
the driveway might be Garnet's. They might be the paper
boy's. They went out the driveway and along the sidewalk.
She imagined they went down the Hawthorne Street hill
and over the bridge, along West Street, and then past the

arena on the way to the highway. Garnet might be there still. Or someone might have given him a ride.

She wiped her face with the back of her hand and lay down on his bed, pulling the sheet up. His pillow smelled of rum, but she turned her face into it anyway. The tears made it wet. If he'd just waited until he cooled down, he might have seen things differently. He might have seen what he was doing to himself. But he didn't see it.

She got up from the bed abruptly. Then she stripped off the sheets, blankets, and pillowcase, releasing the elasticized corners of the mattress cover with a snap. She'd give the linens a good washing and air the blankets on the line, even if it was cold out. It was the smell she minded more than anything.

There came a time when Verna knew Garnet wasn't coming back. After the hailstorm in April. Pellets hitting the roof like shot. When it was all over, the lawn was covered in small white stones. Evelyn went outside in her sock feet and picked up handfuls of them. Pebbles of ice piled up like jewels. Verna got the broom and swept them off the front step.

Allistair stood in the driveway running his hand over the roof of the car.

"Any harm done?" she asked.

"Could have been worse. A couple of dings."

She gazed up at the dark, wintry clouds where the sky was showing through. It had a coppery cast, a strange light. Unpredictable. She took the broom and went around the house to survey the backyard, but there wasn't much damage except a few branches scattered in the grass. The patio was covered with small beads of hail. This was the place where she'd found Garnet once, passed out on the stones. Skin white as paper. Not dead, just drunk.

Verna swept the hailstones off the patio. She swept hard. She swept harder still and they all rolled into the grass.

GARNET

Garnet got out of the car, stretched, and bent to pick a few flakes of rust off the hood. He'd bought the car from Jerry Zyvatkauska for six hundred dollars. It might get him through another winter and it might not. He took his duffel bag out of the trunk and slammed it. Red. Pink. The neighbour's garden was thick with poppies. He set his duffel bag down at the basement door of the cottage. His mother's letter had given him instructions: now he pulled out the crumpled paper and scanned it: "Key under the frog in the garden."

There was a little strip of garden by the shed: a stone frog was sitting under the snapdragons. He got the key and opened the padlock on the shed. All the tools were hung on a pegboard. He lifted another pegboard and saw the keys suspended on strings from tacks, each one labelled. Pocketing one of them, he padlocked the shed door. The woodpile beside the shed was neatly stacked. As he walked around the place, he peered in the windows. A television, a video cassette recorder. A microwave. Someone could break in without giving it a moment's thought. Locks didn't protect anything. A bright yellow finch made an arc over his head and darted to the neighbour's bird feeder, a crooked lighthouse on a pole. He went to the top of the steps where he could see the wide expanse of ocean and the crescent-shaped strip of beach where the waves moved towards the shore in long white rolls. Would he know what to say to them? What would he say to his mother? Or his father?

Another wave formed a lip and fell unevenly.

He didn't know what he would say. At the edge of the water was a damp stretch of sand that seemed pale blue at this distance, shimmering. He rubbed his mouth with the back of his hand. It had been a long time since he'd spent any time at the ocean. It didn't reassure him. The tide came and went, taking things with it.

In the detox centre, the rooms were small. A smell of the pine disinfectant as he sat in a corner, shuddering. The yellow tiles, faintly veined, like marble. The one tile with the cracks in it that he ran his hand over. Shaking. And the sound of a fly buzzing at the top of the window. Not buzzing. Buzzing. Not buzzing. A frenzy that went on all through the day, until the fly finally died on the sill. By then Garnet's whole body was slick with sweat.

And then the DTs.

The worst times were the nights. Something coming out of the water, pulling him down, pulling down his father as they swam together. Something white, a hand, coming out of the dark water. He'd wake, screaming.

When he left that place, the air was sharp as a blade, the day clean and uninterrupted. He moved forward, each step strange to him, even though it was very simple. The movement of his foot off the curb onto the street. The traffic lights: a ruby, an emerald. The feel of his body walking. He recalled a fragment of a psalm that used to hang in the front hall at home: "If I ascend into heaven, thou art there: if I make my bed in hell, behold, thou art there." There was more that he couldn't remember. Something about the wings of the morning, something about dwelling in the sea. His mother had written out the psalm in black ink and mounted it carefully. There were tiny shells glued to the wooden frame. It frustrated him that he couldn't remember more of it. And it was that, more than anything, that made him cry. Walking down the street, his face wet. Right foot, morning; left foot, sea. Heaven, hell.

Garnet didn't have any idea what time the others would get there. It was just about noon, he guessed, looking at the sky. He took off his running shoes and wandered down the steps to the beach where the sand was warm under his feet. It wasn't smooth; it was full of bits of shells. He bent down and scooped up a handful, discovering a few sand dollars the size of sequins. Scraps of mussel shells, pebbles, a sea urchin. He kept the sea urchin, setting it on one side of the bottom step, and discarded the rest.

He was afraid. It was one of the things that had been stopping him all along. He walked along the beach, watching a pink-and-orange kite dip over the ocean and swing back up into the air. A boy was letting it out, reeling it in. He had left home partly because he'd been afraid. Angry. But he'd always known he would go. What was there to do in a town like that? A slim woman in a black bathing suit passed him. There was a gold buckle holding the two skimpy pieces of her bathing-suit top together. He glanced back at her. And then what had he done when he left? It wasn't like he'd done anything with his life. A father was walking a child in a stroller, and the child gazed at Garnet with dark, impassive eyes. Anyone could see he'd made a mess of it.

He stooped and picked up a sand dollar, chipped a little on one side, but still whole. He turned it over. There was a slight rattling of bits inside. The little doves, his mother had told him once. She'd shown him the glass jar on her dresser that contained shells and a few sand dollars. She took out the large one she'd found on her honeymoon, which was pure white, clean as a bone.

This sand dollar was grey. Garnet put it in his pocket. There were things he'd probably have to say to all of them. Things he'd have to account for. That night that he'd come home drunk, for instance, on his father's birthday. His mother speaking to him, her whole body trembling.

"If you speak that way to your father, you can leave this house." Her voice quiet and firm.

Even in his anger, he'd known that she was right. But he'd found a way to hurt them. Far out on the water, a fishing boat was chugging around in circles, pausing while a lobster trap was brought up. Then it chugged on to the next. No doubt he'd gotten back at them, he thought wearily. He wished he hadn't.

Fifth time in the ICU. His skin all yellow: colour of cowardice. His belly grossly distended. By that time, he hardly knew what was happening. Doctors came in, went out. One asked if he knew what day it was.

"No," said Garnet, with an enormous effort.

"So I guess you don't know what year it is, either. What about five times five?"

Zero.

The doctor drew in his breath and began again. "Maybe we should try something easy, like why you're here."

He was dying.

Sometimes a nurse was beside him, moving his body as if he were a rag doll, gently taking the sheets away. Bloody, stained sheets, covered with his own tarry, stinking shit.

They talked about him as if he weren't there.

"Well, he's stabilized. We'll keep replacing the blood and plasma and see how that goes," muttered the one who came most often. He had a gravelly voice.

"Two units," the nurse interjected. "So far."

"So far," repeated Gravelly Voice. "He'll need a hell of a lot more before he's done. We'll need a scope to see where the bleeding sites are. Probably sclerotherapy later on. It's a wing and a prayer with this one."

They asked him if he had any relatives living nearby. He said he didn't.

Did he have any relatives at all?

He wanted to cry.

Because if he had any relatives, the nurses would call them for him.

Was he Protestant? Was he Catholic? What was he? After that it was a priest. Did he want a priest?

A priest came. He sat on a chair by the side of the bed. Waiting.

Garnet lay in his bed, rolled on one side. He was too weak to lift his head to lean over and grasp the K-basin on the bedside table, so when he vomited it spilled out of his mouth onto the pillow and the newly changed sheets. It was dark red. It was his life, rushing out of him.

Garnet circled around and started walking back the way he'd come. The cottages were large at this end of the beach. They weren't cottages at all. One was a rambling cedar-shingled house with blue shutters, a wide porch, and a manicured lawn that sloped down to the stone wall protecting it from the beach. The man reading a newspaper on the porch was probably a neurosurgeon from New York. A financial analyst. Nothing like Garnet.

What was he doing here, anyway? He kicked at a broken piece of blue mussel shell. He didn't belong. Neil had told him when he'd come to visit that Garnet was being an asshole, drinking like a fish and expecting people to bail him out when he got into trouble. Neil wasn't going to bail him out. That was the night Garnet had climbed into the bathtub in his clothes. He'd been a little drunk then, like Cinta, but she was still in the kitchen, laughing with Neil. She liked him; she was flirting with him.

Then Neil had found him.

"What are you, nuts?" he yelled, turning off the water.

"Maybe."

"You might have fallen asleep."

"So."

"Can't you see what you're doing? Don't you have any idea?"

"Yes."

"Jesus. You're a fucking idiot. Get out of the tub, Garnet."

The tide was going out, and the beach looked wider than when Garnet had started his walk. The water was a brilliant blue, flecked with light, and the waves tumbled over and over. He recognized the low roof and yellow shutters of the cottage his parents were renting, which was modest compared to those other places down the beach. But there was no sign of anyone having arrived. He still had time for a swim. Leaving his jeans and T-shirt at the bottom of the steps, he jogged down to the water in his underwear. It was cold. He waded out, letting the waves break against him as he went. He plunged in when he got out to deeper water, shaking his head like a dog when he came up. Laughing, he let a wave crash over him, before he turned and swam with the breakers back to the shore.

"I think we'll keep him on the Vasopressin," Gravelly Voice was saying. "We can do variceal injections until we're blue in the face, but—"

"Time for a shunt, do you think?"

"Well, that's a last resort."

Garnet waded out of the water and walked up the beach. He didn't have a towel so he sat on the steps in the sun. When a riffling of wind chilled him he put on his T-shirt, rolled his wet underwear down his legs, and pulled on his jeans. It was low tide. From this point on, the water would start inching back in. A duckling appeared out of the rocks by the neighbour's steps. Where had it come from? Garnet spread his wet underwear on a rock to dry and watched the bird toddle across the sand as a large gull shrieked overhead. It occurred to him that the gulls might eat a duckling, so he tracked it, hoping to catch it and take it to the tidal pool on the other side of the road. The large gull landed in front of the duckling, making it skitter to one side and fly up, haphazardly, into the air. It escaped to the water, where Garnet couldn't see it any more. He could only see the gull, which pursued it, circling and then plummeting swiftly, where it snatched something up in its beak. Passing over Garnet, it dropped part of the duckling on the sand. He walked over to it.

The head, nipped clean from the body.

What did he know about anything? Life. What did he know about it? He lay down on the sand by the tiny head of the duckling, propping himself on his elbows. The eyes: as if they saw things.

"It's just as well we didn't do surgery. We could have lost him," said the one with a face like bread dough. The one who'd asked him to answer five times five. "But we're not out of the woods yet."

Five more days.

"Well," said Bread Dough. "Maybe we're getting to the edge of the woods."

Six days.

Garnet touched the duckling's tiny, feathered head.

That moment between one thing and another.

"Garnet!"

He turned away from the duckling's head. There they were. His mother coming down the steps. His father. Spike. He got up, brushing the sand away. For a moment he wanted to run, but he stood where he was, waiting for his mother to come closer. Her hair was white, blown up slightly by the wind. She was smaller than he remembered.

He could hear the sound of something beating, which might have been the waves, far off.

"Garnet," she said, approaching with her arms wide open. "Garnet."

JEALOUS

"We're glad you could be here, Garnet," said Allistair.

"We should have had something really festive for dinner," Verna said. "An occasion like this." She cut a bit of chicken and speared it with her fork. "It would have been nice if I'd had time to make an angel food cake, or something like that."

Evelyn stabbed at her peas. She'd been the one to make supper, after doing the groceries. The others had offered to help, but Evelyn had said no, they should go and sit down because it would only take a little while. And now her mother was suggesting more, something that only her mother could achieve. Couldn't they see what a good supper it was? No. They'd wanted candles on the table, the best tablecloth that could be found, which was a blue-and-white one with tassels. Her father had gotten goblets out of a cupboard, washed them carefully, and poured white grape juice into each one. Her mother had opened the oven and given the chicken a poke with a sharp knife. The chicken was doing just fine. But Evelyn hadn't said anything.

Now they sat together at the table in front of the big window in the kitchen. Verna was at one end of the table, Allistair at the other. Robin and Garnet had a view of the ocean, but Spike and Evelyn, on the other side of the table, had to turn around to look at it. The light showed the lines on Garnet's face, the shadows under Robin's eyes. Despite the shadows, Robin seemed to glow with health, while Evelyn knew she herself looked tense and irritated. Since she'd come to the beach, her hair had taken on a life of its own. It was even more frizzy than usual, dark and wild.

The light also showed up the fatigue in Verna's face. She had put on lipstick for dinner and her face was paler than ever. Her hair seemed whiter. Garnet, sitting next to his father, looked severe. His eyes—so very clear and blue—resembled his father's.

"Chicken's good," said Robin.

"Thanks," murmured Evelyn.

A goldfinch swooped to the bird feeder attached by a small suction cup to the window. It gobbled a few seeds, looking rapidly this way and that.

"So you haven't been sick or anything?" Verna asked Garnet. "I just can't get over how thin you are."

"I'm all right."

They looked through the window at the wide skirt of sea.

"Those steps may not last through the winter," Allistair commented. "With the tides. And then you get the storms, too, and there's the combination of the two things. Storms and tide."

Now the light shivered across the surface of the ocean. They still couldn't see the beach, but there might be a strip of sand at the bottom of the steps.

"I think it's going out again," said Verna.

"Well." Evelyn got up, flinging her hair over her shoulder as she took her plate to the counter. The others hadn't finished, but she couldn't just sit there. "There's a couple of pieces of chicken left. And more salad in the bowl." She rinsed off her plate in the sink.

"Here, now don't start with dishes," said Verna.

"Why not? Someone has to do them."

"I'll help you later," said Garnet.

"You?" Evelyn's voice was high. "You never did dishes." She turned back to the sink. "Anyway, I can do them."

"Maybe he does the dishes now," said Spike. "Did you ever think about that?"

Evelyn hunted in a cupboard for a plastic container for the chicken. When she found it, she scooped the remaining pieces into it. Everyone was against her. Robin cleared the plates from the table, putting them by the sink, where Evelyn rinsed and stacked them. They were all in league against her. She cut the pie into slices, putting a scoop of ice cream on each plate.

"Apple," she said as she handed out the plates.

The pie was hard to cut and the apples tasted like plastic. "Get this on special?" said Spike.

"Be quiet," said Evelyn.

They ate the pie in silence. Evelyn noticed that Spike left half of his on the plate, as if to spite her.

"That was a fine meal," pronounced Allistair, pushing his chair back.

It wasn't a fine meal at all, thought Evelyn. The pie was terrible. But her father had eaten all of it.

"Especially the pie," said Spike, grinning.

Evelyn flung her fork down on the plate. "That's it," she said. "What is it with all of you?"

They looked at her.

"Garnet comes home and you fall over backwards. You're overjoyed to see him. You sit here all together, but no one knows what to say to him. Well, what's he ever done for you? I mean, think about it. What's he ever done?"

"Evelyn!" said her father.

"Well, tell me. What's he ever done?"

"Shut up, Evelyn," said Spike.

Evelyn was still looking at her father.

"I never thought that I'd see him again," said Allistair deliberately, "if you must know." Usually it took a long time for him to become angry, but he could feel something rising slowly in him. It had never been his intention to favour one of his children over another. He looked down at the tablecloth, which he pinched between his thumb and index finger. "I'd given him up for dead, in a way. I never thought that—" His voice changed a little. "I never thought he'd come back."

"And then he comes back and you treat him like this. Like royalty."

"Yes." Allistair looked up at her. "And why not?" His voice was dangerously calm.

"You and Mom always loved him best. It was always Garnet, Garnet, Garnet."

"No, Evelyn," said Verna. She stood up, gripping a fork, which she held up at her daughter. The light shone through her white hair, making it almost transparent. Her fine brows were knitted together. "You're wrong there. Each of you have been loved. Each of you. And each of you will always be loved."

"Yes," Evelyn shot back. "Each of us." Even as she spoke, she knew she shouldn't. Especially to her mother. She tried to stop herself, but the words tumbled out. "But Garnet the most. I'm the only one with guts enough to say it. Spike won't because he takes Garnet's side. Robin won't. And Neil's not here. But he'd have something to say, believe me."

"He never liked me much," said Garnet.

She turned on him. "What gives you the right to come here?" Her cheeks were high with colour.

"He has the same right you have," said Allistair. "Any one of you."

Verna made a little noise and they looked at her. She was still standing holding the fork, but she no longer brandished it. She looked older and smaller, as if she'd been punctured and something had leaked out. "You're a mother, Evelyn. You should know what this is all about. This is not about degrees in the way we love you."

A sparrow came to the feeder, pecking at the seeds. They could hear the *hushshwush* of the waves and the metallic sound of the wind chimes that hung outside the front door.

Verna put down the fork. "This is much more than that."

The wind chimes jingled.

"Who says?" said Evelyn.

Garnet got up and started doing the dishes. Evelyn slammed out the kitchen door. They could see her kicking off her Birkenstocks as she crossed the lawn. She pulled off her socks and tossed them on the grass.

"I'll help with the dishes," offered Robin.

The rest of them stayed where they were at the table. Evelyn's red socks blazed, one near the patio and one in the dune grass near the steps. Verna and Allistair both stared at them without speaking.

"What the hell?" said Spike finally.

Verna's mouth was set in a tight line. She sat down heavily.

"You're all right?" Allistair asked.

She nodded.

"Why'd she have to go and do that?" asked Spike, still sitting where he was. "It's like she's jealous."

"Jealous," laughed Garnet. His laugh went high and wild. "Jealous."

He stopped washing a glass casserole dish and turned around. He stood for a moment, drying his hands on a towel. Beside him, Robin continued laying things out neatly on the counter. He tossed the towel over his shoulder, came back to the table, and sat down.

"I can't do this for you," he said. He looked exhausted. He was looking straight out to the water. So clear, those eyes, thought Verna.

"Do what?" asked Allistair. He moved the salt shaker closer to the pepper grinder.

"I don't know," he said blankly. "I can't change things."

"No one's asking you to," said Verna.

They were quiet. Robin stopped putting away the dishes.

Allistair didn't know what to do with his hands. He didn't know where he wanted to put the salt and pepper. He was always so careful. How could he be any other way? Even if he'd wanted to get up and throw something through the window, for instance. "Your mother's right," he said finally.

"I can only change things for myself is what I'm trying to say," Garnet said. He took the dishtowel from his shoulder and sat looking at it, at the red-and-white pattern. "It was my own mess."

"You take people with you when you're in a mess," Allistair said sharply.

"But *you're* still living it."

"Yes, well." Allistair's hands fumbled for the salt and pepper again. "That's what happens. You go over things. You keep going over things."

"But then you're living in the past."

"You've come back," said Verna quietly, "and we're old. That's all. If we're living in the past, it's only because we're old."

Garnet looked at his mother squarely. There were tears in her eyes. He'd made her cry, coming back.

ICEBERG

Verna was taking things out of her suitcase without caring how she did it. She dumped things in a messy pile on the bed, her back to Allistair. He watched her. It wouldn't do for her to get worked up, because then she'd be awake half the night. He went over and put his hands on her shoulders.

"Vern."

"What?"

"Stop it." He spoke gently.

"I don't see why Evie had to say all those things." Verna turned around and sat down heavily on the bed.

Allistair took the things Verna had laid out on the bed, sorted them, and put them into the drawers that had been Verna's for as long as they'd been coming to this cottage. He didn't have any excuses for Evelyn. God only knew why she'd blown up like that.

"She wants attention," said Verna, half to herself. "I guess that's what she wants. But she's a grown woman."

"I know," said Allistair. He stood with a few pairs of rolled socks in his hands. "Maybe it's hard on them having Garnet show up. It's hard on us." He nested the socks neatly at the front of the drawer.

"But it's what's we wanted." Her voice quavered.

"It's what we wanted," he repeated. He turned to put a little plastic bag and a hairbrush on the top of the dresser, catching sight of himself in the mirror. His face looked haggard. There was that tremor again, that almost imperceptible motion. "It's not always easy getting what you want." He recalled how he'd felt that time when Colwell was having trouble with Liz. How Colwell had looked at Verna. How she'd looked at him. As if she couldn't get enough of him. He'd never spoken of it, and Verna had never spoken of it, and they'd gone on together. In the end, Allistair had gotten what he'd wanted.

"But why would it be hard on us?" she persisted.

He sat down on the bed. "Why don't you put your feet up for a bit and have a rest?"

She put her head back on the pillow obediently. He put a soft mohair blanket over her.

"I could turn off the lights and pull the blinds," he offered.

"No. I'll get up soon." She closed her eyes and very quietly he pulled the blind. Her eyes opened. "You don't have to do that."

"But, Vern, you need rest. It's been a trying day."

"It's been a wonderful day," she contradicted.

He sat on the bed. He'd only pulled the blind down halfway; he could see part of the driveway leading to the road at the back of the cottage. On the other side of the road was the Pool and Wood Island Harbour beyond the neck of land. Toy sailboats tilted this way and that on the water. Soon they'd stop moving; the tide would go out and leave them stuck in place. In the west, the sky had turned the colour of a salmon fillet. Then it would turn a purplish red.

Garnet.

For weeks after Garnet left home neither of them could sleep. Verna had gotten up and gone downstairs while Allistair lay in bed staring at the darkness. He could never sleep when she wasn't beside him in bed. One night he went downstairs to find her.

"I wish you wouldn't come down here, night after night," he said.

She was knitting something.

"You don't want me tossing and turning in bed. I'd just keep you up."

"It keeps me up anyway."

She took out a row she'd just purled.

"What are you making?"

"A sweater." She stopped in the middle of taking out the row. "Oh," she cried, "it's all my fault."

"No, it isn't. Come upstairs."

She put away her knitting and they went up the stairs, pausing on the landing.

"I never liked this wallpaper," she said. "What about you?"

He studied the green woman on the swing, pushed by the green man. They were gaily repeated all the way up the stairs.

"I've never really thought about it."

"I think I'll take it down," she said. "I'll put up something I can stand to look at, like a stripe. A yellow-and-white stripe." She ran her hand over the woman on the swing. "That would do it."

It was quiet in the cottage. Verna could hear muffled voices coming from the kitchen, and the tap being turned on and off. She opened her eyes for a moment and saw Allistair staring out the window. She didn't want him in the bedroom with her, but she didn't know how to ask him to leave. There were times in her life when she just wanted to be alone, apart from all of them. Even Allistair, whom she depended on. She closed her eyes, putting a hand under the side of her face so it wouldn't bear the marks of creases from the pillow. Then everyone would know she'd had a lie-down when she'd never really wanted to have a nap in the first place.

She did these things for Allistair, because it was better to go along with him. Let him think he was giving comfort. Marriage was a difficult thing to understand. It was like an iceberg. She shifted a little on the bed. Everyone saw the little white bit that floated on top, but no one had any idea of the accumulated mass under the water. Sometimes it was a luminous, remarkable thing, and sometimes it was heavy with the weight of years.

There was a time she hadn't known this. She and Allistair had come to this beach for their honeymoon and stayed in the small cottage that had once been a fishing-and-hunting shack. It was still there, next to this cottage. There had been only dune grass surrounding it, not poppies in a garden. In the evening, when they sat on the top step above the beach, they could see the nuns from the convent at the far end of the beach. They were dark birds clustered together, their habits lifting out behind them. One was apart from the others, down near the shore.

It seemed to Verna then, as she looked at the horizon, that it was a hinge between earth and sky. It kept opening wider and wider until the sky was on fire and the water jittery with light. They could see all the way from the point at Biddeford Pool down to Fortune's Rocks at the other end. Allistair leaned over and kissed her on the cheek.

"You're pretty," he said.

"Don't ever leave me." She turned to face him.

"I won't," he said. "Why would I?"

"I don't know." She got up and brushed off her shorts. "But don't." She went down the steps and stood facing the water. He went down the steps after her.

"It's so perfect right now," she said. "With the sky like that."

They walked down to the water's edge and a line of sandpipers scurried away from them, leaving delicate marks in the sand.

"There are all kinds of things you don't know about me," she said. "You don't know all the things I'm afraid of, for instance."

"No."

"Sometimes I'm one way and sometimes I'm another. Sometimes I won't love you."

"I know," he said, smiling.

"What? You're laughing at me."

"No," he said, but he was still smiling. "Not at all."

Verna opened her eyes. There was a sound that nudged her awake even as she dozed. A soft, breathy sound. Allistair was still sitting on the bed, but now his face was covered with his hands.

"What?" she whispered.

He didn't answer. His shoulders were shaking.

"Ah, don't," she said softly.

When had she last seen him cry? Years ago. She sat up, taking the mohair blanket with her, and moved next to him. She put her arm around him, but it didn't seem to be enough. Outside, she could see a man walking along the road to Biddeford Pool, obscured periodically by the wild rose bushes. The garden next door was a mass of blooms, all nodding in the light wind. Under her arm, she could feel her husband's body shuddering as he sobbed. "Tell me what's wrong."

"I don't know," he said. He took his hands from his face. "It's more than I know."

"It's Garnet, isn't it?"

His eyes and cheeks were wet. He drew both palms down his face. "It's—well, it's everything."

She felt a disquieting feeling rising in her, a sense of panic. Had she ever seen him like this?

"It's Garnet," he said, his voice sounding strangled. "Yes, I guess it's that. But it's other things." He couldn't seem to stop crying. The tears kept welling out of his eyes. "I keep thinking of my father."

"But you hardly knew him."

"I know," he said, wiping his face again.

She got up and fumbled in her purse for her hanky. "Here," she offered.

"And I was thinking about you," he continued. "About everything I don't say to you. All the things I hide from you."

She leaned against him. "That's all right. I keep things from you."

"I know you do."

They pondered the sky, with the light slowly leaking out of it. It had turned grey, except for a soft band of mauve behind the water tower. But it was mostly the colour of a dead fish, Allistair thought.

"Did you love him?" he asked.

"Who?"

"Colwell."

"*Colwell?*"

They hadn't moved. She hadn't shifted away from him. He was staring fixedly out the window at the mast of one of the sailboats, feeling his head expanding like a balloon.

"Did you?" he persisted.

"I—I guess I did, then."

"And you never said anything?"

"What was there to say?"

His head was still expanding. He felt his body floating up to the ceiling.

"How did you know?" she asked.

"How could I not know?" he said carefully, speaking from the ceiling.

She bent her head.

"Did anything happen?"

"Oh, no," she whispered. She'd begun to rock back and forth. "No."

"You must have wanted something to happen." His voice was quiet, but it sounded oddly harsh. He couldn't be sure what it would do next.

"Once I did."

He didn't say anything. He loved her more than he could bear.

"It was a long time ago," she said. "And I always loved you. Always."

"I know," he said. "I know that." His body seemed to be descending from the ceiling, slipping back into its right place.

She moved to put her hand over his, but he caught it gently and closed both of his hands over it.

It was curious how Verna felt. Her body was warm from the mohair blanket. Her hand was a sleeping bird inside Allistair's large hands. They sat together, leaning against each other.

"Are you all right now?" she asked.

"I'm fine."

This was their marriage, she thought. Outside in the neighbour's yard the poppies were just at their peak. Allistair had asked her; she had told him. It wasn't as hard as she had thought it might be once. But then, she didn't love Colwell now. The flowers in the garden below were red, pink, crimson. There were daisies among them, little clusters of white amongst the fiery colours. And there were some black-eyed Susans. The woman who owned the place next door came from Portland every other weekend just to tend it. All in all, it was quite a garden, thought Verna.

"Maybe I shouldn't have asked you," he said.

"It's all right. It's Garnet coming here and one thing leading to another. Everything comes out." She sat quite still, gazing at the poppies.

He let go of her hand and got up. She knew he wanted her to go with him, back out into the kitchen, but for a moment she just wanted to look at the garden. It was hard to believe that someone could get it all to bloom at the same time—so much that needed attention—especially here, with the sandy soil and the wind. It was a large garden, too. It struck her that it must have required enormous effort, a garden like that. It was an achievement.

BROTHERS

Verna came into the kitchen. Allistair had already pulled a chair out for her.

"Shit," said Garnet softly. "I screwed things up, coming here."

She sat down abruptly. It all seemed like a dream: she felt light-headed. Maybe they were all stuck. Maybe they'd lived years and years of being stuck. It was better to look out at the wide-open sky, though the dark was creeping up. She'd expected it to be different when Garnet came back to them. She'd expected something to feel lighter.

"You didn't screw things up," said Verna, but "screw" was not a word she used. It sounded odd, as if she didn't mean it. She tried to get her bearings. "I tried to find you once, you know. In Boston. I went looking for you."

"Neil came," said Garnet. "There were two things that happened. Neil, and then the whole thing with Cinta."

He was still staring out at the beach, and the light coloured his face with a ruddy glow. But his eyes were like chips of broken china. Blue. There was a little grey in the hair at his temples. The dishtowel was flat on his legs, and his hands were on each thigh.

"Neil fucked Cinta," he said in a hard voice.

There was a little sound behind him. Robin had been leaning against the counter and now she turned to face the cabinets.

"Garnet!" Verna got up and went to Robin.

"Well, that's what happened," Garnet said, glancing over his shoulder at Robin. "You may as well know what happened."

Allistair got up and pushed his chair in, with a heavy, deliberate motion. He walked around the fireplace that jutted out between the kitchen and small living room. He circled the living room. Then he came back, pulled the chair out again, and sat down. His face sagged with age. There were pouches under his eyes. "Are you trying to hurt people, Garnet? Because if you are, maybe you're right. Maybe you shouldn't have come."

No one spoke.

"I think—" Garnet struggled. "I'm trying to say things that need to be said."

"You're not going to go into all the gory details, are you?" asked Spike. It made him uncomfortable.

"Wait just a moment," said Verna. They could hear that tone in her voice they'd heard when she'd stood up during dinner, piercing the air with her fork. "You want to talk about things like this when Robin is in the

room? Don't you think there's something wrong in
that?"

"I want to know," said Robin simply, moving away
from Verna and sitting down in a chair. She had an old
navy blue sweatshirt over her sundress and she pulled at
the frayed wristband. "I think I have a right to know."

"You don't care about him any more, do you?" Garnet
waited for her to look at him.

His eyes were like razors. She couldn't meet his eyes:
she looked down instead. The wind chimes rang outside,
sounding far off and yet close. Lonely. "No," she said. It
was strange to be asked that question. It was strange to
answer it as she had. But it was very clear; it was quick.
No, no, no. She could feel Verna's eyes on her. She could
feel Allistair's silence. But that was her answer. And now
she felt something moving inside, something small, so
very small. And the small thing turned out to be tears.
She wiped at her face. Someone handed her a paper towel
and that same person put an arm around her. Verna. No,
no, no. The tears came running, spilling down her face.

"Garnet," said Verna quietly. "You didn't have to bring
Robin into it."

"Yes, he did," said Robin, wiping at her face with the
paper towel. It didn't do any good; the tears kept coming.
"I didn't want you—any of you—to know how bad things
were with Neil, how bad—" She made a little gulping
noise. "I'm not your daughter, for one thing—"

"Hush, now," said Verna, who had come over to

Robin's chair and stood with her hands on her shoulders. "Don't say things like that—that you're not our daughter."

"Well," said Robin, still not looking at Garnet. "How long was this going on? With Neil and Cinta?"

"Only once," said Garnet. "But that was the end of it for her."

"What do you mean, that was the end of it?" Allistair spoke more harshly than he'd meant to, but he didn't want to hear this, any of this. He wanted to get up and go outside, where the gulls were diving over the water.

"For Cinta," said Garnet. "She wouldn't have anything to do with me after that."

"She was your wife," said Allistair.

"Ha, my wife," laughed Garnet. It was a rough sound, not like a laugh at all. "Do you think that made any difference? It didn't. My wife," he repeated. "You mean the drunk who lived with me. And I was another drunk. I was the scum of the earth and she knew it. Neil wasn't the scum of the earth. Or at least he didn't look like it."

A child screamed on the beach. Evening had fallen and the tide, they saw, had gone out farther. They could see people walking, the child trying to get out of the stroller, the mother trying to coax him back into it. They could see two women walking together, one leaning on the other. The waves broke evenly and rolled away. In places, the sand looked like velvet when the nap is smoothed a certain way. Nowhere could they see Evelyn.

"I know how he looked," said Robin. She thought of
how they'd looked in their wedding photographs. How
young she'd been back then. Cutting the cake with his
hand over hers. And when he'd looked at her, how she'd
trusted his eyes.

"Anyway, I didn't know at first," Garnet went on. "I
was out of it. I'd been sitting in the bathtub with the water
running and Neil came in and turned it off. I remember
that. And then I remember waking up on the bathroom
floor. I got up, all damp and cold and it was like there was
a piece of metal driven into my head. All I wanted was
another drink. I wasn't thinking about Neil or Cinta. And
then I went into the bedroom and there they were—"

Allistair's hand came down hard on the table. He
stood up and his chair fell over. His head seemed to shake
a little, as though he were trembling all over.

"Wait, Allistair," said Verna. There was a calm in her
voice.

"I don't have to hear that," he said gruffly. "I'm going
out."

But he stood still.

"Neil and Cinta. In our bed. I couldn't believe what I
saw," Garnet continued. "I was still drunk. I was still sort
of stupid and I was bumping against things in the hall. I
went into the kitchen and ran water in the sink and put
the plug in and kept running water until the sink was full.
I could do that much. I put my head in it."

Robin turned to look at him.

"Then I knew what had happened." Garnet's voice was hard. "I knew it like something had split me open. And I came up with my face all wet and ran down the hall. I just went straight back into the bedroom and landed on Neil."

"So you fought like a couple of dogs." Allistair walked away from the table.

"Like a couple of dogs," Garnet repeated. "I pushed Cinta away. I'd never pushed her before."

Cinta, saying Garnet's name over and over. Shouting it, to make him stop. As if shouting his name would have done any good.

"Well, and what good did that do?" said Allistair sternly, coming back to the table. "Fighting?"

"I'd never fought like that before," Garnet said. "But I could have thrown him out a window."

Allistair didn't respond.

"We were on the floor," Garnet went on, "all caught up in the sheets."

"But he got the better of you," said Robin.

"He wasn't drunk," admitted Garnet. "He wasn't stupid like that. I was just punching out into air. And he was hitting me every time." And Garnet recalled how after a while he'd slid under the bed just to get away, breathing hard until he came back out and was immediately pounded by Neil. All the time listening to Cinta shrieking into the pillow above him. Cinta. Cinta. Warm Cinta, with her flat face and her sad eyes and flapping sandals and her body that had always comforted him.

Her body, like home.

He sat there as if in a trance. None of them wanted to look at him, except Verna. She saw everything in his face. But she'd never suspected this. That her sons were capable of this. What did she feel? She didn't know. She felt like something had gone that she was used to, like a dam of sticks and twigs in the river, something not quite secure. Whatever it was, she'd had faith in it. Now it was being washed away and she was being washed away with it. She could feel herself floating. She could feel herself letting go. And along with this feeling, she could sense whatever it was that her heart was doing. That weird little flutter.

"Cinta," said Garnet.

The name was there in front of them, round as a plate. The girl that Verna hadn't given much thought to. She'd felt, as a matter of fact, that Cinta wasn't good enough. That girl in the photograph with the heavy breasts and the dangling earrings. Her daughter-in-law. But Cinta had been outside their circle. She'd never entered it.

"So that was it," said Spike. He got up and went to the fridge, getting a beer for himself.

"No," said Garnet.

Spike was at the counter, opening his beer and pouring it into a glass.

"It wasn't as simple as that," Garnet went on. "Don't think you're not a part of it."

"What?" Spike set down the glass on the counter. "I wasn't there. This was between you and Neil and Cinta."

At that moment Evelyn came back in the door, shutting it carefully behind her. Her cheeks were rosy and her hair was blown all over, so that it seemed to have expanded, frizzily, around her head. She leaned against the wall near the door.

"You missed it," said Spike. "And you left your socks outside."

She turned to look at the socks. "Oh." They were strange objects to her. They lay like bright spaceships about to take off. "I guess I should get them."

She put one hand up to the wall as if to steady herself. "I'm sorry for what I said. I'm sorry, Garnet."

Had he heard? He sat very still, as if he were made of stone. He was still thinking of Cinta. But then he gave his head a little shake and something went out of him: the anger he'd been feeling towards all of them. It was true what Spike had said. They hadn't been there. He turned to her—his skin almost translucent, with a faintly yellow cast, his mouth in a firm line. Evelyn could see what he would look like when he was very old. It came to her, how he would dodder a bit, how his face would look pale and sort of waxy, how his hands would tremble. She saw it plainly.

"It's not you who should be sorry," he said quietly.

Evelyn looked away from him, out the window. It may have been that the socks lifted up off the dune grass. They might have lifted once, twirled, draped themselves over the grass again.

"It's me," he said. "I'm sorry for all that happened. I'm sorry for Neil sleeping with Cinta and then Neil going home and Cinta leaving me and then filling herself full of sleeping pills and getting her stomach pumped out and coming back to live with me, and then doing it again, knowing she was going to get her wish the second time. And finding her dead. Finding her—" He stopped. "I'm sorry for that. And I'm sorry for everything from the beginning. I'm sorry for Alice Blaney, because she didn't know what was happening to her. It wasn't her fault. And I'm sorry for Janelle and I'm sorry for Colin and I'm sorry for what she told me and I'm sorry for Spike, because he had no idea. And I'm sorry because somehow this all comes around to me in the end. And I'm sorry you're all in this, too, because you are. And I'm sorry—" But he couldn't finish. His hands had gone up to his face and he was making sounds that didn't seem quite human. But he was still trying to talk. "And I'm sorry that Neil almost killed me and that I wanted to kill Neil." His voice was strangled and they could hardly hear what he was saying. "I've never been sorry for that before. But I am. And I'm sorry that I put you through this."

It was Robin who leaned over and put her arms around him. She was crying, too.

"It's all right," she said.

"No, it's not."

"Yes," she whispered.

He slumped in her arms, right down on the floor, and put his head in her lap, like a child. She stroked his hair, his head. Her face was smooth and her hair was radiant, like something on fire. She stroked him. "It's all right," she kept saying.

"But Cinta's dead," he said, garbling his words. "She's been dead for years. Years. And she was my wife. I loved her. There were people I loved before her. Alice. I loved her." His voice went up and down wildly. "Janelle, too. But she never got over Spike. I was just the one who came after him. I looked a little like him, but I wasn't him. It happened every time. Except for Cinta. But I hadn't figured on Neil." His voice slid strangely. "And he took her away from me. My brother. So even Cinta. Even—"

"Sshhh," Robin whispered. "It'll be all right."

There was nothing the rest of them could say. They could only look at Robin bent over Garnet, listening to the tiny sounds they made: the gasps of his breathing, the murmurs of her voice.

AFTERWARDS

She loved her children. Whatever Neil had done, whatever Garnet had done. And still she clung to this, even though she could see the two of them rolling over and over on the floor. Her eyes were shut, squeezed shut, to keep the tears back.

They could have killed each other. Instead, it was Cinta who'd died.

But Verna wasn't about to lay blame. She took a breath and straightened in her chair. She could still hear Garnet.

Where did blame get them, in the end?

∽

Allistair could feel his anger subsiding. It leaked away.

By worrying about Garnet, had he lost track of Neil? Perhaps he hadn't been a good father to any of them. He had tried, but it wasn't enough.

The horizon was still there. Like a measuring stick. Measuring blue, blue and more blue.

His father. His children.

༄

What? What did Garnet know?

Garnet knew.

There was something of Garnet in all of it. Spike put his thumb in the opening of his beer bottle. He hooked it in, listening to his brother cry.

༄

All of it had happened in her absence. Evelyn had come in from outside and something had happened. What had she started, anyway? It was as though she'd lighted a long fuse and it had burned, snaking along the ground, and then exploded.

Now look at the damage: Neil. Cinta. Robin. Spike. Garnet.

And her parents. But she couldn't look at either one of them.

༄

Where did so much sadness come from? Robin didn't know.

And there was more. There was always more.

∽

Garnet stopped crying. He sat up. Hadn't he put his head in Cinta's lap?

Who were they all?

THE TREE GHOST

After a while, Verna got up and made tea. Good, sweet tea. That was what they needed, she thought, plugging in the kettle. She sighed, exhaling lightly, without making a sound. The sky was a soft darkening blue. The few fishermen who had set out their lines on the beach were packing up their things for the evening.

Garnet had gotten up from the floor and was sitting on the chair again. He had his back to her. She put her hands on his shoulders and bent over, kissing him on the head. She could do that much for him. But she wasn't sure how much he would allow.

"I wish we'd known," she said.

"Well," he said, as if he were waking up, "who knows what goes on?"

"You can't," said Allistair. "Not even people in your own family. My father, for instance." And he flipped up an edge of the tasselled tablecloth, running his hand over the wood beneath. "I never knew him. Not really. And then he died."

"And you've thought about it all your life," said Verna, her head on one side. The kettle had begun to boil and she unplugged it.

"There were things I could have done." Allistair nodded. "Things that might have prevented other things."

"And what do you do with that?" said Spike.

"There's only what you've done or what you haven't done," said Evelyn.

"What you haven't done." Garnet took the cup of tea his mother handed him.

Garnet might have killed him. They were rolling over and over until they were obstructed by the door, their bodies flailing. Garnet's legs kicking out at Neil. Hadn't this happened before? he thought, even as Neil's hand came down to bash him on the side of the face. Didn't he know how it would end? He moved just in time and the hand hit his shoulder instead. He leapt up and ran down the hall, swinging open the door and picking up the heavy doorstop.

"What are you going to do with that, asshole?" Neil was standing in the hall, watching him. His arms were hanging by his side. Garnet was glad to see blood snaking down his face.

"Kill you," Garnet cried.

"Sure you are."

Furiously, Garnet ran at him with the doorstop, but Neil moved out of the way deftly and the doorstop fell between them on the floor. If it had fallen on one of them, it could have broken a bone.

Someone downstairs was banging on a pipe and yelling for them to cut it out.

"Stop it, Garnet," said Neil.

But Garnet wasn't finished. He pinned Neil to the wall, breathing fiercely.

"What now?" One corner of Neil's mouth was turned up, oddly, in a kind of smile.

"I hate your guts. I hate you!" Garnet screamed at him. He could see Neil's eyes, the pores of his skin, the blood seeping out of the cut on his forehead.

"I can't condone what Neil did," said Allistair. "I can't condone what you did, either, Garnet. I won't condone it. But you're both my sons." He drank his tea.

"What would you say about this if one of us had killed the other?" Garnet watched his father.

"Don't test me." Allistair set down his mug. "You didn't." His face was tired. He gazed out at the purple martins— their small dark forms—flicking back and forth in the twi-light as they caught insects. He could still make out the horizon. The window faced east, but in the west the sun was going down. "It's not that you choose family. You're already in it. Like a boat that just gets shoved off into the water, you're in it. And it's not like you can get out. There are ties, Garnet. There are ties that are so strong you can't break them." He'd been speaking quietly, but then his voice became firmer, stronger. "And I'm ready to bet that you couldn't kill your own brother."

Neil had his hands around Garnet's throat. He was throttling him. Garnet could see the tiny broken blood vessels in the whites of his brother's eyes. He could see the freckle on the side of his nose. But there was no air left to breathe and Garnet felt like the top of his head was going to blow off. He slumped against the wall.

"Oh shit," said Neil, suddenly releasing his grip. "What's this?"

Garnet fell down, a wave of darkness coming over him. He lay on the floor, choking. It seemed he was choking for a long time, coughing and choking.

"This is stupid," said Neil, rolling him over. He rubbed Garnet's neck where his hands had been minutes before, strangling him.

Garnet made a gurgling noise.

"I don't know what I'm doing." Neil crouched over him. Garnet listened to him with his eyes closed. "Are you okay?"

Garnet heard him go into the bedroom and talk to Cinta, whose shrieks had diminished into moans. He could hear his brother talking and Cinta's voice, soothing him.

"What am I doing?" Neil was saying. "I'm supposed to help people. I'm a doctor."

"All this time you were thinking I was the one who needed you." Garnet set his empty mug on the table. "And I did, but so did Neil."

"You don't always see what's required of you until after the fact," said Allistair. "I used to think I should have been the one to help my father. You know—" he gazed at the dark ocean— "for the longest time I thought he was still out there somewhere."

"Where?" asked Evelyn.

"Out there," said Allistair vaguely, waving a hand at the window and the water beyond. "But he's dead. The dead can't find their way back."

Garnet thought of all he hadn't told them. He wasn't sure if his father was right about the dead. He felt Cinta near him all the time, though he couldn't remember her face. He felt her body next to him at night, warm against his back.

"I loved him," said Allistair.

"You've never talked about him," said Spike.

"No. Why would I talk about him?"

"But you loved him," persisted Spike.

"Yes." He looked down at his hands, templing them together. "I failed him."

"You couldn't have done anything," said Verna swiftly.

"Oh-ho," groaned Allistair.

"No," said Garnet. He was leaning across the table, looking straight at his father. "He failed himself."

Garnet was Robinson Crusoe.

He'd crept down the stairs when everyone else was asleep, let himself out the back door. The sky was black, studded here and there with tiny stars. He was entirely alone.

He would build himself a hut out of driftwood and live in it, catching fish to live on. With Man Friday. And he would climb the nearest hill and look for passing ships. He leapt for the lowest branch of the oak tree, caught it, and hooked his legs around it, and then pulled himself up. Every day he would watch for passing ships. He sat in the crotch of a branch, feeling the great trunk at his back.

But he wasn't Robinson Crusoe. He was in a tree in the backyard. The breeze was moving through the leaves all around him. The ghost of the tree. It would catch and hold him. It would squeeze the life out of him. And he wouldn't be able to scream. No one would know. No one in the house would hear him. They wouldn't have any idea what the tree ghost was up to.

The leaves shook, rustling slightly. He couldn't move.

And then his father was below him on the grass, waiting for him. His father, with his arms open.

And he scrambled down away from the searching arms, the searching eyes of the tree ghost.

"I'm afraid," he told his father.

"Of what?"

But he didn't know. He didn't know how to speak the words to make the ghost go away.

His father carried him. He carried him across the grass under the black sky, the far-off stars. He carried him into the house and up the stairs. He put him into his bed and kissed him on the forehead and went to the door. Then he came back and kissed him again. It was the kiss that banished the tree ghost that would have squeezed the life out of him.

At some point, Robin was musing, things came together. Not in the way she ever expected. The air was shawled with blue, so it was hard to tell the sky apart from the water. They might have been one and the same.

What had any of them ever wanted but to be loved?

And now. But it was not the sickening feeling she'd imagined it might be. There was sadness, there was damage. But more than that was the sense of relief, that yes, it was finished. Neil was like the rest of them. He wasn't any different. He wasn't better and he wasn't worse. And relief came over her, lightly, almost sweetly.

She could see them all together, as if they'd lifted up from the table and moved out through the window. They were all swimming through the veils of blue. Through the evening. They were moving as one. And every stroke they took moved them easily through the blue, into more blue, a deeper, wilder blue. What had they been afraid of before this? The world was under them, the tiny crests of

waves showing through the blue as they drifted over it.
The ghosts raised up their hands, but didn't call to them.
Farther out. And away.

BONFIRE

Spike was the one to get the wood. Garnet helped him and they carried it to the beach, making trips to the shed, where the wood was piled. They worked in silence for the most part. Spike was thinking over what Garnet had said. Garnet was trying to concentrate on the job at hand. It was dark, though, and once they nearly bumped into each other.

"Christ," said Spike. He had an armload of wood and some of it tumbled out of his grasp when he stopped short.

"Didn't see you," said Garnet.

"This is the last of the wood. We just need the shovel to dig a pit."

"I'll get it."

They worked methodically. Spike dug the pit. Then Garnet selected dry pieces and started setting them neatly in place.

"When did you learn how to do that?" Spike asked.

"What?"

"That sort of teepee thing."

"Cubs," Garnet said. "Or Scouts."

"You must have gotten the campfire badge."

He laughed. "I never got a badge in my life."

Spike started balling up the sheets of newspaper he'd brought down.

"Might not need the newspaper." Garnet took the packet of matches Spike gave him. "Let's see if it works." He lit a match and held it to the base of the teepee of wood. He nearly burned his fingers before a small flame caught. Then he knelt and blew on it to keep it going.

"You've got it," said Spike.

Garnet leaned back on his heels. Once in a while he bent forward and blew on the cluster of flames.

"I'll get the others," said Spike, but he didn't move.

The wood gave a crack and a little shower of sparks flew up into the dark. Brilliant little scrawls of light in the darkness.

"Must have been kind of weird to find out you had a kid," said Garnet.

Both of them stared at the fire.

"It *was* weird." Spike pushed his foot at a log in the pile of wood beside the fire. "She told you and she didn't tell me."

Another flight of sparks went up. One landed on Garnet's wrist and he brushed it off.

"You'd think she could have told me," Spike said.

"Maybe she thought you'd figure it out."

Spike kept pushing at the log until it rolled from the pile. "Once I thought we could start where we left off. You know?"

Garnet shrugged. "Well, maybe. I don't know."

"Shit," Spike said finally. He turned and looked out at the water. "Anyway, she thinks I'm a jerk."

Garnet laughed. He threw back his head and laughed. It was a weird laugh, closer to a howl. "You *are*, Spike."

Evelyn could see Spike and Garnet laughing as she went down the steps with Robin.

"Did you throw gas on the fire to get it going?" Evelyn asked, coming to the fire and putting out her hands to warm them. She turned to Robin. "I can't believe they got it going."

"Garnet spit on it," said Spike, wiping his eyes.

"It's a good fire," said Robin, standing out of the way of the smoke. "We could roast marshmallows." She stared at the flames. Close to the burning wood they were almost transparent, then blue, then yellow-white. "I can't remember when I last roasted marshmallows."

Garnet moved out of the circle of light and they could hear him shifting something. He came back with a piece of driftwood, detached the lengths of seaweed, and put it on the fire. The flames died down, hissing, and smoke came billowing up.

"It's pretty dry driftwood, except for one spot," said Garnet.

"Right," grinned Spike, watching it smoke. "Looks pretty dry."

Robin and Evelyn moved around the fire pit. Then the flames caught one end of the piece of driftwood. There were a few loud snapping sounds and more sparks shot up. The four of them backed off, then resumed their places as the fire began leaping up like tiger paws.

"It feels like years since yesterday," said Robin. "It's strange."

"Years," said Garnet.

The fire crackled again. "Everything's different."

She wondered what she would she say to Neil when she saw him. Would she just pack up her things without speaking to him? No, they would have to talk. They would have to divide things up. She dreaded that. And then where would she go? But she would come to that.

She closed her eyes. She could hear the sharp noises of the fire, but she could also hear the soft *whussshing* of one wave after another.

Evelyn was still trying to get used to it. How could things go back to normal? Well, they didn't, she reasoned. They just seemed to.

Family was a strange thing, she thought. It opened up, it closed. Then it opened up again.

She watched Spike go bounding up the steps to the

cottage. Robin was humming something. Garnet was leaning over the fire, back from wherever he'd been, back from the dead.

Spike didn't find his parents in the kitchen of the cottage. They'd moved into the living room, where they were reading their books. He thought they were two parts of the same thing. Yet they weren't at all. They were sitting across the room from each other, in their own pools of light.

"Are you coming down?" he asked.

"Have they got it going, dear?" asked Verna. How old she was, he thought. How fragile. He thought of what it was to have children. They had the power to hurt their parents. They had all hurt her, in various ways. But she'd weathered it. And so had his father.

"Garnet's got it blazing."

"Can't see it from here," said Allistair, staring into his own reflection in the glass. He got up and helped Verna out of the chair.

"Oh, look at me," Verna laughed. "I'm stiff." She longed just to stay where she was, in the armchair, reading her book. But they needed her. Allistair held her arm as they went out.

Spike stayed behind, hunting through the cupboards above the counter. Then he checked the lower cupboards and found popcorn in one plastic bag, hard marshmallows in another. He took the bag of marshmallows and followed his parents outside.

They hadn't progressed very far: they had their faces up to the sea air. Spike did the same. It was what animals did, he thought. The night breeze was soothing, with its tang of woodsmoke. Then they went along the path to the top of the steps, where Verna paused with her hand on the railing.

Allistair took her arm again, but she wasn't ready to move. She could see them all below her, standing on one side of the fire, while the smoke drifted away in tails of blue on the other side. The flames were white and yellow and gold. All around them it was dark. They looked like figures in a painting, she thought, standing there so quietly, their faces touched with light. Evelyn said something and Garnet answered. Whatever had been going on with the two of them was over now. It was all right to come into it.

Once when the children were young she'd had them down on the beach right there next to the stairs. There had been plastic buckets and shovels and a beach umbrella. The tide was coming in, but Verna had simply moved the children back. They still had some time before the strip of sand was awash in water. But she hadn't counted on one wave that spilled over her in the beach chair and swirled around the toys. It pulled at them all, so Spike and Garnet went sprawling, Evelyn screamed, and Neil clung to her chair.

"My God!" she'd cried, scrambling to get the children. They were all right, just surprised. But she sent them up the stairs anyway, wrapped in their wet towels, and then tried to collect the buckets and shovels. A red one here, a shovel with a green handle sunk in sand, a dump truck upended. The beach umbrella. She hadn't been watching the tide and it had come over them.

Even now, she sensed the movement of the ocean. It was beyond them, darker than the sky. But it couldn't harm them; they were standing around the fire. Now they looked up and saw her at the top of the stairs.

Neil, she thought, as she went down the steps. Neil, Neil, Neil. Garnet had come back. Neil would come back to them sooner or later. It was the way families went. She felt herself larger, as if she were large enough to hold them.

They stood around the fire, waiting for her, waiting for Allistair.

"Well," she said. "Here we are."

NOTES

Earlier drafts of several chapters in this novel were first published in reviews or anthologies. "Snowman" and "The Memory Theatre" were first published in *Event* (25:3, 1997) and *Prism International* (34:3, 1996) respectively. "The Memory Theatre" (then called "The Memory Theatre of Guilio Camillo") was runner-up in *Prism International*'s short story contest in 1995. It was reprinted in *Water Studies: New Voices in Maritime Writing* in 1998. "The Waters of Immortality" was first published in *Riprap: Fiction and Poetry from the Banff Centre* in 1999.

In "The Memory Theatre," there are references to an actual memory theatre conceived of and constructed by Guilio Camillo in the sixteenth century. An effusive letter—though not the one included in this novel—describing Camillo's memory theatre was sent to Erasmus by Vigilius Zuichemus in 1532. For detailed information on these matters, I am grateful to *The Art of Memory* by Frances Yates.

ACKNOWLEDGEMENTS

Most heartfelt thanks to Barbara Berson, my editor, who believed in this novel.

A Canada Council grant helped substantially in allowing me time to write.

To the students in the evening class of English 120 at StFX University in 1990–1991, thanks for helping me imagine Chaucer's *Canterbury Tales* in a different light. For the gift of stories, my appreciation to the people of Antigonish, Nova Scotia, who know that these characters and events are mere fiction.

And to those writers who helped so much with the shaping of versions of the manuscript—Bonnie Burnard, Joan Clark, and John Steffler—I am in your debt. I was much encouraged by the creative spirit of both the Banff Centre for the Arts Writing Studio and the Humber School of Writers Correspondence Program. Thanks also to Eddy Yanofsky, whose hard work helped this book find a home.

Bouquets of freesia to Mary Chapman in Vancouver, Mary Fallert in Ann Arbor, USA, Heather and Andy Martin in Cambridge, UK, and Danielle Schaub in Haifa, Israel. A bubbly toast to Pam MacLean, in whose warm kitchen this book began to be revised. Blue tulips to Jo-Anne Embree, who offered such insightful comments. A bunch of violets to Anne Camozzi, who helped me *see* the landscape of northern Nova Scotia. Several feathers of appreciation to Don McKay, who sorted out the birds. Special thanks to Dr. Leo Pereira and Dr. Leone Steele for assistance with medical information. And finally, a clutch of sand dollars to Anne and Dr. John Atkinson, whose cottage in Maine became a source of inspiration and a special "memory theatre" in itself.

As always, deepest thanks to Jan and Jack Simpson—best of parents—and my sisters, Sue and Jennifer. All my love to my own special family: Paul, David, Sarah, and yes, Shasta, Griffin and Poet too.